The Saturn House Killings

V.J. Randle

BLOODHOUND
BOOKS

Memorial

The sea on the coast of Aegina glimmers purple in the morning. The colour only lasts for a minute or so, and it is a phenomenon that most people miss. But for this minute, the angle of the sun renders the waters a deep violet shade, which is why the ancients ascribed it with the epithet *wine-dark*. The owner of Taverna Dionisiou saw the sea in its morning robe every day on his early run. He liked to tell people that it blushed, as deep as the seabed, when it heard about all the antics from the night before.

This morning, he slipped through the small grove of eucalyptus trees just behind the newly built boundary wall that blocked his route from the coastal track to the beach. The heat had already begun to thicken the air and his breathing was slightly ragged. However, he was never too out of breath to murmur a little curse at the new resort complex, which had forced its way so ungraciously into the landscape, marring what had once been a much-loved public space. The helicopters, the thumping music of parties (to which nobody he knew was ever invited), and those awful luxury yachts had descended like a swarm of long-winged insects; at first, to surprise, then to resentment. Still, the owners never noticed him hoisting himself over the wall, using a conveniently shaped tree as his ladder, to continue his traditional run along what he still considered his stretch of beach.

As he quickened his pace, greeting the purple sea with a familiar nod, he noticed one of the tourists had passed out just by the water's edge. This wasn't surprising: his suppliers had told him about the amount of champagne these people consumed. It was careless – the sea was indiscriminate to its victims, no matter how much one had paid for a room. Luckily, the man's head lolled at an angle facing away; even if he woke up, he wouldn't notice the trespassing jogger. Keeping as wide a berth as he could, he skirted behind the man on the dry land, his stride softening as his feet sank and slid from the sand.

The slow warmth of the morning heated the sky, reducing its orange haze to deep red. Was it the colour that warned him? Or perhaps it was the air; the way that it hung, stiff, more unforgiving than usual. Whatever it was, the restaurant owner looked back. Just a glance, over his shoulder. A quick check to ensure that the tourist was safe where he lay, nothing more.

From this angle, however, the sleeping guest's face was visible. He was not safe. Not safe at all.

The man's face was an awful shade of burgundy, as if he had been dipped and dyed by the sea. The body was still – more still than anything he had ever seen before. He had never realised how much he took the gentle rise and fall of the chest that was present in the living for granted. What lay before him was devoid of life entirely. The restaurant owner fell to his knees. A sound was ringing in his ears, loud and panicked, over and over again. As his throat grew hoarse, he realised the noise was his voice screaming for someone to help.

'Someone come quickly!
At the beach, please!

2

Oh God, anyone – can anybody hear me?'

As if in response to his cries, the sea turned from purple to a crystal blue. Then, the patter of feet arrived along the cedar wood promenade.

Michail fought the urge to nod his head in time to the evzone guards' march. So far, the ceremony was as uncomfortable as he had suspected it would be. There was no reason, surely, for him to be paraded on a platform in the centre of the square. The department had pressing work to carry out; to have them all gathered here, off-duty, for the whole afternoon was brazenly careless on the authorities' part. Plus, he didn't like the way everyone watched him. To the best of his knowledge (and he had conducted thorough research), there were no Hellenic Police Force guidelines about how to behave on a stage. It was impossible to know where to look, where to place his arms and what expression to convey. The best course of action, it appeared, was to stand as still as possible. Hopefully, with minimal movement, he could divert the crowd's attention towards Sofia, who was next to him.

'Michail, try to relax.' Sofia appeared to whisper without moving her lips.

Straining his eyes sidewards, he kept his head firmly facing ahead and replied, 'Relax...?'

'Yes–'

'This is a memorial.'

'Yes–'

'I am attempting to look like I am remembering.'

'Agreed, and that means breathing, Sergeant.'

He forced himself to take a deep breath, counting to three as he inhaled, then exhaling for the same amount of time. The action made him feel a little dizzy, which under normal circumstances would be suboptimal. However, seeing as remembering the events of last summer was precisely the opposite of how he intended to get through the day, the sensation proved quite useful. Of course, the victims deserved proper and meaningful commemoration, but all this pomp, the crowd, the press, the speeches... it felt too close to...

His chest tightened. He pushed his shoulders back to convey a sense of solemnity and strength, gripping his jaw against the ascending live music. This appeared to please Sofia, because she gave a quick nod, before noting, 'I'm up at the end of this march.'

'Correct.'

She sighed and shook her shoulders, as if she was trying to wriggle free from something.

'I do not think that there is a requirement for you to dance–'

'Yes, thank you, Michail.'

The music stopped and the guards gave their final salute. Sofia cleared her throat and stepped forward to take her place behind the lectern, her heels making a deep percussive sound over the platform as a silence shrouded the square. Michail squinted above the heads of the spectators as she began her speech, finally resting his gaze upon the line of guards who had assumed their position before the old Royal Palace. A small bead of sweat trickled down his forehead. It seemed that large crowds had become a small (and, he assured himself, a perfectly surmountable) problem for him. It was a perfectly reasonable response: mob mentality had been the cause of last summer. The department was still combing through the scores of people who had allowed their senses to be ripped apart by catchy rhetoric and a sense of superiority. Crowds, he had decided, must be treated with extreme caution.

Sofia continued to talk into the microphone. 'Of course,

today is mostly about the innocent victims of the terrorist movement, the so-called Awakening...'

Staring into the middle distance, he felt the muscles in his throat twitch as Sofia worked through the list of names. Each syllable was like a sharp pierce to his skin. Although the force had saved many lives, he had missed the signs he should have seen. The person working alongside him, smiling and laughing.

'...the Hellenic Police Force feels that both the victims' families and the public are owed transparency. You will, no doubt, be aware of the culpability resting within our institution itself. Rest assured, we have taken – and continue to take – a most severe action in response to anyone found guilty of soliciting the...'

Yiorgos shifted pointedly behind him. Michail clenched his hands at his sides, that familiar guilty jolt shooting its way through his stomach. He had planned to stick to the facts at Katerina's inquiry; he had always operated according to the truth. Yet, his testimony reverberated through his bones like a wayward siren.

'Sergeant Mikras, did you ever see any evidence of Katerina Galanis's involvement?'

'I arrived at the cave and found her tied up and in danger.'

'But did you suspect that she had been working in collusion with her boyfriend, Theo, or anyone else?'

'Not in collusion, no.'

'You believe that she was unaware of her boyfriend, Theo Kounos's, crimes?'

'I believe that to be correct. She was completely unaware until I found her.'

'Two of your colleagues in the Special Violent Crime Squad say that you suggested she had involvement at the time...'

'Did they provide any specifics?'

'No. Neither of them is a witness. In fact, the only thing that *either of them witnessed is Katerina fighting on behalf of the Special Violent Crime Squad. However, Major Sampson told us that you'd provide us with all the information we needed. Your testimony is key. We're facing unprecedented levels of work here. To be honest, without your account, the charges against Officer Galanis will be dropped without further recourse. We were hoping that you...'*

'I've told you everything I know. She was a victim. That must be what Major Sampson meant...'

He gulped, tasting sourness. Sofia was beginning to reach the end of her speech, reiterating how the values of freedom and tolerance were always at the forefront of the force's mind. A slight ripple of voices sounded from the back of the crowd. Sofia paused for a moment, before continuing in a slightly louder voice. Michail squinted to see what the disruption was – surely, people had the decency to wait until the end of the speech before chattering? This wasn't a social event.

Again, another flurry of voices, this time from nearer the platform, interrupted Sofia. Michail watched her head jerk upwards in response. As he scanned the crowd, he saw that people were looking at their phones. What could be so important that they were more interested in that than honouring the dead? He twisted around to look at Yiorgos, who gave him a gruff, non-committal shrug.

'So, thank you for allowing us to be a part of...' Sofia's voice echoed into the square, laced with her characteristic stern inflection. Michail gave a satisfied nod – if anyone could recapture their attention, it was her.

Unfortunately, she never got to finish her sentence due to a shout from the area just below the stage that was reserved for photographers and press. 'Major Sampson! If I could just–'

A few disgruntled groans occurred from the crowd. At least some people had a sense of decency. Michail pursed his lips, feeling his cheeks grow red with anger. This was intolerable. Questions were surely not permitted at memorial events, let alone interruptions. He looked to the constables on the ground to try and gesture for them to intervene, however, their heads were also tilted downwards looking at their screens. Unbelievable.

'I don't think press questions are at all appropriate,' Sofia began. 'If you need more information regarding the internal police inquiries, then please–'

'I'm sorry!' It appeared that the shout was coming from a young female journalist. She took a deep breath, as if to steady herself with confidence, and continued, 'I wondered if the Special Violent Crime Squad had any comment to make about the body found on Marathon beach at Aegina?'

Michail blinked as he digested the woman's words. Sofia's shoulder blades tensed together beneath her dress. Yiorgos murmured something that sounded like a swear word underneath his breath.

Sofia paused for a few moments and then leant back over the microphone. 'That will be all. Thank you.'

Her parting words caused the press area to fall into a frenzy of clicks and flashes and further shouting. Sofia turned towards Michail and Yiorgos, shaking her head. 'Cars. Now.'

Lost Wax

Sofia's fingernails pressed into the seat as the boat catapulted through the water. There had been no time to change, which meant that she would be negotiating the sand in her heels. There had also been no time to have the very urgent conversation that she'd been putting off having with her team. A new wave of nausea caught her as the boat swerved violently against a wave. She hung her head, attempting to gather herself. The announcement would need to wait.

'All okay?' Yiorgos asked, offering her a bottle of water.

'Fine.' Her voice was clipped, and she forced herself to sit up straight. She eyed both Michail and Yiorgos carefully. 'I don't have many more details other than what was revealed at the ceremony. Apparently, it's a private beach–' She stopped mid-sentence as the boat hit another wave, the force throwing her head back against the plastic headrest. She swore loudly and, taking a deep breath – as well as Yiorgos's water bottle – continued, 'Some expensive hotel – the desk manager made the call.'

'Yes.' Michail had barely looked up from his phone since

they'd left the square. 'I've compiled a small collection of photographs already posted by tourists–'

'Vultures,' said Yiorgos.

'A good comparison.' Michail nodded, showing them his phone. 'It's a place called Saturn House; they own a large stretch of the beach.'

'Saturn?' Yiorgos asked.

'I agree,' replied Michail. 'I think that they should have used Kronos too – Saturn's Hellenic counterpart. We are in Greece, after all.'

'Oh, yes, that's the main focus here...' Yiorgos mumbled.

'Obviously, the main focus is the male corpse,' Michail said without a hint of sarcasm, before going back to scrolling.

Sofia shot Yiorgos a warning look as she swallowed down a small gulp of stomach acid. These two needed to get along, especially today.

'It's part of an extortionately priced members' hotel group,' Michail continued without looking up. 'There's a Balcombe House in London, Village House in New York, and an East House in Berlin.'

Sofia looked longingly through the window to see how close they were to the island. She had never experienced a longer forty minutes in her life. 'I've heard of them,' she said. 'Reserve of the rich, beautiful and famous? I suppose it explains the public interest. Oh God, please tell me we don't have a celebrity victim on our hands?'

'No reported name yet. Although the people in these photographs aren't all conventionally beautiful,' said Michail.

'Let me guess,' Sofia said, 'the women all look a good twenty years younger than the men?'

'For the most part, correct.' Michail's phone vibrated and, upon checking his screen, his frown grew deeper.

'What is it?' Sofia pressed, exhaling in relief as the boat began to slow. 'Michail?'

He looked up, suddenly seeming like a much younger version of himself... the version that Sofia realised she had only met a year prior. 'I've received a message,' he said.

Sofia glanced at Yiorgos, who shook his head, apparently as clueless as she was.

'That's the beach,' the coast guard called from the front. 'Get ready to disembark.'

The boat's engine churned and spat as it slowed in the shallows. Were it not for the police cordons and the body tent, the setting would have been idyllic. A small crowd, phones raised before their faces, had gathered behind the police ribbons on what was presumably the boundary between public and private land. When the boat ground to a halt, Sofia allowed herself to imagine for a few moments that she was not here to inspect a corpse, but instead for a holiday. As soon as the thought entered her head, she tutted, irritated at herself, and looked back at Michail. He was still staring at his phone. She narrowed her eyes as she noticed his feet: three taps on the right, three taps on the left.

'Michail, we're about to inspect the scene. Good to go?'

He took a deep breath through his nose and raised his eyes to meet hers. Although they were wide with anxiety, he seemed to force himself to hold them steady. If there was one thing that she liked about Michail, it was that he always took his job seriously – albeit sometimes a bit too seriously. She raised her eyebrows expectantly.

'It's her,' he said, his breathing becoming shallow and fast. It was all he needed to say. If she was honest with herself, she should have managed the situation better. She had uncharacteristically let this situation simmer without much management. Yiorgos would have a problem with it too. Hell, *she* wasn't exactly sure what to make of it... a feeling which had unfortunately been the theme of the last year.

Yiorgos shook his head whilst letting out an impatient sigh and swung himself through the door of the cabin. 'I'll talk to the island police,' he said in a voice that was clearly supposed to indicate he didn't think she should be wasting time babysitting.

'I'll be there shortly,' Sofia called after him, listening to the soft splash as Yiorgos's feet hit the wet sand. 'We both will.'

Now that the engine had been turned off and the air conditioning had stopped, the boat's plastic cabin was stifling. The boat bobbed gently upon the water. 'Let's go onto the deck,' she said.

Michail did not move, apparently unfazed by the heat. He watched her with an odd expression – one of amazement and... anger?

'Mich–'

'Did you know?' he said, his voice very insistent and certain. 'It is reasonable to assume, as the person in charge of the squad, that you knew it would be today.'

She tilted her head to one side and tried to find the words. For a while, she'd suspected that the matter was far more delicate than she understood. She took a short intake of breath, her head beginning to ache from the heat and seasickness. 'Yes, Michail, I knew. Ideally, we would have held a formal reintroduction back at headquarters and... I didn't think she'd text you directly, but, well, we didn't account for a possible murder victim today.'

She left out the part about how she should have raised the issue with him weeks ago but had decided against it, mostly out of concern for him, slightly out of having no idea how to navigate the situation. He remained impassive and she stood, trying to coax him to follow her outside. She said, a little defensively, 'You must have known that Katerina would be returning to duty soon? Her name was cleared months ago.' She didn't add: *entirely thanks to your testimony.*

He sat perfectly still for a few seconds, his eyes moving from one side to the other as if he was thinking very carefully. Finally, as if reaching some silent resolution, he slapped his knees and stood up. 'Yes. This is, of course, the logical outcome,' he said. 'Evidence was given and, based on the facts, a decision was made.'

She wasn't sure what to say to this, so nodded, gesturing for them to move onto the deck. He followed her in silence, his breathing a little heavy. Then, rolling his trousers up high to his knees, he looked at her and said, 'I have a responsibility to tell you that Katerina's reintegration may be a little tricky for me, Major Sampson. We have not communicated since last summer. However, the smooth functioning of our team comes first, so I will remember to put my feelings to one side. They are irrelevant.'

'I wouldn't say that–'

'Irrelevant,' he repeated. 'When will she be joining us?'

Michail marched to catch up with Yiorgos, trying with every stride to put Katerina out of his mind. Yiorgos had already dispersed the bystanders who were now traipsing along the other end of the beach.

'They just needed telling.' Yiorgos folded his arms as Michail approached. 'Everything all right?'

'Certainly,' Michail said. 'It would be unhelpful for me to panic.'

Yiorgos frowned and looked like he was about to ask something more but was interrupted by the sound of a shrill and piercing voice.

'Hello, hello!'

Michail turned to see a blonde woman approaching them with an enormous smile that seemed out of place, given the circumstances. Inexplicably, she had gone to the trouble of wearing a tightly fitted crochet dress that was completely see-through, revealing the black bikini underneath.

'Hi, oh, there we are.' She flashed a smile at two constables who, rather unprofessionally, gawked back at her. 'Lily Woodstow, oh gosh, I'm sorry...' Michail noticed that her eyelashes seemed unnaturally long as she looked at him from beneath them. 'Do you speak English?'

'Yes,' Michail replied, at the same time as Yiorgos replied, 'No.'

'Fabulous, and, sorry again... you'd think I'd have learnt the language more quickly what with me living here.'

'Quite understandable. Greek is a very complex language that only the most intelligent of visitors manage to master,' Michail said.

She looked momentarily offended, her smile faltering for a second, before she snapped her face back into a toothy grin. 'I'm the PR and events manager at Saturn House, I've been with the company for over a decade. We have a lot of high-profile guests, you see, and they, of course, expect an elevated, personalised sort of service.'

She spoke so quickly that Michail was forced to close his eyes to focus. He nodded in reply, confused as to why she thought any of this was important at this given moment. Unfortunately, she took his silence as a prompt to continue speaking.

'Obviously, this incident... Teddy... well, it's upsetting for everyone, particularly since we're preparing for the event of the year... it's a highly exclusive thing, well-known in these circles if you catch my drift. We've blocked out most of the hotel for privacy, including the penthouse.' She gestured behind her to a large balcony overlooking the beach. 'Very alarming, as you can imagine, not at all good for creativity, nor the pre-event socials. There's an associate of ours staying here running the publicity pre-game, extremely VIP... and all this...' She wafted her arms about in the air. 'I was wondering when Teddy – the body – would be moved away from the beach? I don't mean to be a pain, it's just–'

'Good,' Michail cut in.

'I'm sorry?'

'It's good news that you don't wish to be a pain, as you say. The best place to wait is inside the hotel building as I am sure you have been instructed by my colleagues–'

She stepped closer to him, her lips moving into a gentle pout and said in a lower voice, 'Look, I didn't want to disclose the VIP name but it's Alek Knox...'

She paused as if she was waiting for Michail to respond. He looked at Yiorgos, who rolled his eyes. 'Alek Knox?'

'Yes.' Lily nodded, in a strangely serious manner. 'So, you'll understand...'

Michail turned to Yiorgos. 'Who is Alek Knox?'

Yiorgos sighed and replied, 'Famous. I think he started on social media and now he has his own television series. Thalia used to watch it. It's sort of a mix of lifestyle and travel show, with some inspirational life advice thrown in. He's had trouble recently, though, with spurting some male-centric crap–'

'Oh gosh, boys will be boys!' Lily gave a small giggle. 'You name me one powerful man who hasn't made an enemy or two along the way, eh? Look, if the body could be moved as soon as possible, like I say, that would be wonderful.'

Michail frowned, trying to follow Lily's line of argument. 'If I understand correctly, you would like us to remove the body from the beach so that this... this Alek can continue his holiday in peace?'

'Yes!' Lily clapped her hands, apparently relieved.

'Out of the question,' said Michail, before her misunderstanding of the situation's severity continued.

'But–'

'A man is dead and the proper course of action must be taken.' Michail opened his notebook. 'You mentioned that you think the deceased is named Teddy?'

'It *is* Teddy.' She nodded. 'A guest.'

Finally, yet completely out of the blue, she started to show signs of distress. Her veneer seemed to crack, and her large blue eyes filled with tears. 'It's sad, so sad, I know... you don't need to tell me,' she said, her arms fluttering about her face. 'He'd had too much to drink and taken too much of God knows what, everyone could see that. It's just the most awful accident... I am just trying to protect the vibe here, you know? It's horrible, but that's PR for you: disaster control.'

Michail stared at her, careful to keep his face impassive. He reminded himself that she didn't yet know this was a possible murder inquiry. Based on the current facts, even he was struggling to calculate why the Special Violent Crime Squad had been called. Either way, they needed Lily to remove herself.

'Please return inside,' he said, a little more gently. 'We will most likely have a few questions.'

She took a final look at the body tent, the temporary flimsy tomb, and eventually nodded before disappearing back up the beach.

'She seems sure that this was an accident. Do we know why the island police thought this was a murder?' Michail asked Yiorgos.

'Yes.'

Michail jumped as Sofia's voice sounded from behind him.

He spun about to see her, a little red in the face, barefooted, her shoes dangling from her hands.

'Now, if you've finished with your celebrity gossip, perhaps you'd like to see the body?'

Michail stood back as the photographers did their work, his breath hot behind his mask. Sofia stood opposite him on the other side of the corpse. She had her arms folded, which, based on his previous interactions with her, meant that she was one of two things: concerned or angry. It was perfectly possible, all things considered, that she could be both.

'Found by a local restaurant owner on his morning run,' explained Sofia. 'He screamed, alerting the desk manager at reception, Iraklis Barlas, who phoned the police. There's no reason to think that the body has been moved since its discovery. This is how it was found. As you've already heard, we're looking at Teddy Menkopf, a British national on holiday.'

'Alone?' Yiorgos asked.

'Yes.' Sofia nodded. 'Booked in to stay another two weeks here, apparently for some big party. The only other guest staying here apart from Alek Knox and his girlfriend. Oh, and a couple of models here for some sort of promotional shoot.'

Michail knelt and observed the position of the body carefully. Teddy's dark hair fell in wet undulations over his discoloured forehead, covering one eye. Were the circumstances different, he would have seemed almost styled to look like some mythical sea creature. The young man was rolled onto his side, the muscles of his abdominals still chiselled in death. His left ear rested against his left bicep. One of his knees was bent so it looked like he had rolled over in his sleep. Both of his wrists were cut, the flesh folded about them in a creamy, discoloured –

yet meticulous – incision. He was naked apart from a silver chain necklace around his neck formed in the shape of a volute 'T'.

'Toxicology will verify whether he was inebriated,' he began. 'The slit wrists–'

'There's very little blood loss, if any, judging from the colour.' Sofia crouched down to join him. 'I agree with the island police – it's likely that these cuts occurred after he was dead. That'll need to be confirmed, of course. They were right to treat this as suspicious.'

Michail kept his eyes steady on the thin wounds. Before he could stop himself, he realised that his fingertips were tapping three times on his right thigh, then three times on his left. He clenched his hands, trying to control the old compulsion. 'Did they say anything about the direction of the cuts?' he asked.

'The direction?' Sofia leaned further forward.

'The flesh is slightly puckered towards the outside of the wrists.' Michail tilted his head, trailing his eyes along the delicate lines.

'Why does that matter?' Sofia asked.

Michail pursed his lips together and reached for his pen. Then, he held it over the body, moving it close to the flesh.

'Michail–' Yiorgos started.

'There is no need to worry,' Michail replied, waving the pen. 'Imagine that this is a knife. See the way I'm holding it? It would be awkward, if not impossible, to slice both wrists at an outwards trajectory... unless someone else was doing it for me.'

Sofia nodded to Yiorgos. 'Make sure that's reiterated. It certainly looks suspicious, but until we have confirmation, it's not a murder. Obviously, we'll search his room and the grounds in the meantime.'

Michail followed the two of them out of the tent into the bright sunlight. He placed his hands on his hips and hung his head so that his chin rested upon his chest, before they set off for the hotel. Another body. Another blow to the justice scales, skewing them off-kilter, placing the world out of focus once again. Last summer's victims half-emerged behind the moisture in his eyes. They floated, silent, vaporous, but somehow so loud, so vivid and broken. His eyes swelled and he shook his head, attempting to make any sense out of it. His counsellor had suggested that his adverse reactions to violent crime scenes were because he did not like gore. This was preposterous, of course. Gore was an integral part of being on the Special Violent Crime Squad.

'Feeling all right there, Sergeant Mikras?'

'I'm fine, Yiorgos, thank you for your concern. I am merely having what my counsellor would refer to as a mild anxiety attack. Unsurprising, given the recent trigger.'

Yiorgos exhibited signs of some type of discomfort, despite there being no apparent cause, before Sofia raised a pointed eyebrow at him. Michail had noticed an odd dynamic between these two over the last few months. Quite frequently, Sofia would intervene where she never had before; often nudging or glancing at Yiorgos to convey what seemed to Michail to be a sort of secret code.

Whatever the message Sofia had intended for Yiorgos, he suddenly responded in a strangely loud voice. 'Oh, another one, well... uh... that's good you're recognising them, I suppose. Erm... did you want to talk about it?'

This was precisely the sort of topic that his counsellor encouraged him to speak about. 'I would. Death is an inalienable, immovable truth. Whether accidental or through natural causes, it will happen. Murder is not an inescapable truth – it spins on the whim and the will of another person. A murderer takes a universal rule and moulds it to their own twists and turns. They take what is black and white and make it blurry. I detest that.'

Michail exhaled. This new method of 'externalising' was proving to be very useful indeed. Previously, the confusion, the tension, the colours, the noise would have built in tremendous proportions like a pulsing balloon pressing against his skull. Now, he was learning to use words as a funnel; he had worked on a very accurate and detailed metaphor for his counsellor, which he hoped to present to her. Now seemed like a good opportunity to test it out.

'Have you ever heard of the lost wax method, Yiorgos?'

'Erm, no...'

'It was the way in which ancient bronze sculptures were made.'

'I see...'

'I think that my brain might be like the lost wax. You see, to get an accurate rendering, molten wax was poured into a cast, resulting in a hollow wax sculpture.'

'Umm...'

'Then, clay was pressed around the wax sculpture, making another mould.'

'Yes...'

'This mould was placed into the kiln and the wax melted away, leaving space for the good stuff – the molten bronze. My brain is like that. It must have a syphon for bad stuff, like stress, to allow room for the good stuff, like solving crime.'

'Right...'

'You asked, so I thought you would be interested.'

'I asked?'

'Yes, remember? You asked whether I wanted to talk about it, so there you have it.'

'Oh, yes, thanks for that, Michail.'

Michail couldn't help but feel that Yiorgos had not quite

understood. Perhaps the metaphor needed more work. For a fleeting moment, he pictured himself telling Katerina the same thing. She would have been more enthusiastic, he was sure. Most likely, she would have made some silly joke, but she would have listened properly. He found that his fists were clenched again and he forced himself to relax his fingers one at a time.

Sofia was waiting at the hotel entrance, her red lips pressed more tightly than usual. Michail knew what was coming before she said it. He held his face as still as possible as the words he'd been expecting for months flew from her mouth like tiny arrows into his heart.

'Katerina's here, Michail. In the lobby. She'll be running interviews with you.'

Michail could not speak. He left a spluttering Yiorgos behind him for Sofia to placate and stepped past her into the lobby. There, looking precisely the same as she had a year ago, was his old partner.

Something In Between

K aterina had obsessed over a thousand times about how she would greet him. There was too much to say, to explain. Most of all, she wanted to thank him, but had no idea how to do it without sounding like she was being flippant. He stood framed by olive trees, which flanked the enormous doorway. Their eyes locked for a few seconds and, briefly, she thought they might go back to old times; that she might give him a hug and make some joke and he'd push her away and tell her to focus. But, as Mama had warned her, there was no use chasing old times. *It is not possible to step in the same river twice, Katerina. Things have moved on; you must move on too. React and repair.*

She took a deep breath and stepped towards him, a hand outstretched. 'Michail–'

He moved forwards, but instead of greeting her, walked straight to the main desk without so much as a glance. She stood, unsure where to look, as Sofia and Yiorgos entered. Yiorgos's face was thunderous, Sofia's lips were set in a straight, taut line. She knew that she should have been prepared for this, but a rising shame boiled from the middle of her chest, firing along her neck and face. She opened her mouth to speak, but nothing came out. Michail rang the bell on the reception desk with three sharp taps. The sound, reverberating against the thick marble walls, seemed to taunt her. Perhaps she shouldn't have come back. Perhaps this had been a mistake.

'Welcome back, Officer Galanis. I'm sorry that your first day couldn't be more typical.' Sofia observed her with sharp eyes, as if she was waiting for her to do something terrible, something treacherous.

'It's fine,' Katerina mumbled.

'You'll be with Michail. Sergeant Mikras, will you fill her in?'

Michail, who rang the bell with three taps again, audibly exhaled before turning to face her. His expression looked as if someone had forcibly pulled his face into a smile. His eyes were glassy and large. 'Officer Galanis, good to have you back.'

His tone was so monotonous that Katerina flinched. She looked at the floor; her face felt like it had gone up in flames. 'That's kind of you to say, thank you,' she managed.

The four of them hovered in the lobby, caught in an awkward silence. Eventually, Sofia spoke. 'Obviously we all have a lot of catching up to do, but for now, I need us all to focus on the matter at hand. Understood?'

Katerina looked to Michail, who, although his hands were clenched into two tight balls, shot Sofia a stern single nod.

'Oh, I can't wait to catch up,' Yiorgos said, the disdain thick in his voice.

Sofia clapped her hands together. 'Good. They've said we can use a couple of rooms for interviews. Let's get started, shall we?'

The room was amazing. A terrace, complete with a private infinity pool, stretched its entire length, overlooking a lush pool area filled with shrubbery. The living space was big enough to house an entire family, complete with a desk, a sizable bar, and a sunken seating area. It had that smell about it – a mixture of heady spice and lavender – that Katerina associated with extreme wealth. Michail had insisted they rearrange the room to make the process seem more formal. Katerina had agreed, feeling that she was in no position to argue with him. So far, he had not mentioned the inquiry, nor his evidence, nor anything to do with last summer. She helped him move the furniture in silence, pushing a sofa into the centre of the room.

She watched Michail write studiously in his notebook for a few minutes, before gathering up the courage to ask, 'Should we ask for the first interviewee?'

He closed his book and his eyes simultaneously, as if forcing himself to think very carefully about what to say. 'Alek Knox is the first on our list. I'm told he is very important. Apparently, this means that we must wait for him.'

Katerina couldn't help but let out a small squeal. 'Eww. Alek Knox! You know who he is?'

'As I said, I am aware of his fame, however, it is essential that we both maintain a high degree of professionalism. Remember, none of the guests know that Teddy Menkopf was murdered.'

'Unless one of them did it.'

'Correct. Obviously, that person would know.'

Without being able to help herself, Katerina's lips twitched into a small smile. She had missed this. Slipping into their familiar back and forth was like wrapping herself in a comforting blanket. The tension about Michail's eyes softened slightly and she wondered – hoped – that he might be feeling the same. However, before she could say anything else, a rap at the door signalled they should stand up.

'May I present to you both Mr Knox.' An attractive woman who looked like she was in her mid-to-late thirties announced the man like she was appearing on a gameshow, shimmying into the room wearing little more than a bikini. The past year had afforded Katerina enough time to recognise the tell-tale signs of a few Botox injections too many.

'Lily Woodstow.' The woman flashed Katerina a bright smile before pouting at Michail. 'And we've met.'

Behind Lily followed a short man in sunglasses, wearing a robe and swimming trunks. It took Katerina a few moments to recognise him.

'Mr Knox, thank you for your time,' Michail said. 'I'm Sergeant Michail Mikras and this is my colleague, Officer Katerina Galanis. Please take a seat.'

Katerina did a double take as Michail smoothly gestured to the sofa before shaking Alek's hand without even the smallest jitter. She had never seen him so comfortable. She supposed that he had enjoyed a year of duty, of practice, of professional improvement while she... while she'd not. As she sat down, she glanced at her old partner, an odd mixture of pride in him and embarrassment of herself curdling thick in her veins.

Alek Knox removed his sunglasses and leaned forwards, setting his signature steel-blue eyes in line with Michail's. 'You probably know I'm half Greek – happy to speak it.'

His body language was almost textbook toxic masculinity. He spread his legs, his hands resting on his thighs, and almost aggressively cocked his head towards Michail. She may as well have been invisible, which suited her.

'I'm afraid I probably can't help you.' Alek massaged his chin, taking a slightly longer than needed pause before continuing. 'No idea what happened. Best guess is that the poor lad decided to go for a night-time swim.'

He sat back, placing his hands back on top of his thighs,

which were spread unreasonably wide. 'Makes you think though, doesn't it? How it can all end, in... well, in the click of a finger. Live in the *now*.' He took a purposeful breath, his chest rising noticeably. 'It's the only way. Right here, right now.'

'Yes, the present is the most logical time on which to focus,' Michail replied. 'We are, however, trying to piece together the final hours of Teddy Menkopf's life. Did you see him at all yesterday?'

'Absolutely. We all spent the afternoon down by the pool–'

'All?' Katerina noticed Michail shift as she interjected. She gritted her teeth and pressed on. 'Sorry, who was there? Can you give us the names?'

'Sure.' Alek stood, rubbed his temples, and walked towards the terrace. 'Mind if I get a little air? It was a heavy one last night.'

'You were intoxicated?' Michail asked as they followed him onto the terrace. As soon as the sun hit his skin, Alek removed his robe and plunged himself into the pool. He emerged raking his fingers through his hair and moaning in relief. Only then, did he answer Michail's question, chuckling. 'Last time I checked that wasn't a crime, Sergeant?'

'It depends on the substance,' replied Michail, bending over to wipe water droplets off his shoe. 'Alcohol is permitted.'

'Awesome,' muttered Alek, leaning back against the side of the pool, his arms stretched wide. 'So, you wanted names? Sure. You had me, Lily, Innes–'

'Innes?' Michail confirmed. 'Your romantic partner?'

'That's right and then just the girls–'

Katerina frowned. 'Girls?'

'Yeah, models, actresses. Here to promote the Saturnalia... follow me about like kittens...' He grinned and gave a soft meow, grotesquely imitating a cat. 'Social videos, photos. Nobody can resist a bikini shot, right?'

'The Saturnalia?' Katerina whipped her phone out, sure that she had heard it before. 'That's right, it's quite the event?'

Alek shrugged. 'For the lucky few. Anyway, that's about all I can tell you. We partied – fairly hard – Teddy joined in with our group. Easy to see why: he's alone, we're having a good time, then he leaves to see some girl. Jesus...' He rubbed his forehead. 'Reckon we can order some drinks up here?'

'Inadvisable until you have completed my questions,' Michail replied. 'Alcohol clouds the memory. You say that Teddy left? Do you remember at what time?'

Alek laughed and pushed himself out of the pool, the water sloshing down his front in careless swathes. 'Somewhere between the vodka and the dancing. I wasn't paying attention to him. Avoided him, to be honest. That party was the first time he'd actually managed to muscle his way in.'

Without drying himself, he padded back into the room towards the bar and began inspecting the bottles. 'But I can't give you an exact time,' he said, pouring himself a liberal measure of rum. 'It was dark, I remember that much.'

He took a swig from his glass and looked to and from Michail and Katerina. 'Are we finished here? Like I said, I don't really know how he ended up drowning himself.'

As he took another sip, Katerina narrowed her eyes; the healthy-living affirmation lifestyle seemed a world away from the real Alek Knox. The persona he portrayed over social media was alcohol-free, she was certain.

'Teddy travelled here alone according to Lily. Was he helping organise the Saturnalia too?' Katerina asked.

Alek downed the remainder of his glass. 'He said he worked in finance or something? Youngish, rich... they litter these sorts of places solo; always looking for the next score, the contact, the deal, the girl. He must have thought he'd died and gone to heaven when he found out he was the only other guest here. He didn't waste any time in trying to hang on–'

'But what was his role?'

Alek stared at her for a couple of seconds, presumably shocked to have been interrupted. 'You'll need to ask Lily, she's the admin girl. Like I say, he was a money guy – probably making sure everything we were putting out there was investor friendly. That'd explain him hanging about.' He shrugged. 'But I didn't talk to him more than necessary. I don't know, he was probably keen to get a load of selfies with us, boost his reach, poor guy really. Feel for him, you know?'

'Must be difficult being so popular,' Katerina said.

Alek looked at her for a moment, his eyes suggestive of something that she couldn't quite put her finger on. What was it? Greed? Pride? Whatever it was, it made her feel that she wanted to appear taller, stronger, in his company.

'Not as difficult as it is being a nobody,' Alek finally said, speaking for the first time like he wasn't putting on a bravado. He waved a hand over his face, as if trying to dispel the cloud of gravitas and laughed. 'Anyway, Teddy was the only other guest here, it's not like the sycophants outnumbered us.' With that, he placed his glass on the coffee table and raised his eyebrows at Michail. 'All good, then?'

'Not at all,' replied Michail. 'Your answers have been vague at best.'

Katerina jumped in before Alek could respond. 'You're free to go,' she said. 'Enjoy the rest of your stay.'

'Got a ton to get on with,' he mumbled under his breath, before sauntering out of the room.

As soon as she was sure he'd gone, Katerina collapsed onto the armchair, inhaling deeply. 'Quite a first day,' she said, more to herself than Michail.

Michail seemed to be unsure of what to do in response. He walked behind the chair, then in front of it, then checked the terrace, before returning with a firm expression on his face. She opened her mouth, but he spoke first, holding out a hand to silence her – a gesture that she used to hate, but now felt oddly grateful for.

'Katerina,' he began. He brought his elbows to his sides and pointed his hands towards her simultaneously. She suspected that this was his way of focusing his attention upon her, but he instead resembled someone doing a robot impression.

'You're back.'

'Yes,' she said. 'I–'

'No.' He stepped forward and then back again. She stared up at him, holding her breath at what he was about to say. 'I would like to speak, if it's all right with you. You see, things have changed since you have been gone. I must melt my mould's wax–'

'What...?'

'Katerina, please, listen.' His voice grew small, far smaller than she ever wanted to hear it. The ugly claws of guilt groped through her guts, and she crossed her arms, as if she could defend herself from what she had done, the lies she had told. The danger she had placed everyone in. He lowered his arms and focused his eyes, she could tell, at a point just above her left shoulder.

'You lied to me,' he said. His words stuck in the air between them like spiky rock formations.

She lowered her eyes to the ground. 'Michail, it's no excuse, but I was terrified. Theo, he did things–'

'I know.' His voice softened and she raised her eyes to try and meet his, yet he continued to avoid looking at her directly.

'I didn't ever want...'

'I understand,' he said simply.

'Michail, I–'

'I need to finish,' he said, walking behind the chair as if trying to put an obstruction between them. He gripped the back of it and spoke to his hands, a muscle in his chin twitching. 'I heard about the unimaginable position that Theo put you in,' he said. 'He deserves the most severe sentence possible for what he put you through. That's why I...' he swayed forwards slightly, '... that's why I said what I said in my statement.'

'You didn't need... I didn't expect...'

'I am responsible for my own actions,' he said. He hung his head low so that he resembled a wilted flower struggling for water. She felt the hot burn of tears begin to swell behind her eyes. 'I did what I did, said what I said. But I am not sure that we can be what we were. That–' he shifted his weight to one foot and then another, '–that will prove difficult for me, Katerina.'

She stared straight ahead, the tears now pushing to the front of her eyes. She blinked, and felt a trickle slide down her cheek. 'I... I get it,' she said. She wiped her face and added, 'Thank you, though, Michail. I didn't get a chance to thank–'

'No.' He swayed again, blowing through his teeth. 'Please don't thank me.'

'Okay.' She nodded and made for the door before the sob she could feel brewing in her chest exploded from her.

'I would like it if we could remain professional,' he said. 'That would be good, since my integrity has been compromised.'

She didn't turn to face him. She didn't want him seeing her like this. 'Okay,' she whispered, her voice torn. Then, before she fled from the room to find a corner to hide in, she said, 'The wax melting thing – it's an analogy, isn't it? I'm glad you're talking about your feelings, Michail. That's brilliant.'

He didn't reply, so she closed the door gently behind her and covered her face with her hands before running down the corridor.

Sofia narrowed her eyes as Yiorgos helped himself to a gin and tonic from the bar, before deciding that the day had been long enough and asked him to pour her one. The pool area made a fairly pleasant makeshift meeting place whilst they waited. They had been offered rooms for the duration of the investigation, and, in lieu of finding suitable last-minute accommodation during high season, she had accepted. After taking a long sip, she leant against the back of her barstool and addressed the team. 'The Aegina station's too small for us, so it looks like we'll be running the investigation from here–'

'Highly irresponsible,' said Michail. 'We could be amongst potential suspects.'

'No,' replied Sofia, trying not to lose her temper. The return of Katerina seemed to have propelled Michail to new heights of professional enthusiasm, something she had not thought possible. Unfortunately, this meant he seemed to feel the need to interrogate her every decision. She sighed. 'All the guests' stories match up – Teddy left Saturn House at some point last night, most likely to head into town – there was a small gig on the harbourside. Nothing suspicious has turned up in his room and all the guests have willingly submitted DNA and prints. We still don't know if he was meeting anyone, and, if he was, whom. If you're worried about being amongst suspects, then you'll need to apply that logic to the whole island. Plus, remember this is only a suspected murder – we don't know anything for sure yet.'

'There's something odd about Alek Knox,' Katerina piped up. Sofia had noticed her face was a little puffy after returning from the interviews, but judged it best to let her get on with it. Today had always promised to be difficult. 'Least of all his drinking. He preaches sobriety constantly on his social media accounts.'

'I concur,' said Michail. 'He was very vague even though I specifically asked him not to be.'

'The girlfriend was frustrating too,' Yiorgos said. 'Too much money, too little sense, if you ask me.'

'Noted. Although being an idiot doesn't make you guilty of anything,' Sofia replied. 'They'd been partying a lot.' She glanced down at her notes to make sure she'd got the name correct. 'Innes, the girlfriend, attested to that–'

'The models who Alek thinks follow him around like kittens,' Michail said. 'Did they add anything to the picture of last night? A detail that we don't yet know?'

'No.' Sofia shook her head and folded her arms. 'The main theme seems to be that everyone was too drunk, too out of it, to remember anything specific. Until forensics comes back to us, I'm afraid we might need to call it a night.'

A 'coooooey!' sounded from the path that led from the hotel to the pool area. Sofia grimaced. 'Oh not her again.'

Lily emerged from the path, now changed into a black silk kimono and – it did not escape Sofia's notice – very high, very expensive stiletto heels. 'Here you all are!'

She eyed Yiorgos's and Sofia's drinks and, not altogether convincingly, added, 'Please do help yourself to the bar. We want you to feel like guests here at Saturn House, Domenico insists.'

'Domenico?' Sofia asked.

'The owner of the members club group,' Michail interjected. 'He is a self-made millionaire and lives in London, although he's from Rome originally.'

'You've been doing your homework.' Lily laughed. 'But yes, we spoke this afternoon and he's keen for you to settle in.'

She flitted behind the bar and took out five glasses. 'Here, try some pistachio liqueur, it's my own brand. Domenico is always super keen to kindle our entrepreneurial spirit! So, whilst living here, I started this since the island's famous for pistachios... it's selling unbelievably well back home... anyway, *yamas*, everyone!'

She held her glass up to the sky and waited for them all to follow suit. Reluctantly, they raised their glasses. Sofia eyed Lily's concoction with suspicion before tasting it. Yiorgos smacked his lips as if it was the most disgusting thing he'd ever drunk. Sofia wondered what the locals thought of this woman's butchering of their prized delicacy. Of course, Londoners would lap this sort of thing up – she had a feeling that Lily might have a knack for successfully marketing unoriginal products for twenty times its worth to people with the right amount of cash.

'Another?'

'Definitely not, Ms Woodstow, we are technically still on duty,' Michail replied.

'Oh... yes... about that...' Lily rifled about in an expensive-looking white leather handbag and pulled out a memory stick. 'The security footage you asked for,' she announced proudly, handing it to Sofia. 'For the time you said – the last week, all the way up to this afternoon.'

'Thank you.' Sofia took the memory stick and reached for her laptop. 'Any idea when the rooms might be ready?' She waited for the files to load.

'Oh! Yes! Any time now. The cleaners are just finishing their rounds.'

'Cleaners?' Sofia drummed her fingernails impatiently upon the marble bar. 'We didn't interview any cleaners.'

'No, you didn't,' replied Lily.

Sofia tried her best not to seem irritable, but this woman seemed intent on rubbing her up the wrong way. She couldn't work out whether she was being purposefully obstructive to protect her oh-so important guests, or was just genuinely dense. Sofia removed her sunglasses so she could give Lily her best imperious stare. 'We need to interview everyone who has access to Saturn House,' she said, slowing her words so she could be sure that Lily would follow. 'That includes the cleaners.'

'Oh!' Lily brought her hands to her mouth. 'I see – my bad, totally my bad! To tell you the truth, I didn't even think to ask them... I often forget they're here at all!' She gave a short tinkle of laughter which stopped short when Sofia pursed her lips. 'That can be arranged. I'll send you a list of the names who were here last night,' Lily confirmed, moving her head in a manner that reminded Sofia of a demented lapdog.

'Good.' Sofia looked at her screen. 'Hang on, before you go – there's only one file on this memory stick called "Lily's office". I need footage of the entire complex.'

'Oh!' Lily's hands flew to her mouth again – a gesture that was wearing thin, to say the least.

'Oh?' Sofia pressed.

'Well, you see.' Lily raised her eyebrows as if she was letting Sofia into a much-coveted secret. 'This is a highly exclusive place. Our high-net worth guests wouldn't want cameras in their private space.'

Sofia stared at her for a second, before clasping her hands into a tight ball. 'But the pool area, the corridors, the various bars dotted about the complex – that's not private space, it's public–'

'It's private,' said Lily breezily. 'A home away from home, that's what we provide at Saturn House. It's the same for all our residences.'

'You mean to tell me that we have no footage at all of Teddy Menkopf's last hours in the hotel?' Sofia heard the quiver of frustration in her own voice.

'Oh... oh, well no, I'm sorry, I didn't realise it was so

important... but if it was just an accident then what does it... I mean, surely we can imagine...'

A buzz sounded from Sofia's handbag. She ignored Lily while she stuttered through a long line of unintelligible sentences and answered it, turning her back to the bar. After a minute, she nodded, a firm, sharp movement, and hung up.

Spinning about on the bar stool to face them all, she said, 'It matters a great deal.' She looked at her team. 'That was forensics – this is officially a murder investigation. Which means, Ms Woodstow, you can tell Domenico we'll be staying indefinitely.'

Michail stood before his new whiteboard and gave a satisfied nod. Yiorgos sat with his legs outstretched on the bed, Katerina on the floor, her knees drawn to her chest. Sofia came out of the bathroom, a cold, wet towel pressed against her forehead. 'Michail, why are there paintings on your bathroom floor?'

He had taken the liberty of removing the artwork from the walls and storing them in the bathroom. He understood that art was a matter of taste – he would never question that – but the garish mishap of bright colours and strange digital shapes (complete with a QR code, preposterously telling him that he could purchase an NFT version) had done nothing but distract him. The only piece of art he had approved of thus far was what looked like a Roman sculpture of the god Saturn in the corner of the lobby. At least the hotel had committed to their anti-Hellenic preferences in this respect, meaning it made some sort of logical sense at least.

'Whoever oversaw the room's interior design clearly did not consider the rich artistic and archaeological history of the island. The paintings seemed out of place; blank walls are preferable.'

Sofia regained her position at the desk by the French

windows. She didn't respond and he sensed an unusual air of distraction about her.

'Where did you get a whiteboard from at this hour?' This, from Yiorgos, a fatigued slur blurring his vowels and consonants. Michail's eyes stung with the lateness of the hour, however, he jogged energetically on the spot, attempting to infer a sense of exuberance and tenacity into the sluggish room.

'Ms Woodstow sourced it for me,' he said. 'She has proven herself quite useful, despite her other irritating tendencies.'

Sofia laughed drily, running her hands through her hair. 'Right, Michail, let's get to it – no time like the present.'

'Indeed, just as Mr Knox explained to me earlier...'

He removed the lid of his pen with a slightly exaggerated arm motion to show that he meant business. 'Now, whilst I realise that, for reasons previously discussed, my Myth Buster Unit will not be reinstated–'

'Michail,' Sofia interrupted him. 'As I have explained on numerous occasions, we don't need a Myth Buster Unit because not every crime is connected to a myth.'

'Correct. However, the reason and logic that our cultural history inspires is surely always a good place to...' His voice trailed off as he identified a 'Level Critical' scowl appearing on Sofia's face. This, he knew, was a strong signal for him to stop talking. Over the last year, he had developed a useful grading system based on the specifics of her facial expressions. When her eyebrows moved so close that they were almost touching, he knew to relent.

'...while I realise that it will, beyond question, not be reinstated, I would like to propose that we hold regular meetings here, in my room, as we have done in the past. I feel that this way of working–'

'Yes, yes, that's fine,' Sofia interjected again. The 'Level Critical' moved to 'Serious' – an improvement. 'Can we just get to it? It's late. I'm tired. This shouldn't take long, it's not like we have any suspects yet, as the powers that be have kindly reminded me.'

Michail nodded and turned to his board. 'Preliminary observations: the substantial number of recreational drugs found in Teddy's blood make it seem, to the unobservant eye, that he drowned due to intoxication. However, there are two things that indicate this not to be the case. The first, the atypical slashes to his wrists–'

'Didn't you say they struggled to identify what sort of instrument was used?' Katerina spoke very quietly, raising her head as if scared to draw attention to herself.

'That's right.' Sofia nodded. 'The wounds are too precise for a knife; the report suggests that some sort of scalpel could have been used. Odd.'

'–imply an unconventional weapon, as well as the fact that the wounds were administered post mortem.' Michail scribbled notes on the board as he continued. 'The second thing is the detail about the windpipe.'

Sofia read from her screen. 'Slight compression to the windpipe consistent with light strangulation but also force being applied from above the shoulders... here, they've included a diagram.'

'Seems a strange angle to strangle someone at.' Yiorgos yawned.

'Unless you're doing it whilst holding the person underwater.' Katerina squinted at Sofia's screen. 'That's what forensics is suggesting?'

'I believe so,' Sofia agreed. 'So, someone drowned him before slashing his wrists?'

'Precisely.' Michail stepped back from the board. 'It makes no sense.'

'Someone was obviously trying to make it look like a

suicide,' Yiorgos said, his eyes half closing. 'Oldest trick in the book.'

'That's exactly what doesn't add up,' Michail said, trying hard to inject a healthy amount of disapproval in his voice at Yiorgos's lackadaisical approach. 'Why go to the trouble of cutting Teddy's wrists if he was already dead? Surely, with the drugs in his system, an accidental drowning would be plausible. Forensics may not even have looked for signs of foul play had his wrists not been cut. The question we need to ask is why the killer decided to overcomplicate matters.'

Sofia was massaging her temples. 'I see what you mean. If it was premeditated, then they certainly didn't think it through. Perhaps a crime of passion? Although, that doesn't explain why someone would mutilate the body. It feels like a straightforward murder until you look more closely and then–'

'It leads you one way and then another,' Michail finished. 'Not quite planned, not quite unplanned. Something in between.' Michail drew a large question mark on the board before turning to Sofia again. 'No DNA traces? Items on his person?'

Sofia shook her head. 'Nothing that gives us any clues, just his necklace. Oh, and another "T" tattooed just above his right ankle, we wouldn't have been able to see it on the beach. A bit egotistical if you ask me. I'd love to see if Teddy returned to his room that night, but, thanks to this place's frankly ludicrous attitude to security cameras, that'll take a while. We'll talk to local taxi firms tomorrow, see if any of them remember a man of his description, as well as see if we can access the hotel's key card records. His room search turned up absolutely nothing of note, and no sign of his phone. Oh–'

Her phone buzzed and she looked at it, again with the same withdrawn expression. Usually, she was the sharpest and most pertinent person in a room. Today, something seemed to be dragging her away. Michail waited to see if the message related to the case. After a few moments of silence, it appeared not.

'If he was naked, then surely he must have returned to his room?' Katerina asked. 'Who's wandering about like that?'

Sofia nodded absent-mindedly. Again, Michail noticed that she was slow to tear her eyes away from her screen. He wished that everyone would remain focused.

'Remember the clothes the other guests said he was wearing?' Sofia asked. 'A pretty memorable pink shirt and skinny salmon chinos – they haven't turned up in his room, nor in the wider search of the resort grounds.'

'So, someone disposed of them?' Katerina asked.

'Obviously, the murderer stripped him, wherever they did it,' Yiorgos added.

'Again, that doesn't make sense,' Michail said. 'There's no evidence of sexual violence consistent with someone stripping him and if you were trying to make the murder look like a suicide, why would you bother removing his clothes? It's a further complication, more evidence to hide. Teddy could easily have drowned in his clothes – him being naked only makes the death more suspicious.'

A fatigued silence filled the room. Michail scrunched his eyes tight, trying to squeeze the last drops of concentration from his brain. Eventually, Sofia pushed herself from the chair.

'We're tired. Let's re-tackle this first thing. Yiorgos is heading back to Athens tomorrow so let him know what clothes you want shipping over, he's happy to help. It's best if most of us remain here, keep an eye on things. There's a lot to do.'

'Very sensible,' replied Michail.

'I'll leave early in the morning to ask local businesses if they have cameras,' Katerina said. 'Security cameras on the island seem a bit sparse to be honest.'

Michail gave her a restrained nod, careful not to catch her

eye, and turned promptly to view his board again. It was important that he maintained a professional distance from her, which meant keeping communication as unemotive as possible.

'Good.' Sofia flexed her hands so the joints made a soft crack and gestured for everyone to leave. 'Michail, remember to get some sleep.'

'Of course,' he replied, unable to take his eyes from the board, which was already resembling an intricate puzzle of ideas that pushed and pulled upon his mind. 'As soon as I have gone through the footage of Lily's office.'

Sofia rubbed her forehead, displaying what Michail identified as a 'Moderate' expression. 'That can wait until tomorrow; I need you on top form, really. It's been a long day. Anyway, I'm not sure how much use–'

He held his breath, torn between a strong suspicion that she wasn't in the mood for arguments and the pull of responsibility to explore every available thread before bed. She placed her hands on her hips, awaiting his response.

'Order received,' he replied finally, his cheeks growing a little red. Sofia narrowed her eyes and, caught in a wide yawn, let him be.

In his underwear, Michail sat upright in his unreasonably large bed, laptop balanced on his legs. It turned out that Sofia had been correct: the footage of Lily's office revealed nothing but the fact that she often worked late into the night posting pictures of her pistachio liqueur bottles on social media. The tug of sleep encroaching, he reached over to turn off his bedside lamp. Just as he moved, he caught a flicker of movement on the screen. His head snapped back towards the laptop, his fingers tingling with excitement.

A blur of movement whipped across the office in a stream of smoky action. It took Michail a moment to realise the figure was a small woman propelling herself forwards with tremendous force. Her hands were outstretched, reaching for Lily. He paused the video to make sure he wasn't making an error. Indeed, the woman had thrown herself across Lily's desk. The still image allowed him to see the utter shock upon Lily's face: her mouth was slack and open, her eyes bulging. Pressing play, he watched the woman attempt to claw at Lily's face in wild, animal motions, over and over.

Lily opened her mouth in a silent scream for help, before the woman yanked a handful of Lily's hair in a brutal fist. The force pulled Lily onto the desk, her legs kicking, her laptop flung to the floor, as she was dragged over it. Michail flinched as the first kick landed in Lily's abdomen. Then another. She curled her body into a ball, her eyes scrunched closed, her mouth pressed tight in a resolute mound as if waiting, resigned for the attack to be over.

Eventually, the woman stopped. She backed away from Lily's trembling body, her lips moving, her eyes steady. Whatever she was saying, Michail was willing to guess that it wasn't pleasant, because Lily, who had wrenched herself to a sitting position, began to weep. The tears seemed to anger her attacker because, taking a breath large enough to make her chest visibly swell, she raged towards Lily once again, taking her by the side of the head and pulling her face towards hers. Lily tried to pull away, but the woman shook her like she was a rag doll, her mouth pressed close to her ear. Then, she released her and Lily fell to the floor, covering her face with her hands as the woman left.

Michail's heart pounded as he processed the scene. He rewound the footage, watching the vicious blows play out in reverse, until he got a clear, frontal view of the attacker.

Zooming in, he studied the image before cross-checking it with the named photos Lily had provided earlier. Then, he kicked off his sheets and hurried to the whiteboard. Next to the large question mark, he drew a large square and wrote within it: *The hotel cleaner (Irene Kanatas) assaulted Lily Woodstow at 12.30am on the night of Teddy Menkopf's murder.*

Sick

The water rushed along the sides of Sofia's body as she pushed herself through the pool, her head submerged. Holding her breath, she closed her eyes and let her mind drift to where it had been threatening to go yesterday. Had he needed to tell her in a text? She wasn't upset – she wasn't the type to get upset about things she had no control over. Least of all ex-husbands. But a text? Surely the news warranted a phone call at the very least. Short. Sharp. The news of the child, his child, condensed to a few digital silent characters.

The thought sent a nervous jolt through her muscles, her skin seeming to tighten and shrink, as if it was trying to extinguish the memories. Her head snapped backwards and she resurfaced, her arms flailing above her head, her mouth gasping for air. Why had he told her? There was no need for her to know. He could have done this without her ever finding out. She didn't plan on going back to London. It wasn't as if she'd met the wife. She didn't need to meet the child. It was cruel. Cruel and tactless and reckless. As if he had forgotten. As if he was trying to forget.

She wafted her arms in the water and drifted to the middle

of the pool, watching the sky. She hated how blue and innocent it was, gaping down at her with its fluffy dimples. It saw the horrors of the world. How did it keep returning with the same optimism, day in and day out? She closed her eyes, wishing the sky and the pain and the dead bodies away.

Sofia. Her name penetrated her memories. She hadn't visited them for a long time. They felt too smooth, too well-formed. *Sofia*. There it was again. His lips, so pink and uncracked by time. *Sofia*. His arms, just past the point of fleshy toddlerhood, firmer, full of potential and promises. *Sofia*. But he didn't call her that, *Sofia*. He never called her that. He never would have.

'Sofia!'

She opened her eyes and flopped her head to one side. Katerina stood, in full uniform, at the side of the pool. It occurred to her that she could tell Katerina to find her later, that she was having some alone time, that it was too early. Of course, she didn't voice any of these things. Instead, she swam towards the edge of the pool.

Katerina started speaking in a fevered manner, her words garbled and rushed. 'I couldn't sleep after Michail called last night–'

Sofia felt her lips twitch: she had been certain that the office footage wouldn't have thrown up anything significant – Michail's discovery would only serve as further incentive for him to push himself to the limits. On top of everything, she could do without worrying about him. He'd been making good progress up until now. To throw him into this situation unprepared had been a mistake. She hadn't thought that his reaction would be quite so dramatic.

Sofia sighed, squinting up at Katerina's drawn face. 'That makes two of us. I highly doubt that Lily simply "forgot" about the cleaner, like she said. I'll be interested to see how she explains that.'

'It looked like a pretty violent attack, maybe she's frightened of her?'

'Maybe.'

Sofia gestured for Katerina to pass her a towel and hoisted herself from the pool. She patted herself dry in silence, keeping her chin dipped and her eyes lowered. Before Aegina, the last time she had seen Katerina had been at Theo's trial, thin and fragile, purple half-moons beneath her eyes, hunched in the back row, her mother's arm unwavering about her shoulders. Katerina's shadow shifted upon the white tiles like a half-formed memory; it was like she expected Sofia to acknowledge the situation, her return, the past year. But what was there left to say? Were the shoe on the other foot, would she want to be reminded of what Theo had done to her? To be forever painted as the victim? That wouldn't help. The best thing Katerina could do was move on and forget. The mind was more powerful than most people thought – with enough willpower – it could block things out. Roaring, painful things. It could diminish them to a whimper, then a muffle, and then to silence.

Sofia wrapped the towel around her wet hair. 'It'd be better if you and Michail worked together, you are partners. Where have you been?'

Katerina gave a small intake of breath at the mention of Michail. Clearly, both parties were finding their reunion difficult. 'He's, er, he's talking to the manager about the key card records. I went to catch the local cafés at opening time to see if they remembered a man of Teddy's description... nothing yet.'

Sofia narrowed her eyes and sighed. She hadn't pictured this conversation happening in her swimming suit, but needs must. 'Do you think you're up to this, Katerina? I hadn't anticipated your first case to be a murder investigation on an island. It's a lot, given the circumstances. If you're finding it too much–'

Katerina's eyes widened, the whites forming desperate circles around the deep brown of her irises. 'Too much? No... no... I'm so grateful to be back. I'm grateful to you for having me and to Michail for–'

'No need to retread old ground.' Sofia's voice was clipped, and she cut her off with an iron gaze. She had chosen to ignore the inconsistencies in Michail's story surrounding the cave that night. If she had thought for a second that there was a chance Katerina couldn't be trusted, then she would have taken the issue up. She was old enough to know that things were rarely clean cut, and, in the end, Katerina had risked her life for the right side. As far as she was concerned, the inquiry's result was final: Katerina was innocent. There was nothing more to it. There would be nothing more to it.

Katerina didn't reply. Instead, she hung her head and mumbled, 'Well, thank you for letting me back.'

'It wasn't my decision,' Sofia replied. Please, God, she did not have the energy for sentimentality. 'The charge was dropped and you've recuperated as a victim of a terrible crime. That's all.'

Katerina gave a weak nod before her bottom lip began to quiver. Enough was enough. She folded her arms and looked her squarely in the face. 'Dwelling won't help, you know. Wake up, do the job, take the snide remarks, grit your teeth if you must, but don't dwell. It will eat you up. And I need my team strong.'

'I don't think Michail and Yiorgos will ever like me again.' Katerina whispered the words as if she was afraid they might come true if uttered too loudly.

'You don't need them to like you. Anyway,' Sofia pulled her

robe over her shoulders, 'Yiorgos will come around, you know what he's like, takes a while.'

'And Michail?'

Sofia pressed the back of her hand against her forehead to wipe away the beads of sweat that had already formed. 'You know him better than me, but he'll be thinking of nothing else but the case. Use that as your starting point, perhaps.'

Katerina exhaled and rocked backwards on her feet as if releasing a great tension. Then, although her eyes were glassy, she managed to smile. Very briefly, Sofia saw a glimmer of Katerina's former spirited self. Happiness hadn't completely deserted her, then. She was lucky. She should kindle her second chance, let it burn and crackle and cling on to it with all her might. Because for some, the flame did little more than smoke from the ashes, black and dusty.

Michail started as a young woman catapulted into the lobby, her mouth open and panting with breathlessness. Her eyes fell upon him and she charged forwards, face slack with panic.

'Have you seen him? My *baba*? He works here, please – I need–'

'I... if you tell me his name, then I am certain I can help...'

'He works here – look, I don't have time to explain – I just... someone's *died*, you know! It's all over the news!'

'Yes, I am aware of–'

Before he could finish his sentence, she pushed past him and made for the manager's office behind the main desk, her sandals slapping erratically against the floor. He darted to block her way, spreading his arms wide to make it clear that she was not permitted to enter. 'This is the desk manager's office and, due to the recent murder, I cannot allow–'

'It's fine, she's my daughter.' Cigarette smoke wafted over Michail's arms as Iraklis, the desk manager, appeared in the doorway behind him.

Michail remained in position. Daughter or not, the office was off-limits until he had collected the key card records. There was a long pause, throughout which the woman stared at Michail, wearing what he identified as an expression of intense curiosity. He shook his head, realising that he might need to explain. 'There is zero possibility of you entering the office until the police have carried out the required investigations–'

'It was ransacked by your team of orangutans yesterday,' Iraklis breathed through another cloud of smoke. Michail's arms had begun to ache, but he kept resolute. It was important that he maintained an aura of authority.

'You must mean the constables, most for whom an orangutan is an unfair comparison,' he replied. The woman's lips in front of him twitched as if she was mildly amused. He kept his face straight, although noticed a tiny fluttering sensation in his chest that he had not experienced for a long while.

'We can talk here.' The woman stepped back and Michail dropped his arms, pleased that he had dissuaded her. 'I just wanted to check in, anyway; you haven't been answering my calls, *Baba*. I was worried sick. I got the first boat over.'

They moved into the lobby, Iraklis continuing to emit an unreasonable amount of smoke. 'It's been busy,' he rumbled. Michail couldn't help but notice that the man's chest sounded volcanic; he would be well-advised to stop smoking immediately. 'The place has been swarming with police.'

'Good, well that's good.' His – far more sensible – daughter nodded. 'It's good they're taking it seriously, *Baba*, the news said his death was suspicious.'

Michail gulped down the irritation at the media for being so clearly reckless with their reporting. They'd not been permitted to share anything significant.

'Hmph.' He took another long drag. 'Lily's been buzzing about like a fruit fly, as you might imagine...' Michail did not interrupt, pleased that Iraklis had selected a much more pertinent animal comparison this time. His daughter rolled her eyes and laughed softly – apparently, she thought so too.

Michail held out his hand to her. 'Sergeant Mikras of the Special Violent Crime Unit. You have nothing to worry about in terms of your father, he is perfectly safe. The team is residing in the hotel as we complete our investigation.' He shook her hand rigorously to convey a sense of direction and steadfastness.

'Oh. Thank you, I'm Maria.'

Sofia and Katerina appeared at the main entrance. Astonishingly, Sofia had opted to wear a white robe complete with dripping wet hair. A morning swim was acceptable, of course, and arguably good for the brain; however, Michail couldn't help but worry about her. Just like last night, her behaviour was falling short of her usual whip-smart professionalism.

'Any progress on the key cards?' Sofia padded towards them, her eyes moving between Maria and Iraklis.

'I have been busy meeting Maria,' Michail replied, gesturing to his side. 'She arrived only a few moments ago to check up on her father, although I have assured her that we have everything under control.'

Sofia's eyes narrowed and, in response, Maria elaborated. 'Sorry, I probably overreacted. I don't live here and I heard the news and my mind... well...'

Iraklis took a wheezy drag from his cigarette, his eyes growing dark and small. 'I'm sure the police know what they're doing, Maria, they don't need your life story. Come on, let's get a coffee. I'm exhausted already–'

'Mr Barlas, before you go, it's imperative that I access your key card records.' Michail stepped towards him, attempting to seem casual, but acting upon the distinct impression that Iraklis was trying to hide something. Sofia folded her arms, her eyes now resembling two serpentine slits. Despite her unconventional sartorial choice, she evidently detected something similar.

Iraklis shrugged, the weight of his large shoulders sending a ripple through his rounded belly. 'Sure,' he mumbled, smacking his lips. 'It'll take a few seconds, in here, come on.'

'What records are those?' Maria asked. 'Can I help at all? *Baba* isn't always the best with technology.'

Although her interference was out of the question, Michail found the edges of his mouth twitching upwards. It was a nice change to encounter somebody so proactive and thoughtful. He wished the same could be said of his team. 'Thank you, Maria, however, I am technologically adept, so will be able to find the information we need.' She smiled back at him, her cheeks puckering into tiny pleasant dimples.

'Are you local?' Katerina produced her notepad and jabbed a pen into the air, directing the question to Maria with a slight strain to her voice. He agreed that it was a good idea to conduct some background questions with Maria, but there was no need to be quite so acerbic. Perhaps she needed to be reminded of the proper interrogation conventions.

Maria nodded, then shook her head, then nodded again before giving a nervous giggle. 'Sorry – yes and no. I grew up here, but now I live in Athens.'

'And why did you think that your father would be particularly affected by the murder?' Katerina's question was so sharp that even Sofia raised an eyebrow.

'I... well... wouldn't anyone?' Maria's dimples smoothed over as her face fell, ironed flat by what seemed like a dark memory moving behind her eyes. She looked at her father, who simply shrugged and took another drag from his cigarette. Clearly, her concern was unreciprocated.

'I can imagine that the news was a shock,' Michail interrupted, shooting Katerina a look that he hoped would encourage her to think more carefully about how she conducted herself. Assumptions should never be made, of course, but there was no reason to suspect that Maria was anything other than a dutiful daughter checking in on her father – she had only arrived on the island this morning. Random questions weren't useful in this scenario. He turned his attention to Iraklis once more. 'The key card records, Mr Barlas.'

Iraklis nodded and made for the office as Michail followed. 'Just here...' Iraklis typed his password with his index fingers and began clicking on various tabs to find the records. Maria needn't have worried – although he was slow, he seemed capable of navigating the system. 'Here... and then... ah, yes, here...' A long list of key card entries appeared on the screen.

'Could you print it out?' Michail asked, already scanning the list to find the entries for the day before yesterday.

'Er, yes... hang on...'

Michail spotted the correct date on the screen. 'Room twelve – this is Teddy's room?'

'That's right,' Iraklis replied, tearing the wrapping off a wedge of printing paper. 'You'll see all the key cards used to access his room that day. The names show up next to the times.'

Michail nodded. There was the cleaner, Irene, then a couple of entries from Teddy throughout the day, but none after mid-afternoon until 9pm. Michail leaned over to scroll downwards. After that, there wasn't another entry until 11.06pm that night. He stared at the name, blinking to make sure he was correct. But there was no doubt about it; there it was on the screen. Michail felt his fingers tapping against the side of his leg. His brain whirred as it sifted through the information being presented to it, attempting to draw conclusions, though landing instead upon question after question. *Why was he so calm? Why would he willingly show him this?* There could, of course, be a reasonable explanation. He cleared his throat, keeping his eyes upon the name as he spoke. 'Mr Barlas, it appears that you entered Teddy Menkopf's room late on the night that he was murdered.'

Katerina lay back on her bed, staring at the ceiling. The hot breeze carried through the open windows bringing with it thumps of music from Alek's poolside party. Michail and Sofia had accompanied Iraklis to the local station, leaving her behind. She closed her eyes and blew gently through her lips. Perhaps it would be better if she just slept. It wasn't as if she was bringing anything to the table. Sleep. The word was almost alien to her now. Like luxurious silk slipping through her fingers, it evaded her, tantalising her with its false promises.

Maria's face emerged at the top of her thoughts. She was beautiful – that was undeniable. Why did it matter? It didn't. Not even slightly. She groaned as she recalled the way she had questioned the poor woman. She groaned again when she recalled the look on Michail's face. Why had she cared that Michail had looked at her in that way? She didn't have a monopoly on him. She was nothing to him. He no longer considered her a friend, let alone anything more. Sofia was right – she had to focus on earning his respect again, not getting him to like her. It seemed easier said than done. A good start would be to talk to Maria properly. The look on her face when her father had been marched out of the office had been interesting – both Michail and Sofia had been preoccupied with calling the station ahead of arrival, but she had watched Maria: her eyes had flashed with the sort of panic that seemed a bit misplaced. Granted, Iraklis's key card entry was suspicious, but it was hardly the most incriminating discovery; there was nowhere near enough evidence for the police to hold him. Yet, his daughter's mouth had trembled like a child's, her hands had flown to her cheeks, her fingernails pressed against her flesh as her father had been led away.

Perhaps Maria was just dramatic. Or perhaps she was seeing things that weren't there.

The music grew louder as cheers erupted from outside. Katerina rolled off the bed and shuffled to her terrace. Alek and three women danced at the pool's edge. The women stretched their arms above their heads, elongating their already tight torsos, as Alek grinded alongside them, glass in hand. The woman with dark hair – the model Rita, as Katerina remembered from the notes – threw her head back and closed her eyes, her lips parted in an ecstatic smile; Katerina faintly heard the tinkle of laughter above the beat of the music. Was it genuine? Could she really be enjoying herself? Or was she just posing for a photograph? Alek goggled at her like he was weighing up fruit. Yet, all the girls accepted his hands, his febrile fingers, with uniform white smiles.

Alek took Innes, who seemed completely unfazed by her boyfriend's behaviour, by the waist and brought her in close. He leant in for a deep kiss, his hands raking hungrily at the back of her head. When he pulled away, they pressed their foreheads together, sharing a knowing, glinting look. She'd seen couples exchange the same look in nightclubs after kissing and it made her strongly suspect the use of some sort of illegal substance. It was good to know. Again, drugs were at odds with Alek's public persona.

Innes pulled away from Alek, her snow-blonde hair

glistening, and jumped down from the pool's edge to answer a phone call. She checked the number and her face suddenly grew serious. Katerina cocked her head to one side, her attention piqued. Innes looked over her shoulder, her hair swishing like a platinum curtain, and mouthed something to Alek to which he nodded. Then, she disappeared, phone in hand, down the walkway of olive trees.

Katerina moved quickly. As quietly as possible, she ran down the stairs opposite her room and scooted through the lobby. From the entrance, she could see Innes leaning against a pillar, holding her phone up before her, speaking in a very animated manner. Katerina carefully pushed the glass door open and slipped through it, keeping herself obscured behind the oversized potted plants that lined the steps. Crouching down, she strained to hear what Innes was saying.

'Sick? Yes, look, I'm serious. He was sick... I'm telling you...'

Innes paused and adjusted the AirPods in her ears, as if the person on the other side of the call was raising their voice. Katerina pushed herself onto all fours to try to see who was on the screen, but the sun was too bright.

'Look, I think I would know. He was sick, okay? But there is honestly nothing for you to...' Katerina's heart began to pound. The conversation didn't make much sense, but she felt a great weight of significance in the words. What was Innes talking about? 'No, no, I'll let you know. You can relax, I mean it. I don't think it has anything to do with it.'

Innes hung up and exhaled loudly, staring into the space in front of her for a few moments. Then, she readjusted her bikini and strutted back down the path to rejoin the party, leaving Katerina crouched behind the plant pot wondering what on earth she had just heard.

Sofia rested her forehead against the back of the front seat of the car. She could feel Michail's expectant eyes upon her; he was waiting for her to offer some wisdom, to lead. The weight of the phone in her pocket was heavy with the restless tug of the message that she hadn't yet devised a reply for. She closed her eyes and sat back, folding her arms.

'Did you buy any of that?'

Michail, already sitting with an iron-rigid back, consulted his notepad. 'It is difficult to know for sure,' he said. 'Mr Barlas was adamant about his key card having been stolen. His alibi is strong; it appears he did indeed leave work at 5pm, as he told us, before heading to the café. The staff have corroborated his story. We were right to let him go home. I don't believe we would have uncovered anything sufficiently incriminating. However, I have the feeling that he is not telling us everything.'

'Exactly,' Sofia agreed, looking out of the window at the turquoise sea. 'My gut tells me he's telling the truth about the key card. I don't see why else he would so willingly hand over the records. But it feels like there's something else. I think it's wise to assume that whoever entered Teddy's room that night has something to do with his murder. Unfortunately for us, if they have any sense at all, they'll have wiped the card for prints even if we could find it.'

Michail sat very still, as he usually did when he was thinking deeply. Eventually, he said, 'I have a strong feeling that we are misinterpreting something that we have already come across.'

'Oh?' Sofia widened her eyes. 'Any idea what that is, then?'

He shook his head, completely ignoring her sarcasm. 'Usually, the facts begin to work together. One leads to another and then another until the mystery is solved. However, for this case the board is still a random mess.'

'Your whiteboard?'

'Yes.' He nodded and sunk low into his seat, his chin pressing against his chest. Clasping his hands together, his brow furrowed. 'What did you think of Maria?'

The question completely threw her. 'Maria? Iraklis's daughter? What did I think of her?'

'Correct. Maria Barlas. Did you form an opinion?'

'I... well, I only spoke to her for a few minutes.' She tried to picture the scene in the lobby. 'Katerina certainly wasn't enamoured.'

'No,' Michail said, his face giving nothing away. 'Her questioning methods followed absolutely no protocol – I have already made a note of that.' He stared straight ahead, blinking at slow, methodical intervals.

'It makes sense she was concerned about her father's well-being,' said Sofia. 'Iraklis is all she has left family-wise – the station police confirmed that.'

Michail pressed his lips together, still apparently lost in his thoughts.

'Is there something else?'

'Yes,' he answered quickly, giving a sharp nod. 'Yes. I have conducted a thorough audit of Teddy's public social media posts. It seems that Alek represented him accurately. His recent photos are all of the resort. He gave the impression that he wanted to impress people.'

'I see...' She didn't comment on the abrupt change of subject.

Michail pulled out his phone to show her. 'His final post, a selfie, shows him wearing the pink shirt and the salmon chinos by the pool.'

She studied the image. Indeed, Teddy posed, looking up to the camera, his face beaming with self-satisfaction. 'His clothes still haven't shown up. We've searched everywhere.'

Michail frowned. 'We're missing both the key card and the

clothes. They've either been destroyed, hidden, or they're still with the culprit.'

'Yes.' Sofia leaned back, stretching her legs out as far as she could in the footwell. 'If I were the killer, I'd have burned them by now, but, as we know, killers don't always behave sensibly. Unfortunately, we have no profile to work with.' She observed him closely, his serious profile thrown into stark contrast against the bright seascape glittering past the window. She bit her lip, dubious as to whether now was the time to bring it up, before saying, 'How are things going with Katerina?'

At the mention of her name, he visibly tensed. 'Very well, thank you for checking, Major Sampson.'

Sofia sighed, wishing she could create some space between her legs and the hot leather of the car seat. She hadn't had a chance to shower after her swim and chlorine lingered on her skin, making her clammy and uncomfortable. 'You should tell me if you're experiencing problems, Michail. I wasn't expecting it to be plain sailing.'

'You have noticed that I am not performing sufficiently?' he asked, his forehead screwing up into what looked like deep concern.

She shook her head. 'No. But I have noticed that you are becoming more reserved, less of a team player. You've achieved a lot, Michail, and you've made huge professional leaps over the past year. I wouldn't want anything to ruin that.'

He looked as though she had slapped him in the face. She shifted against the leather seat, sweat pooling at the small of her back. 'This isn't meant as a criticism—'

'I am allowing personal feelings to get in the way of solving the crime?' His words filled the car so earnestly that she didn't know how to reply.

Eventually, she said, carefully, 'I'm not blaming you. But Katerina is back and, for this case at least, you're partners. I would think about trying to find a way to work together again, even if it's only temporary. For your own good, just try and find a way?'

The car pulled up on Saturn House's drive, past the row of olive trees. She exhaled, looking forward to her impending shower. Before getting out, she said to Michail, 'Does that make sense?'

'Yes,' he said. 'I must find a way to work with Katerina. So far, my efforts have been insufficient.'

Something about the way he said this didn't fill her with a great amount of confidence, but, before she could respond, Lily appeared at the top of the marble staircase, wearing yet another pair of designer stilettos and a silk kimono wrapped around a white swimming costume. Sofia reluctantly opened the car door.

'You wanted to chat?' Lily descended the stairs, her pink lips puckered with anxiety. 'That's right, isn't it? You wanted to see me? That girl said...'

'Officer Galanis was correct.' Michail strode around the side of the car and levelled Lily a concerted stare. 'We have some further questions for you. Officer Galanis and I will interview you in room nine in approximately ten minutes, if you are free?'

Sofia noticed a slight tremor in the corner of Lily's jaw. That was interesting – what did she think Michail needed to ask her about? Lily had handed over the footage of her attack – she must have known that they would watch it. And anyway, she had been the victim, not the perpetrator. Lily took a small breath and checked her phone, giving a prim nod.

'I'm meeting with some press ahead of the Saturnalia in half an hour... if we can make it quick...'

'We will be as efficient as possible,' Michail said, walking past her briskly and flexing his knuckles as if preparing for some sort of physical fight. 'As you might imagine, we consider finding

Teddy Menkopf's murderer a greater priority than your summer event.'

———————

Michail stood alert and ready in the same makeshift interview room as they had used yesterday. His conversation with Sofia had proved very useful indeed: he had clearly allowed his judgement to be clouded by his personal feelings about Katerina's return. Worse than that, he had not seen how he had allowed his emotions to interfere with the smooth running of the investigation. Unacceptable. Luckily, he had already identified a clear course of restorative action. Difficult as it would be, he had to find a way to ensure that he and Katerina worked well together. Although he suspected his counsellor would disagree, this meant hiding away all Katerina-related emotions somewhere unfindable. There would need to be a blockage in the syphon where they were concerned. Then he could return to making rational and useful decisions: the balance of his mind would return. This method would allow him to keep his emotions completely hidden: the cave... the lies... he would box them away. Sofia was right: he must do everything within his power to ensure an efficient working partnership.

'Thanks for calling me up.' Katerina was by the window, her arms folded, the hot breeze blowing her hair in gentle wisps about her face. Michail had decided to leave the windows open in favour of turning the air conditioning on – not only was it better for the environment, as he had explained, but he was growing fond of the sound of the sea and its soothing effects.

'It is no trouble. We are a team and, therefore, we must work as one.' He arranged his face in the most encouraging expression that he could muster, without adding that Sofia had insisted that Katerina join him in the interview, despite her English not being fluent. For some reason, instead of matching his new optimism, Katerina dropped her eyes to the ground. He opened his mouth to clarify his position – she seemed to have misheard – when Lily opened the door.

'Ms Woodstow, please take a seat,' he said, assuming his place on the sofa as Katerina joined him.

Lily flashed them both a smile and held her index finger up as she read a message on her phone. Then, she folded her legs and leant back on the chair. 'Honestly, it's been a day already.'

'Yes.' Michail frowned: it was only 3pm. 'We watched the security footage from your office...' He paused to allow enough time for Lily to react. She blinked, her eyes widening before her chest rose as she inhaled.

'You saw it then? Oh God...' Her hands flew to her mouth. Michail looked to Katerina who had cocked her head to one side, wondering how much she had understood.

'You gave us the footage,' she said, to his surprise, in impressive English. 'You must have known that we were specifically looking for any events in the lead-up or on the night of the murder. This can't be a shock to you.' Katerina leaned in towards Lily, her elbows resting on her knees as Michail fought to seem unsurprised at the assuredness of his partner.

Lily nodded in tiny sparrow-like flinches, as if every one of Katerina's words came as an expected blow. 'Yes, yes, I know... I suppose... I suppose I didn't want to draw attention to it... obviously I knew you'd see eventually...'

'Attention to what?' Katerina asked.

It seemed impossible, but Lily's eyes opened even wider. 'Oh God, I feel so bad... you must think I'm an idiot.'

Michail cleared his throat. 'At the moment, perhaps, until you can offer us a reasonable explanation.'

Lily's wet eyes froze, and, for a moment, the watery swell of her bright blue irises glazed over. Then, she bit her bottom lip and replied, 'She wanted more pay. I... we don't pay the support staff at all well here, actually. It's something that the locals have been going on about for a while. She started asking for a raise and I wouldn't give it to her.' She shrugged and shook her head. 'It's head office's call anyway, not mine. I kept telling her.'

'So, she attacked you because she wanted more money?' Katerina asked, her voice landing flat against the coffee table between them.

'S-she has a short fuse,' Lily stuttered. 'I didn't know what to do. I... well, I sacked her immediately after that.'

'You didn't tell us because you were ashamed that you didn't pay her enough?' Michail pressed.

'That, and... well... I didn't want a fuss made... causing trouble for Irene. I know what it looks like, but she's a good person really, at heart.'

'How do you know that?' Katerina stood and strolled around the back of the sofa.

'She's just a cleaner!' Lily exclaimed.

'You were protecting her?' Michail asked. He opened the laptop on the table and tapped the space bar. The attack played out before them, Lily's silent cries, writhing helplessly on the screen. 'Why would you want to protect someone who did this to you?'

'I was embarrassed, okay?' Lily began to cry. Reaching into her bag for a tissue, she dabbed beneath her eyes. It came away smeared with black and beige streaks. 'I drove this woman, this person to do... that! She just wanted more money and I didn't do anything. I didn't even send an email. So she...' Her words broke into a small sob. She sniffed, throwing her shoulders back. 'It's not a big deal, is it? I mean, I gave you the footage... I knew you'd watch it. I know I should have told you immediately, but I... I just didn't think it was relevant with everything going on!' She sobbed again, this time more loudly.

'A violent attack on the night that one of your guests was murdered is very relevant,' replied Katerina, making her way back to the sofa. 'What is she searching for?'

'What?' Lily's eyes darted up, filled with confusion.

Katerina pointed to the screen. 'She's looking for something, see? What's she looking for?'

Lily shook her head. 'Money? Probably money, like I said.'

'Is that what she's shouting about too?' Katerina pushed the laptop closer to Lily.

'Yes, yes...' Lily answered, closing her eyes as if the memory was too painful for her. 'She was shouting about money. I couldn't understand everything...'

'I see.' Katerina looked to Michail who gave her a small nod. 'Where does she live? Irene? We'll want to question her.'

'Near the Temple of Aphaia. I'll get you her address.' Lily sniffed.

'We will need that immediately,' Michail prompted, standing to open the door. Lily nodded and pushed herself from the sofa, her ankles unsteady within her high heels. 'If there is anything else that you have neglected to tell us, we will need that too,' he added.

Lily dabbed her cheeks with her fingertips. 'There is a teeny-weeny thing, that I don't think is relevant but–'

'Everything is relevant,' Michail interrupted, flicking open his notepad. 'Go on.'

Lily looked hesitant, her mouth hanging open in mid-breath, Michail nodded expectantly, which seemed to prompt her to begin. 'I heard... crying. A woman crying on the night that Teddy was murdered. I was in the office, before Irene's visit, and I could have sworn that I heard weeping from outside. I had a poke about, you know... I thought it might be one of the models or something... but by the time I'd followed the sound, it had stopped.' She shrugged. 'That's it.'

Michail stared at her to ensure she had remembered to tell them everything.

'There's nothing else! Oh God, I feel so stupid...' Lily cried. Neither Katerina nor Michail contradicted the feeling, and there was a short pause before she flicked her handbag over her shoulder and left. Michail listened to the sharp click of her heels as she disappeared down the corridor before turning to Katerina.

'Your English has improved significantly.'

Katerina gave him a sad smile. 'I've had a year to brush up,' she said. 'A lot of time on my hands.'

'Congratulations for putting it to good use,' he said.

Katerina looked at her hands, which were laced over her lap. 'Michail, you don't have to... you don't have to be nice to me. I understand–'

The box labelled 'Unfindable Katerina Feelings' gave a tempting shudder from somewhere deep inside, but he shook his head, forcing it to stay locked and still. Sofia had been clear: for them to work effectively, he and Katerina must get along. 'Please consider what I said yesterday as irrelevant. We need to try and push through our past. It is the only way that we will be able to focus fully.'

Although he had been very clear, Katerina seemed stunned. She stared up at him, her lips slightly parted and limp, devoid of words.

'Sofia has instructed that we be friends again,' he clarified, ignoring the jolt in his abdomen as he uttered the word. He remembered, all too clearly, what it had been like to have Katerina as his friend. And he remembered, all too clearly, what it had been like to lose that friendship. But he could not ponder upon these things: he packed them into his box immediately.

'Sofia,' she repeated. 'I see–'

'Precisely. Like I said, please disregard everything I said

yesterday. We must move forward to solve this case.' To solidify the sentiment, he stepped forwards and held out a hand to her, as a gesture of goodwill.

She observed him for a moment and stood up to face him. 'Michail, I don't think–' For some reason, she seemed upset.

'I am certain that this is the best course of action,' he said, waggling his hand to remind her of its presence. She sighed and extended her own hand to meet his. He wasn't sure how to process the sensation he felt when their palms touched, their thumbs entwined. It wasn't unpleasant, yet it wasn't entirely comfortable either. He arranged his lips into a smile and nodded. The job was done. He had cemented their friendship afresh, just as Sofia had asked him to do. Everything could now run as normal.

'Good,' he said. 'Now, what did you think about Lily?'

Katerina blinked a few times before answering him. 'Erm, right. Good. I mean, she was all over the place, wasn't she? She seemed genuinely embarrassed. I just don't understand why she didn't mention the attack before. Seems odd, although she initially didn't realise that we were investigating a murder. Maybe she's frightened of Irene. She could have thought that giving us the footage was a way of telling us without having to *actually* tell us?'

'It's possible.' The soft wash of the sea drifted through the windows, and he exhaled, setting his thoughts into order. 'So far, we have two instances of clues being handed to us on a plate. Iraklis claimed ignorance, Lily claimed... incompetence. Do we believe either of them?'

Katerina gave a small laugh. The sound danced in tandem to the sea's low hum. 'It's not a problem we usually have, is it? People offering up clues willingly?' She shrugged and made for the terrace, rolling up her sleeves. 'I didn't go easy on Lily. Her story, as silly as it is, was consistent. And she's happy for us to visit Irene.'

She rolled her shoulders back and made for the terrace. He followed her outside and joined her in watching the sea. 'In addition to your English, your interview technique has also improved. You were pertinent and precise.'

'Thank you for the appraisal,' she said in a small voice. Then, looking into the distance, she added in a quieter voice, 'I'm trying my best.'

He glanced at their hands placed on the balcony, not far from touching, a sliver of whitewashed stone separating them. Katerina's little finger tapped absent-mindedly in time to a solo bird singing into the breeze.

'Nothing is impossible to those who try,' Michail replied, noticing that his finger, too, had begun to tap in time with hers.

Smiling Soldier

Katerina checked the address once again, shielding her eyes as the sun reflected off the tiny whitewashed house. 'It's here,' she said, as Michail parked the car at the side of the dirt track, his head protruding outside the window to check he didn't lodge the wheels in the ditch.

She stepped beneath the dappled shade of the sparse olive trees planted at scattered intervals over the small patch of land that led to a small blue front door. The low single-storey building seemed to squat, glowing defiantly amongst the mountain setting, proud in its decrepitude. A single window, dark and placed at a random point in the wall, peeped back at her from the right side of the door. The sill was filled with broken colourful ceramics placed before the backdrop of a net curtain. Numerous vases of the same style were placed randomly outside, giving the impression of an abandoned workshop. A black cat rolled on its back beneath the porch, its legs luxuriating in the soft, balmy breeze.

'The Temple of Aphaia is close, as Ms Woodstow indicated,' Michail said, standing next to her. 'A prime specimen of the late archaic moving into early classical sculptural styles.'

Katerina suppressed a knowing smile. Michail's historical titbits never failed to amuse her. However, today, she wanted him to know that she was taking him – them – seriously. Although he had only offered an olive branch because Sofia had ordered him to, she appreciated his attempt, no matter how forced. He'd never been the best at giving himself the required space, nor time. Although, her return to work had hardly given him much of a choice.

'She certainly has a thing for pots,' she said, skirting around a collection of broken water jugs.

'The village of Mesagros is famous for its water jugs,' Michail said, seeming glad that she had spotted this detail. 'The white and yellow argil used in pottery is found in abundance throughout the island.'

The cat bolted upright as they neared the door, its ears wide and alert. Katerina stroked its head and it purred gratefully. 'If she has a cat, she can't be as bad as Lily made out.'

'Even the most evil of humans are capable of loving pets,' Michail whispered as they heard a shuffle from inside. 'Putin has four dogs whom he adores.'

The door shook back and forth on its hinges before opening with a screech. Behind it, hidden by the shady interior, stood the woman from the footage. In person, she seemed a lot smaller and frail.

'Irene Kanatas?' Katerina asked, squinting into the darkness. 'Hellenic Police Force – we'd like to ask you a few questions regarding an assault upon Lily Woodstow.'

The woman sagged further forwards, as if hearing Lily's name placed a great burden upon her shoulders. Her eyes were yellowing at the sides and her skin was marked with deep, leathery lines. She patted her white-flecked hair, flattening it at the top of her head. 'Am I in trouble?' she asked. The voice wasn't what Katerina expected at all. It was scratchy and uncertain: a million miles away from the screaming attacker that she had witnessed on the video.

'We just need to ask some questions,' Katerina replied. 'Lily's not pressing charges though, so no.'

Irene's eyes fell to her cat who was meowing at her ankles. Clicking her tongue, she picked it up and disappeared into the house, turning her back on them with the door open. Katerina raised her eyebrows at Michail who nodded: apparently, they were supposed to follow her. It was marginally cooler inside. An electric fan whirred in the corner of what seemed like a single room, complete with a bed in one corner, a kitchen in another and a television with an aerial stuck onto the wall with tape.

'I made *kolokythokeftedes*.' Irene waved a hand to a dish covered by a tea towel on the narrow kitchen counter. 'Have some. Cassio won't eat them.' The cat jumped onto the counter and sniffed disapprovingly at the dish.

'Thank you.' Katerina eyed the food cautiously, fairly certain that Cassio had already helped himself. She spotted some fold-out chairs propped up against the counter. 'Do you mind?'

'No, please...' Irene helped them arrange the chairs in a small circle between the bed and the refrigerator. 'What's Lily said?'

The way she said the name almost made Katerina flinch. Perhaps this was a woman to watch out for, after all. 'You, er, had a disagreement about pay?'

She shook her head. 'I don't work for that place anymore.'

'No, Lily told us that you were sacked–'

'Did she?' Irene chewed on the side of her mouth, her head tilting to one side. She shook her head in a way that seemed like she was untangling herself from a thorny memory.

'Yes,' Michail interjected. 'This morning. You were recorded, Mrs Kanatas. We have seen the attack in Lily's office.'

There was a thick silence, only filled by Cassio's rhythmic tongue strokes as he licked his paws. Irene closed her eyes and exhaled deeply, blowing a musty aroma of coffee and mint through her dry lips. 'If she doesn't want to press charges, then why are you here?' she asked, without opening her eyes.

'Could you explain why you attacked her?' Michail asked.

Irene opened her eyes slowly, her hand groping for the silver crucifix hanging about her neck. 'Greed,' she said. 'Greed. I wanted money. She wouldn't give it to me.'

'That's all?' Michail looked at Katerina. She could tell what he was thinking: it seemed unlikely that this old woman would have descended to blows all for a pay rise.

Irene must have picked up on their doubts because she added, 'It was a strange night. The preparations for this big party are making Lily manic. She's working everyone to their bare bones. You'd think with there being no guests that it would be relaxed, well... everything was so up in the air, urgent. I snapped. I should have been stronger.'

'Did you hear anyone crying that night?' Michail asked.

'Crying? Who?' Irene's knuckles whitened around the crucifix. 'Why all the questions? I've told you everything.'

'A guest was murdered on the night you attacked Lily,' Katerina said carefully, not taking her eyes off the woman's face. 'That's why we're here.'

Irene stooped forwards, like her head would collapse beneath the news. 'My God, my God... murdered? One of the guests?'

'Correct,' replied Michail. 'If you recall anything unusual, then it is of paramount importance that you tell us. We have had a report of somebody crying in the hotel – did you hear anything similar?'

She seemed to freeze, her face turning to cracked clay. Her

eyes closed again, the flicker of them flitting beneath her paper eyelids. 'Yes... yes... now that you ask me...'

'You heard somebody crying too?' Michail asked, his pen poised in the air. 'Was it a female or a male voice?'

Her eyes flew open, and she opened her mouth to reply, searching Michail's face as she spoke in short, succinct strokes. 'I think it was a girl.'

'A female voice? How could you tell?' Michail's free hand began to tap against his left thigh.

'I could tell, just from the sobbing. She seemed very upset.'

Katerina looked to Michail, who was wearing the same concentrated expression that she must have been. 'Seemed? Did you see her?'

'I... no, no... I mean, from the sound of it, she seemed upset...' Irene's hand began to tremble as it gripped the crucifix. 'Just from the sounds...'

'Irene.' Katerina stood and placed a hand on the woman's shoulder. Beneath the cloth of her tunic, it felt brittle and thin. The old woman's breathing quickened, rising in ripped intervals between confused mutters and yelps.

'It's okay.' Katerina knelt before her. She peered up at her face, which had crumpled in on itself. 'You can tell us...'

'It is imperative that you tell us,' Michail added, before Katerina shot him a sharp look.

'I... I may have seen her.' She wavered, rocking backwards into her chair. 'D-did you check the security footage?'

'No,' Katerina lied swiftly. 'Not yet, but we have it.'

Irene nodded and rocked forwards towards Katerina again. 'I... I do remember. I saw a girl, a young woman. She was weeping, terribly upset. I... I assumed that she was just another one of Lily's casualties... someone she was forcing to work late... perhaps a new cleaner. I didn't speak to her. Perhaps she's what tipped me over the edge – someone else being treated poorly by that awful woman.'

'Can you describe the woman?' Michail jumped to his feet, watching Irene intensely.

'Oh...' Irene's hands fell from the crucifix to her lap, her fingers moving in tiny spirals. 'Yes... young, very beautiful. Long, dark hair.'

'Did you get a name?' Michail asked.

'No, no, no. I didn't speak to her, I've told you!'

A large vein running up through Irene's temple pulsed at an alarming rate. Katerina placed her hands over the older woman's. 'Okay. That's okay, Irene. That's really useful.'

Irene nodded vaguely and rubbed the tips of her fingers together, signalling for Cassio to pounce from the counter and lick them. Katerina sat back on her ankles and watched Michail as he scanned the room. He stopped in front of a small photograph hanging on the wall above the television. 'This is you, Mrs Kanatas? And who is this?'

He stepped to one side to reveal a picture of two women at the beach: one of them was unmistakably Irene, although looking noticeably less haggard, the other was a younger woman, with a heart-shaped face and a wide, remarkably symmetrical smile. She reminded Katerina of the sort of women she saw posing on social media, with impossibly pinched waists and smooth faces.

It was almost as if Irene hadn't heard his question. A glaze spread over her eyes as she grew very still, her hand unresponsive to Cassio's licks. 'Irene?' Katerina prompted.

The older woman flinched at the question and hoisted herself from the chair to join Michail before the photograph. 'My daughter,' she said. 'Tatiana.' She drew the photograph from the wall and gazed at it. 'She's beautiful, isn't she? It's a wonder she's mine...'

Michail's eyes were set and focused on the photograph. He nodded, a short, sharp movement, before turning abruptly to Katerina. 'I think that's all, Sergeant Galanis, unless you have any more questions?'

Katerina shook her head as she watched Irene place the picture back in its spot. She stepped back to admire it, a strange, ethereal smile on her face. 'Nothing more from me.'

'Excellent,' replied Michail. 'I have another visit in mind, since we're here.'

Sofia traced her fingernail along the plastic countertop as she took a small sip of tea. In the near distance, a speed-boat revved its engine and swung in the opposite direction. Water lapped, giddy and helpless, in the rock pools at the edge of the decking. It was a nice spot; the sort of restaurant British people pictured when they imagined the idylls of Greek islands. Here, however, most likely due to its location being tucked about the corner, hidden from the main drag of Aegina town, were mainly locals. She wrinkled her nose; the tea, as expected, was under-brewed.

'Sofia Sampson?' Maria raised a timid hand above her head to get her attention as she approached. Her linen skirt rippled against the outline of her legs in the warm sea breeze. Sofia let out a wry laugh – it occurred to her why Katerina had taken a dislike to such a woman. Maria was every inch what Katerina had been... well, before.

'Maria, thank you for meeting me.' She stood and pulled out the chair opposite. 'I wouldn't recommend the tea, but please order what you want.'

Maria glanced at the menu and called to the waiter for a coffee and an iced water. He replied like they were old friends, which, she surmised, was likely. Then, she took a deep breath and looked Sofia straight in the eye. 'It wasn't my *baba*, you know. If you have any sense, you'll know that.'

Sofia raised her eyebrows and leaned back against her chair. The woman before her was one of those rare people that had a natural magnetism. Her dark eyes suggested a deep intelligence, and, although she spoke directly, she seemed able to get her point across without being aggressive or rude. The combination was precisely the sort of personality type that Sofia wished she had more of on her team.

'We're exhausting all lines of enquiries,' Sofia replied, adjusting her sunglasses as the waiter arrived with the drinks.

'Back for long, Maria?' he asked, a boyish grin spread over his face.

'Hopefully not.' Maria gestured to Sofia. 'That all depends on this lady.'

'Ah...' The poor man clearly had no clue how to respond, so instead changed the subject. 'You sold three this week, by the way! Two mountains, and the temple.'

'Oh, really?' She clapped her hands and smiled. 'That's great. I never thought that anyone would buy them.'

He shrugged. 'True talent sells, always. There's room on the wall now, if you have time to do more.'

She nodded, giving the impression of deep consideration. 'If I find myself hanging about, I could do with the creative outlet. I'll bring them around.'

'Great!' He bobbed his head towards Sofia and sauntered back into the restaurant. Sofia waited for Maria to explain, comfortable, as always, to wait for as long as it took for the other person to speak.

Maria took a sip of coffee and looked back at the restaurant. 'He's just being nice – we grew up together. It's his dad's place and they let me hang up some of my artwork here.'

'Oh?' Sofia raised her eyebrows: she hadn't pegged Maria for an artist.

The surprise must have shown on her face because Maria added, 'It's just something I do for fun, mostly when I'm back home. I don't visit that often so it's just a hobby.'

Sofia stirred her tea. 'It's not so far from Athens, why don't you visit much?'

Maria sighed as if she'd been expecting the question and ran her fingers through her hair. 'Work is busy. I run an advertising firm which can be relentless, to say the least.'

There was something in her voice that told Sofia that she wasn't telling the whole truth. 'Your father must miss you? He said your mother died when you were younger–'

Maria's eyes darted up to meet hers momentarily before she regained composure and folded her arms. 'Of course, he would have told you all that when you arrested him.'

'It always helps to get a clear picture. The more details, the better.' Maria looked at her lap, although the movement didn't indicate weakness as it did for most people; instead, she inhaled as if commanding the warm air to fill her lungs with strength. 'It bothers you, talking about–' Sofia pretended to flick through her notepad for the name.

'Okay,' Maria cut in, her eyebrows drawing together. 'And yes, it bothers me to talk about my dead relative. That's not unusual.'

'No, not unusual,' Sofia agreed. She looked out to the vast blue expanse, hoping that it would somehow guide her to the next question. Maria managed to walk the line between being an open book and shutting down the defences. That, thought Sofia, was unusual.

'You still don't understand why I rushed back to Aegina?'

Maria's question interrupted Sofia's thoughts. She flicked

her eyes towards her and nodded. Perhaps it would be better to let this one lead the conversation.

Maria gave her a sad smile. 'I want to look after him, to love him, but... well, it hasn't worked out that way. At least, not like I imagined.'

Sofia drew her gaze from the sea to Maria and nodded for her to continue. 'That's how it is for *Baba* and I. We're not close, but I want us to be. When I heard the news about his workplace, all I could think was that he'd be alone, frightened. I thought... I thought he'd need me.' She chuckled, although the sound was low and heavy. 'You saw, of course, he doesn't need me at all.'

'What made you think he'd need you?'

'Look, I know what you're getting at and you're so wrong.'

'And what do you think I'm getting at?' Sofia asked, keeping her voice low and steady. This was good. It was good to pinpoint the interviewee's anxieties, their fears. They often gave more away than people thought.

Maria laughed, a barbed sound, and placed her hands on the table. 'Listen to me, no, really listen. *Baba* would never hurt a soul, never in his life. He had nothing to do with that man on the beach. Anyway, you didn't charge him, did you? You can't. You won't find any real evidence because he's innocent.'

'You seem very certain of that.' If she was being honest – not that she placed much weight in intuition – Sofia highly doubted that Iraklis Barlas had killed Teddy Menkopf. There was no obvious motive, an alibi, and, apart from the key card, no indication that they had had much, if any, interaction at the hotel.

'Yes.' Maria's face softened. 'I'm certain.'

'You just said you weren't close. How can you know for sure?' Sofia made sure to make it sound nothing more than a pleasant question, although the muscles in the back of her neck twitched as if signalling her to push Maria on this point.

Maria held Sofia's gaze for a second longer than necessary before replying. 'I've told you. He would never do anything like that. Apart from anything else, why would he?'

'But you hardly ever visit,' Sofia pressed. She had expected the change in direction would throw Maria, but, instead, she sighed and leant back in her chair. She looked up to the sky, her eyes closed, her face bathed in the sunlight. The question didn't seem to have ruffled her at all.

'No, I don't, but that doesn't mean I don't know him.' She brought her head down again and tilted it to one side. 'You must have people in your life that you know, really know, without seeing them regularly?'

The question's wraithlike fingers reached out across the table, and groped their way through the silent ghosts that had whispered to her through the sea's translucent spray since arriving on the island. Texts, the news, the face of the man she had known better than anyone else and... *him.* Half-grown teeth, half-grown bones, half-grown memories. It was like liquid pulsated in her chest, engulfed her heart, filled the folds of her lungs. Her gaze did not waver. 'Perhaps. I suppose I'm wondering why you'd allow work to get in the way of somebody whom you clearly love. Is there another reason, apart from being busy?'

'Losing a family member is... unbearable. It was for us, anyway. You know, I often thought that it would have been easier had I lost them both. Then I would have had only my pain to deal with. Is that selfish? Probably, it feels selfish. But seeing him so consumed, so changed... death possesses the living.' She straightened her back. 'It never leaves. So, I understood.'

'Understood?'

'He needed space.' Each word scraped against the next, her voice hoarse. 'Everyone grieves in their own way and he... he likes to go it alone.'

'And when you returned?'

'He asked me not to–' Her fingers gripped the table as if she was remembering herself. 'Oh God, I know how it sounds, but it's not suspicious. He wanted to work. To keep busy.'

To be honest, it made perfect sense. Sofia gestured to the soft, undulous mounds of land stretching into the sea. 'It's a beautiful place to call home. That must have hurt.'

Maria shrugged, following her gaze. 'I suppose. It wasn't like I was banished or anything. It just... felt like he needed a break from me. Grief doesn't behave in the way you think. I guess sometimes it needs distance.'

Sofia bowed her head in grim agreement. 'There's nothing else you can think of that might help? In terms of Teddy Menkopf?'

'No.' Maria shook her head and raised her hand to grab her friend's attention for another drink. 'I don't have much to do with this place anymore, especially not that hotel. Did you want anything else?'

Sofia inhaled the salty thick air through her nostrils and checked the time on her phone. 'A glass of wine,' she replied.

The afternoon heat beat steadily down onto the dust. A sweet, earthy smell of pistachio trees laced through the air as Katerina huffed her way up the slope. At Michail's heels, dust circulated as he strode ahead, reeling off facts about the temple excitedly.

'The remains of the temple which we see today date to about 500 BC,' he said, his legs working in a steady rhythm. 'Of course, you will have noted that Aphaia is not a typical goddess

– in fact, her origins are somewhat mysterious: her identity is actually thought to be linked to the lesser-known nymph, Britomartis, the daughter of Zeus, whom...'

Katerina shook her head, a nostalgic smile twitching at her lips. Some things never changed. And that was a good thing. A lovely thing.

'...of course, as the interpretation of the goddess's identity evolved, she came to be associated with Artemis–'

'Michail, is there a reason why we're here?'

'We are on Aegina. This temple is arguably the most important site on the island.'

'Yes.' She puffed out her cheeks, wriggling at the trickle of sweat running down her back. 'But is there any other reason?' Michail turned to look down at her, his mouth poised and ready to launch into more explanation. 'Apart from it being fascinating,' she added quickly.

He waited for her to catch up. When she reached his side, he gestured up the hill. 'What most visitors fail to comprehend is that this temple sits at the threshold of a significant artistic turning point. It will be obvious from the date, of course, as to what this turning point is...'

He stared at her expectantly. 'Erm... something to do with...' she plucked a word from the blurry recesses of her memory, '...the sculptural scheme?'

'Correct. Absolutely, Katerina.' He beamed, his open, gleeful expression making her forget, just for a second, his coolness towards her that morning. 'The disparity between the east and west pediments are key in academic discourse.'

Without elaborating, he inhaled as if something had satisfied him greatly, and turned on his heel to continue the rest of the way up the slope. By the time she caught up with him, he was sitting, straight-backed, palms placed flat against his thighs, on a rock, gazing at the temple. He didn't move his eyes when she wiggled onto a rock next to him, but he said, 'This is better.'

She nodded, caught between having no idea what he meant, yet somehow knowing precisely what he meant. The columns stretched high to their scarred and crumbled entablature. In the low afternoon sun, their shadows laid upon the ground in perfectly even stripes.

'It is simple,' Michail said. 'People have forgotten the beauty of simplicity, I think.'

Katerina looked at her shoes which were covered in dust. 'This case seems anything but simple,' she said.

'I agree.' Michail bowed his head. 'However, our meeting with Mrs Kanatas has balanced the pattern somewhat, even if we don't yet know how.'

'Are you going to tell me what you noticed about that photo?' Katerina asked tentatively. She had been wondering since they had left Irene's hut, feeling stupid that she hadn't worked it out herself. To her surprise, Michail cracked a crinkly smile.

'I do not need to tell you how I feel about coincidences?'

He certainly didn't. 'You don't believe in them.'

'Precisely. There is a reason why philosophers view coincidence as paradoxical. Probability theory can predict the overall outcome of events with uncanny precision, even if the events in themselves are unpredictable. Since we investigate events that we already know have happened – and are therefore entirely predictable – coincidence is almost an impossible consideration. It would be ludicrous to entertain it.'

Katerina fought the urge to place her head in her hands. 'I think I'm following, but what does this have to do with the photograph?'

'Ah.' Michail looked at the temple as if he were gulping its stones, the equations that went into constructing it, through his eyes. 'Her daughter, Tatiana. She was wearing a necklace with a "T" on it.'

She squinted as the sun grew lower, its orange beams bathing her face. 'The same as Teddy's necklace? He was wearing a necklace with his initial too.'

Michail nodded, a low hum beginning to emit from his throat. She looked at him and saw that the sun had also hit his face, but that he had closed his eyes, and his expression was perfectly calm. 'You think there's a connection?'

He opened his eyes and stood, brushing the dust from his trousers in three distinct strikes. 'Inevitably,' he said. 'We just need to look in the right places.' He turned back to Katerina, who remained seated. 'That's why I wanted to come here. Apart from the temple's obvious beauty, which is evident to anyone, I thought that the Temple of Aphaia would assist me in viewing things from a different perspective.'

Katerina pushed herself up from the rock and traced her way along the ancient, uneven ramp leading into the main structure. 'Right, so is it working?'

Instead of replying, he swung his rucksack from his shoulders and placed it on the floor, before pulling out an old, heavy-looking book. He then silently counted a *one, two, three* of the tiny, coloured placeholder stickers and knelt, placing the book before him. 'Here,' he said, pointing to a double-page spread showing the temple, 'is an illustration of what the temple used to look like: pedimental sculptures intact.'

She skirted around him and crouched down. 'You brought this all the way–'

'Of course not, Katerina. We left for Piraeus straight from the ceremony – the potential murder enquiry superseded my desire to fetch my Aegina books. Thank goodness there is a lovely second-hand bookshop in town with an excellent archaeological section.' He shook his head in amazement over the page. 'Remarkable...'

'You couldn't pull this up on your phone?'

'It would be too small to see the details,' he said. Katerina, knowing it was unlikely that Michail would be dissuaded, gave in and looked at the pictures. On it were two large triangular images, presumably showing the sculptures that used to exist in the triangular pediments on both ends of the temple. Both showed a similar scene: a war. Based on her rudimentary efforts in the classroom, she made her best guess. 'It looks like they're both, the east and west side, scenes from the Trojan War?'

'Precisely.' Michail's finger tracked the images, before he raised it into the air, pointing it towards the temple. 'The western pedimental sculptures, here and in this photograph, were made in 490 BC. The eastern...' he pointed to the opposite side of the temple, '...a decade later, in 480 BC.'

He sat back on his heels and looked to and from the book and the temple in quick, regular movements. Eventually, he let out an aggravated groan. 'There is something!' he cried, pushing himself back so he sat on the dusty ground. 'There is something I am missing, something visual, that isn't quite right... there is a piece out of place, something amiss... I thought that coming here...'

Unsure quite how to help – or how indeed the temple might help – Katerina picked up the book and walked closer to the temple's huge steps. 'So... so... right, so the earlier sculptures, they look less...'

'Less natural,' Michail called after her. 'Scholarly discourse focuses on the dying warrior on the edge of the pediment. You will see that he looks far too happy to be dying; he wears what is known as the "archaic smile". His hair also falls in unnatural beads and his body is carved in a way that is too perfect, too formal, too precise to be mistaken as human.'

'And then a decade later–'

'The same scene is depicted on the west but it's altogether transformed,' Michail continued. 'Ten years of progression in skill and style, ten years that captures the acceleration of craftsmanship.'

'Oh I see, yes. The dying warrior is in the same pose but...'

'He is more human.' Michail spoke in quick, concentrated bursts. 'The style moves from archaic to early classical. He is no longer smiling, his hair is not beaded, his body is rendered with more naturalism, his flesh is no longer a vehicle for shape and pattern, but a representation of the human form. Both tug at the spear that pierces their chests, but they are worlds apart.'

Katerina turned her back to the temple to face him. He looked small, dejected, huddled on the ground as if in hiding. She stepped closer to him. 'Michail, why did you think this temple would help? What made you want to come here?'

He looked at his feet. 'I realise it must seem very strange to you, Katerina,' he muttered.

'No! No, that's not what I meant. I'm asking genuinely – what pulled you to this temple? There must have been something. Something hiding inside your brain, somewhere, that told you to come.'

For a second, she thought he might not reply, but then he raised his head and met her eyes. A tiny frisson shimmied from the bottom of her spine to the base of her skull. She recognised that look: a piece of the puzzle was falling into place.

'A pertinent question, Katerina, thank you.' He jumped up to stand in an awkward jolted movement and ripped the book from her hands. 'Unbelievable!' He examined the page again. 'Sometimes, we just need the right environment to see what we need. Thank you for your encouragement, Katerina. It is lucky that you're here.'

She blinked, her eyes flooding with unexpected tears. With

his back to her, she looked up at the sky to dry them. *He was lucky to have her*. Lucky. She knew it was stupid to place too much hope in his words – she could tell he was ignoring what he really felt, pulled along by his sense of duty. And anyway, it was just a throwaway comment, barely meaningful at all. Still, the words lit up the air around her for now.

'You... you think you've got something?' She rolled her shoulders back and moved to stand next to him. 'What is it?'

'Tell me...' He held the book before her. 'What is it about the earlier, the archaic sculptures that makes them look less real?'

She studied the dying warrior again. As Michail had said, he didn't look like he was in pain at all – his smile was puckered and perfect, his eyebrows carved in the perfect arches. His body showed no hint of writhing in agony as the weapon penetrated his chest: he was perfect. Too perfect. Too well-proportioned. 'He's too manicured, like he's an imitation of a man dying, but that's all, he isn't natural.'

'An imitation, yes.' Michail's face scrunched up in thought. 'I feel like I am so close to filling the gap, but... I can't quite see what I need to.'

'The gap?' Katerina struggled to keep up as Michail began to stride in a frustrated lap around the temple, his book promenading proudly before him. 'If I could just...'

He tutted, and held his head to one side, lost deep in thought. 'There was something else about the incisions that didn't make sense to me... although I'm struggling to put my thoughts in order – I am afraid that I am failing in this respect, Katerina...'

'Oh, well, I wouldn't say–'

His head drooped. 'The connection is here, I can feel it. The mystery behind Teddy's murder is here... I just can't...' He let out a frustrated yelp and stamped his foot in the dust. Before she began to comfort him, his phone rang.

She stepped back to give him some space, taking in the pinks and the reds of the sky, all swirling together, spread above like icing on a cake. The *tzitzikas'* song lifted in applause at the early evening's colourful offering, as if they had gathered especially. She closed her eyes and imagined herself weightless, drifting above the tree-covered valleys, sinking into the soft air, learning to recognise only the passing of the days and the drapery of the skies. The *tzitzikas*, the sky, the sea, they did not care for matters past or present or future. They were in timeless, perpetual motion; a detached, uncomplicated existence.

'Certainly, Major Sampson. We will come with the utmost urgency.' Michail's grave tone penetrated her thoughts. She opened her eyes to hear him walking towards her spot at the edge of the hill.

'Urgency?' she asked, watching the colours begin to bleed into grey.

He folded his arms and followed her gaze as the sun's long fingers extended for their final stretch before folding behind the horizon. His lip quivered and he bowed his head before taking a deep, shaky breath. 'They have found another body outside a restaurant by the harbour.'

Michail counted to three, nausea gripping his intestines. Bright lights flashed, red and blue, as more vehicles arrived at the scene. Sofia was speaking in quick, directive tones to the head of the Aegina station.

We know exactly what we're doing.
Get your team knocking on doors immediately.
I want them patrolling the area.

Any gawkers, any press, escort them away immediately.

The churn of a helicopter encircled up ahead, its white searchlight stripping sharp segments of air from the darkness. Michail forced himself to look at the body. *One, two, three. One, two, three.* He had never seen anything like it. Alek Knox sat upright at the restaurant table as if in the middle of a conversation. The only indication that something was deeply wrong from this angle was the small, red circle which stained the front of his white shirt. Michail swayed slightly backwards and exhaled, feeling his fingers begin to tap on each side of his leg alternately. *One, two, three. One, two, three.*

The photographer gave him the nod from behind Alek's shoulder, the soft lick of the camera's flashes abating, signalling that it was his turn to inspect the exit wound. He edged around the empty chairs and tables, the whirring of the helicopter growing thunderous, his throat dry and tight.

The view of Alek's back was incomprehensible. Michail stared for a while as he waited for his brain to organise the mess before him. But it was devoid of reason. A monstrous wet hole gaped where his spine should have been. The bullet had not discriminated between types of matter: muscle, cartilage and bone blended into a thick pulp. The bullet must have just grazed the spine itself, because a line of vertebrae, gleaming impossibly white, chewed along one side of the wound like a line of oversized teeth.

'Oh my God!' Katerina stepped next to him. 'It's...'

'Professional,' Michail whispered, unable to pull his eyes away. He clenched his hands at his sides, forcing himself to remain analytical. 'The bullet required to do this type of damage is professional.'

'Afraid so.' Sofia emerged from behind a group of officers. 'Forensics will identify the bullet, but, judging from the wound, it looks like modified special service. Sniper, most likely.'

'What? So, a hit-man?' Katerina asked.

Sofia nodded, her eyes trailing along the top of the strip of restaurants and bars that lined the harbour. 'Seems like it.'

Michail's chest tightened. A radio crackle, the spit of speed-boat engines, the slam of a car door, the smack of Sofia's lips, helicopter whirring, camera clicking, zip undoing, shoes pounding. The sounds magnified, congealed into one, roaring cacophony. He stepped back, *one, two, three. One, two, three.* The numbers sank beneath the chaos, meaningless and vapid.

'Michail?'

He tried to respond, but his words could not rise above the roar between his ears. Lowering himself onto a chair, he hung his head, breathing in and out, just like he had been told to.

'Michail, is everything okay?' Katerina crouched next to him.

He shook his head, his eyes drawn yet again to the wound: the hole which slurped and spat at any attempt of his to see the logic, understand the rationale behind this catastrophe. 'We need a meeting,' he decided. 'As soon as we're finished here. This body is very real indeed. He is not a smiling soldier at all.'

Phantom Iterations

Michail listened to Yiorgos's voice sound from Sofia's handset. 'We've got the whole team on this at headquarters as directed, Sofia. Send us anything you have; tech's working on his social media accounts as we speak. You'll have seen the message from forensics? The entry wound looks likely to have come from one of the top windows of the neighbouring restaurants.'

'Well, we assumed that anyway—' Sofia replied.

'Nothing turned up in the search?'

'No. Whoever's behind this is clearly skilled in leaving no trace. We've got a trained killer on our hands.'

There was a short silence from the other end of the phone before Yiorgos replied, 'It's good you've got his phone, at least. The team at Aegina station are going through it right now, they'll keep us all in the loop and have been instructed to deliver it to you in the morning after taking prints. On that topic, any sign of Teddy Menkopf's?'

'No.' Sofia let out an exasperated sigh. 'Apparently, it's untraceable. Wherever it is, there's no signal, no GPS, nothing. My best guess is that it's at the bottom of the sea somewhere.'

'Right...' A tapping sound signalled Yiorgo was typing. 'The latest from the social media companies is that they'll get back to us *as quickly as they are able* regarding the release of Teddy's private messages on his accounts. It'd be quicker if we had his phone, but that's all we have for now. How's the hotel? Are you all still staying there?'

'Oh, Lily's super glad to help, even considering her *extra busy* schedule in the lead-up to the party,' Sofia snarled. 'And very eager to let us know how grateful we should all be. Thank God for billionaires like Domenico.'

Yiorgos chuckled on the other end of the line. 'I don't need to tell you to keep your wits about you. Second guest and—'

'We're looking into accommodation. It's all rammed,' replied Sofia. She rubbed her forehead and picked up the phone from the bed. 'It's not actually terrible that we're here; there's something in being in the eye of the storm. We've obviously scanned our briefing room for devices.'

'I assumed they'd cancel the Saturnalia,' Yiorgos said. 'Distasteful, isn't it, holding a festival after two guests have been killed?'

'To most people, yes,' Sofia responded. 'But to the clientele of Saturn House, it seems it's not a big deal.'

'Right, just let me know the outcome of your meeting tonight,' he said. 'I'll be here.'

Sofia mumbled in assent and hung up. She glanced from Michail to Katerina. 'This is quickly becoming an embarrassment,' she said. 'Two guests dead, one under our watch. We'd better come up with some theories and fast.'

Michail took this as his opportunity to jump into action. He tapped the whiteboard with the tip of his pen to ensure he had everyone's full attention.

'He who has the feeling of shame is afraid,' Michail said helpfully, nodding at Sofia. Strangely, the useful proverb did not seem to lift her spirits. He explained further, 'Plato posits that shame is merely an expression of fear, specifically regarding the fear of one's reputation. We, Sofia, cannot be afraid. We must stay strong and rational.'

'Fascinating, thank you, Michail. Now the theories, if you can spare the time?'

'Of course.' He scribbled on the board as quickly as he could. 'The first question is whether we assume that Teddy Menkopf's and Alek Knox's murders are connected?'

'They must be,' murmured Katerina.

'Teddy's was made to look like suicide, Alek's wasn't, but I have to agree with Katerina, here.' Sofia pinched her chin. 'There must be some relation. Guests at the same hotel, both youngish men. Similar socio-economic situation.'

'A sensible assumption,' replied Michail, thankful that no one had made the ludicrous suggestion of coincidence. 'And yes, their demographic similarities are worth noting.'

'Has Innes been informed?' asked Katerina. 'We'll need to speak to her.'

'She's been told, yes, but was in no state to answer questions tonight.' Sofia checked her phone and blew through her lips. 'It's almost morning. I told her we'd want to talk to her today.'

'There was that weird thing she said by the pool, too–' Katerina said. 'Something about someone being "sick"? What could that have meant? I'm right about it meaning "ill" in English?'

Sofia nodded. 'That's right. It also used to be a slang word to describe something as good but I don't think Innes is the right type, also she's Portuguese so hardly likely to use niche colloquialisms.'

'Perhaps she was talking about a relative?' Michail suggested, writing the word 'sick' on the board. 'You said that she exchanged a significant look with Alek before taking the call?'

'Yes, like he knew what the call would be about. I don't know... it was as if they were both expecting it.' Katerina shook herself. 'Ugh, I wish I could explain this properly... look, it just seemed weird. Before Alek's murder, it was just a strange thing to say. Now, I can't help feeling that something wasn't right. I'd love to know who was on the other end of the conversation.'

'We can ask for her phone,' Sofia said. 'We're investigating the murder of her boyfriend, after all. Let's not reveal we suspect anything – if she has something to hide, we don't want her to know that we're onto her.'

'Speaking of people who may or may not have something to hide, I think it's safe to assume that neither Iraklis nor Maria Barlas are suspects.' Michail circled their names in red on the board. 'Nothing relevant was revealed during Iraklis's interrogation–'

'Maria seemed happy to help today,' Sofia interjected. 'She's overprotective of her father – perhaps understandably – but I agree that it's unlikely either of them has anything to do with Teddy or Alek. The involvement of a sniper points to a more organised operation, a professional perpetrator. Also, neither of them has a motive.'

'Excellent. I will remove them from the list.' Michail tapped a second point on the board. 'Now we come to Irene Kanatas, a former cleaner here at Saturn House.'

'How did it go?' Sofia asked.

'Two minor progressions,' Michail replied. 'The first was thanks to Katerina's quick thinking and ability to lie smoothly–' His hand hovered in mid-air, frozen, as he realised what he had said. He looked at the ground, trawling through his brain for a suitable solution to his oversight. Disastrously, he felt his face begin to grow hot and suspected that his cheeks were growing a deep red. After two excruciating seconds, Katerina broke the silence.

'Um... yes.' She cleared her throat, her cheeks also glowing. However, despite her clear discomfort, she persevered. 'Yes... Irene asked whether we had security footage of the corridors. I pretended we did, and, interestingly, only then did she admit to hearing a woman on the night of Teddy's murder. It was like she was going to lie about having heard anything at all but then changed her story. Apparently, she heard crying too.'

'Tallies up with Lily's account,' Sofia said. 'Could she describe her?'

'Very vaguely – young, dark hair. Clearly, she didn't know her, which rules out anyone associated with the hotel. What I can't work out is why she'd bother lying about *not* hearing her? Why admit it when she'd clarified that we had proof?'

'It's odd,' Sofia agreed, her eyes shifting slowly from Michail to Katerina. 'Maybe she's hedging her bets, working out what we know and don't? Although, I can't figure out what she has to hide. What else?'

Michail straightened himself up and gripped the pen tightly between his fingers, which were clammy. 'The necklace.' He drew a 'T' on the board. 'Irene's daughter, Tatiana, wears a necklace displaying her first initial, the same as Teddy Menkopf.'

'Right...' Sofia folded her arms: a sign that she was unimpressed. 'It's not exactly what I'd describe as a breakthrough. Both names begin with a "T".'

'Perhaps not yet,' Michail replied, circling the letter on the board again to ensure that its presence was not overlooked. 'But sometimes the tiniest of details can pierce the heart of a case like a spear.'

'I'm sorry for your loss,' Sofia said, handing Innes another tissue. She looked at Katerina, whose eyes were scanning the sprawling hotel room.

'I... I just don't understand... why? Why? How could anyone do this to him! Alek! He's famous, for God's sake!' She curled forwards, her hardened abdomen folding in on itself, preparing for another round of sobs. Sofia sat back against her chair and rubbed her lips together, levelling out the lipstick she had hurriedly applied. She had met her fair share of grief-stricken friends and family; the only way to get through without becoming a quivering wreck herself was to adopt a certain distance, develop an immunity. It was harsh – she of all people knew that helpless falling feeling, like being suspended in air, unable to breathe, to see, but it was necessary.

'That's what we're trying to work out,' Sofia said. 'Run us through it, if you can? You left Alek at about 8pm?'

'Yes! Yes! Here, you can check my Uber receipt!' She scrolled, her fingernails clicking frantically against the screen, and shoved the phone in front of Sofia's face. Indeed, the receipt confirmed what they'd already checked: she'd taken an Uber at 8.03pm from *Tsias*, the restaurant at which Alek had been found outside.

Sofia pushed the phone gently away from her face. 'This isn't an interrogation, Innes. We're just trying to confirm some details.'

She sniffed, pressing a tissue against her mouth. 'I... I never even wanted to go out. The food here is amazing, so much better than anything in town. You know the chef is from Milan? Two Michelin stars. Alek liked the local stuff, always going on about community options. He's so humble.'

'You didn't return together, though?'

'No, no. He gets talking... used to... used to get talking.' Her voice wavered dangerously, but she pushed on. 'It's part of his

91

personal brand, isn't it? Inspiring nobodies, embracing authenticity... It's not my thing. I often went home alone, left him to it.'

'You have no idea who would want to do this to him?' Sofia asked. 'Anyone who would want him dead?'

'He has over ten million followers and speaks the truth,' she said. For the first time in their conversation, her turquoise eyes flashed with anger, the moisture in them shimmering as she held Sofia's gaze. 'He received death threats every day.'

Was this jealousy? Frustration at being asked repetitive questions? Or did she have an idea about who might have done this?

'Anything stick in your mind? Perhaps he mentioned a particularly threatening message?'

Innes shook her head; her bottom lip trembled but her eyes continued to gleam. 'No... I... I would have told you! Look, it's your job to find out who did this. I don't have the answers! There must be witnesses you should be talking to!'

There was no good in explaining that the witnesses had all reported the same horrific scene: one moment Alek was there, leaning back, laughing, reaching for his beer. The next moment... the descriptions varied in vocabulary but not grisliness: splatters of blood, flesh exploding, blind panic.

One account had even described the sound of the bullet as being like a nut cracking – the back of the ribcage splitting as the bullet exploded inside Alek's chest. None had seen, nor even been aware of, the shooter.

The restaurant's security footage had made for eerie viewing. Sofia was, of course, accustomed to the strange, uneven films that captured the most depraved of crimes in stark, almost perverse, silence. However, the lack of obvious perpetrator, the way Alek's body had awkwardly jolted backwards, as if pushed by an invisible hand, the almost undetectable shudder, the cloudy mist engulfing those sitting behind him as the front of his body remained intact, his mouth sagging.

Sofia sighed. 'We're of course speaking to everyone we need to. On that note, I wonder if we can take a look at your phone?' Sofia didn't miss the reflex: Innes's fingers tightened around the device. Sofia glanced at Katerina who had settled in the chair next to her.

'My phone?' Innes pulled back her shoulders and tautened her cheeks, forcing her lips into a sad smile. 'Of course. I'm not sure how it will help–'

'It probably won't,' Sofia interrupted smoothly. 'It's just protocol. We'll get it back to you as soon as possible.'

Innes nodded, fresh tears erupting from her eyes as she handed it over. 'I... I just can't believe it.'

'I can't imagine how difficult this must be for you.' Sofia raised her eyebrows at Katerina's low, soothing voice. She was reminded of her younger colleague's knack for winning people over. It had been one of the main reasons that she and Michail had made such a good team.

Innes's head dipped forward, her hair tumbling about her shoulders as they shook in unbridled, tumultuous wrenches. 'No,' she spluttered, the words barely audible through her ragged gasps. 'No, you can't. Just... just find who did this?'

'It's what we plan on doing,' Katerina said, her tone still comforting and velvety. Only then, did she gesture towards the large marble bar in the far corner of the room. Various expensive bottles were arranged on its top, most more than half drunk. 'You've drunk a lot from the bar, I see.'

Innes raised her face to Katerina's, her eyes glittering in acidic flecks. 'So? Until recently, there were two of us in this room. How is that relevant?'

'Oh sorry.' Katerina held up her hands, as if she were apologising. 'I didn't mean to be judgemental. It's just I was under the impression that Alek didn't drink? Wasn't one of his main messages to practise abstinence from alcohol?'

Sofia watched as Innes took in the question. She blinked; the motion reminded Sofia of a reptile moistening its eyes as it lay flat and still against a rock. Waiting no more than a second, Innes licked her lips and replied, 'Yes. Things aren't always as they seem on social media, you know? He was – we were – stressed. I stopped drinking when I met him because he believes women shouldn't drink, and kept to it. This isn't exactly a typical time.'

Katerina and Sofia couldn't help but exchange a look. 'Stressed?' Sofia pressed. 'What about?'

'The Saturnalia.' Innes's voice had grown sharper, almost acerbic. 'It's a huge deal. Half his sponsorships last year were from the posts he made at Saturn House. Anyone who's anyone is invited. It's basically the most exclusive event in the world. It was his personal brand on the line – he wanted it to go perfectly.'

'He was drinking to cope with the stress?'

'Yes.'

An uncomfortable pause followed. It was plausible, of course, that she was telling the truth. Plenty of people's public image was a far cry from reality. Although, there was a defensiveness in the way that Innes now presented herself, like something was being wound tighter and tighter inside of her. Perhaps it wasn't the party that Alek had been stressed about? Sofia cleared her throat, her head beginning to throb from fatigue. 'What's your password?' she asked, thumbs poised over the phone.

'It's 81726,' Innes mumbled, concealing what Sofia thought was a small petulant roll of the eyes.

'Thank you.' Sofia tapped the numbers in with the tips of her fingernails and immediately swiped through to the call log. Innes didn't receive many calls, which wasn't unusual nowadays. Scrolling down, it was easy to identify who had called her on the date and time that Katerina had overheard the phone call: Domenico, the name of the owner of the Balcombe House Group and surely not a coincidence. Sofia clicked her tongue against the back of her teeth and passed the handset to Katerina, who frowned when she saw the name.

'Is there a problem?' Innes asked.

'Not really...' Katerina began, looking to Sofia who nodded, giving her permission for Katerina to lead this part of the questioning. 'This incoming call from a certain Domenico a few days ago... is he a friend of yours?'

The skin around Innes's eyes twitched – a miniscule movement – before she shrugged. 'Yes, he's a friend of mine.'

'Domenico Bonarelli? The owner of this hotel?'

'That's right. He and Alek–' She choked and closed her eyes, before gritting her teeth to continue. 'They were good friends. Domenico is a very well-connected man. He got Alek his first television opportunity. He's always been very supportive of Alek's mission.'

'Must be nice to have such a powerful friend,' Katerina commented.

'Of course.' Innes wiped a tear from her cheek. 'What's this about? I took a call from a friend, why do you care?'

'Do you remember what you spoke about?' Katerina asked.

Sofia watched Innes's face very carefully. Her thick eyebrows drew close together and she shook her head, as if trying to retrace the conversation. 'Er, I don't know, the usual things.'

'Usual things?'

'Yes. I was involved in Alek's branding, the messaging direction for socials, content calendar, everything like that.'

'Did you discuss anything not work-related?' Katerina asked.

Innes's eyes shifted between the two of them. Either she was genuinely nonplussed or an excellent actor. 'I don't understand what you mean?'

'Just out of interest,' Katerina pressed. 'Did you discuss anything that wasn't related to work? It would be useful if you could try to remember.'

'I'm not sure what you're getting at.'

Innes looked to Sofia, who sighed – this was going nowhere. It wasn't what they had planned but they couldn't afford to waste any more time on this. 'Innes.' Even Sofia heard how sharply her voice cut across the space. 'You were overheard on the phone that day.'

'By who?'

'It doesn't matter,' Sofia replied. 'But you said something about someone being sick. Do you remember that?'

'Sick...?' Innes laced her fingers together and hung her head, as if the answer was in her lap.

'If you could answer the question quickly, that would be good,' Sofia said, trying her best not to snap. This was beginning to grow tiresome.

'Sick...' Innes shook her head, sending her hair tumbling about her shoulders. Had the circumstances been different, Sofia would have thought that she was posing. 'Oh!' Her eyes widened and she gave a breathy, sad laugh. 'Sick... yes...'

'Yes...'

Innes unlaced her fingers and stretched them out wide against her thighs. She took a deep breath and nodded. 'Yes... yes... I was talking about Alek. He... he had been feeling unwell, and Domenico was concerned about him.'

'It didn't sound like that–' Katerina began before snapping her mouth closed. 'I mean... it sounded like–'

'You were listening in, then? It was you?' Those electric eyes flickered again as she glared at Katerina. 'I didn't realise that I was being spied on.'

'You weren't... I... I just overheard,' Katerina began. Just as Sofia was about to intervene, Katerina pulled her shoulders back and met Innes's gaze straight-on. 'It sounded like you were talking about someone Domenico didn't know, not Alek,' she persevered. 'You said the word "sick" repeatedly, as if you were trying to convince him that whoever you were talking about was unwell but would be okay.'

Innes stared at Katerina for a few stunned seconds before letting out a ragged, throaty laugh. 'I don't know what you want me to say. I've told you who I was talking about. Who else would I be referring to, eh?' She stood and made for the door. 'If you don't mind, I'd like to be alone. Unless, of course, you'd like to arrest me for... what is it? Oh, receiving a phone call from a friend.'

Sofia pushed herself from the sofa and gestured for Katerina to follow. 'We'll keep a hold of your phone, unless you have any objections,' she said as Innes stalked to the bar and opened a bottle of mezcal. 'You never know what might be helpful.'

Innes waved a hand in the air. 'Fine. Fine.'

Sofia tugged on Katerina's arm; she seemed unwilling to leave, her arms folded, her eyes boring into Innes's back. 'Thank you again, Innes,' Sofia called as the door closed behind them.

Katerina swore softly under her breath. 'I am sure... *sure* that there was something weird about that conversation,' she hissed, striding down the corridor. 'It wasn't about Alek... I know it!'

Sofia could feel the frustration writhing with every step Katerina took. She understood: she would feel that she needed to prove herself. This had seemed like a lead, and perhaps her opportunity to make amends. 'Look, I agree, from what you say it didn't sound like she was talking about Alek.'

'Alek didn't show any sign of being ill, certainly not enough for someone like Domenico to be checking in on. It doesn't add up!'

'I know. Right now, though, all we have is a vague suspicion that Innes is lying about what she meant. We don't have an idea and we don't have anything we can pin on her.' They entered the lift and Katerina jabbed at the button to take her to the lobby in frenetic, irritable movements. Sofia added in her best soothing tone, 'I'd like to meet this Domenico in person. I'll make some inquiries.'

Sofia considered her reflection in the mirrored wall. She looked haggard. The morsel of time for sleep that she could have enjoyed last night had been spent drafting responses to texts, deleting them, then drafting them again. Her eyes stung and her belly gurgled with that weary nausea that seemed to rush through her every breath. This had to stop. She had to decide either way: speak to her ex-husband, celebrate – somehow – his new life, wife and child, or cut him from her life completely. Neither was an attractive option, but this limbo was intolerable. She hung her head and brought her mind back to the matter at hand. 'Good spot on the alcohol, anyway,' she said.

'It didn't turn much up,' Katerina said, her bottom lip pouting. Typically, Katerina's propensity to revert to childlike sullenness irritated her, but now – and perhaps it was the severe lack of sleep – she felt an impulse to encourage her.

'It was still a good observation,' she insisted. 'Innes said that they were stressed about the party, but I'm not so sure. They would have attended hundreds of events like it. So, what were they worried about? What spooked two non-drinkers to work their way through half the bar? Her reaction to your question makes me think that it's more than just someone not practising what they preach.'

This seemed to cheer Katerina up a tiny bit. 'Teddy's murder?' she suggested. 'A guest at the same hotel's murder. It would have been a shock.'

'Maybe...' The doors opened onto the lobby, where Lily was speaking at volume, arms in the air, at a man wearing a baseball cap.

'The speakers have to be on the beach! It's a must, a must! We're putting on boats from the private airport... that's the whole point! It's the first thing they'll hear when they come around the headland. The sound quality must be second to none! Have you thought about clearing the sand? Has that occurred to you?'

Skirting around them, Sofia finished her sentence in a whisper. 'A stranger's murder is sad, even shocking, but it doesn't normally incite such an extreme response. Something was eating away at them in the lead-up to Alek's murder. I'd like to find out what that was, and I think Domenico Bonarelli might be the answer.'

Michail sat on a bench at the far end of the olive gardens, his shoulders hunched. He'd already examined Alek's posts twice over, but, whilst waiting for his phone to be couriered, there was no harm in trawling through them again. The case so far presented as a frustrating compendium of the smallest, random puzzles – all of which may well be connected in some way, if only he could see how the pieces fell. Clearly, perseverance and a balanced mind would be the quickest route to solving this. Fortunately, due to his successful closing of his wax syphon, he was certain that his mind was regaining its old knack. Indeed, the block was working. Katerina and he were effective colleagues once again. His counsellor, were she here, would likely not approve, despite his success. She would advise him to arrange a blunt and truthful conversation with the aim of airing past traumas. Clearly, he had found a better way. Plus, he did not have the words for this particular situation. The lost wax technique worked remarkably well for talking through his thoughts about crowds and bodies. It did not work when it came to Katerina. It was much less stressful, and an order of magnitude more sensible, to bury those feelings away. They were too messy, too big to unleash into the world. With them neatly boxed up, he could continue to get on with what he needed to do. The slight, at times imperceptible, agitation in the pit of his stomach, was worth it.

The sensation reminded him of when he was sixteen, just after his mother had died. He had not cried. People had thought him strange. The accepted expression of grief was tears, and yet his eyes had remained dry, barren. His father, he remembered, had attempted to speak to him.

'Michail, your teachers, they say that you don't want to talk about Mama...'

'There's nothing to say.'

'But you must want to speak about it. If not to me, then maybe to a friend...'

Even if he had had a friend, his father's suggestion would have been impossible to enact. Then, like now, there was no language through which to describe the gurgling, tendinous insect that pulsed somewhere between his belly and lungs, growing larger and bristlier with every breath. There was no word for that creature then and there was no word for that creature now. He had never mentioned it in his therapy sessions. So, he had decided to do what he had done as a child: ignore it. Swallow the indefinable creature down again. No matter how much it wanted to climb out of the syphon in wordless grunts. No matter how much it pressed against his throat.

He clicked on yet another video of Alek speaking into a tiny microphone, framed by an impressive view of a city Michail identified as Rome. 'Only you are in charge of your life,' Alek said, his eyes filled with a sincerity that Michail struggled to believe. 'You oversee your destiny. Stop blaming others for your mistakes, your weaknesses. Whatever it is. Money problems? Love problems? Diet problems? Whatever – it's on you. Only you. As soon as you accept that; that's when real change happens.'

The video cut into a montage of him and Innes posing at various tourist spots in Rome, ending with Alek lifting her over his shoulder to carry her up the Spanish Steps.

'Don't forget to hit follow and look out for my new show, *Your Best You,* coming soon.' Alek signed off the video with a nod at the camera.

Michail blinked, sure that he must have missed something. The video had opened with the very clear and sensible promise of self-improvement and discipline, yet had suggested no tangible advice, nor practical information for the viewer. He shook his head and clicked on the next video. It opened with Alek in the pool area of what Michail immediately recognised as Saturn House.

'As you can probably hear, there's a bit of a party going on...' Indeed, pumping music and splashes sounded in the background, as Alek laughed at something happening behind his phone. As a professional videographer, it seemed an unwise choice of setting. 'So, I'm here at Saturn House on Aegina ahead of the Saturnalia party. Keep watching for more updates. To those of you with tickets, look, all I can say is that it's going to be epic, you have no idea how beautiful it is here. Like always, bring your best self and I can promise you the time of your life...'

A squeal of delight and a splash sounded from off-camera and Alek threw his head back, revealing his set of perfectly straight white teeth. 'All right, pool's calling! Later!' He placed the phone so that it was face up – presumably a stylistic attempt to seem authentic – and the words 'Follow to be your best self!' appeared on the screen to the backdrop of a loud splash and more shrieks of laughter. From this angle, the camera caught the edge of a large-rimmed cocktail glass, looming like a translucent moon in the corner of the shot. Michail was unsure why it caught his eye – perhaps it was the slight shudder the glass gave as Alek pushed off his lounger towards the pool. Or perhaps it was the fleck of incongruous colour against the brash saturated blue of the sky. He paused the video and zoomed in. It was there. It was most certainly there. Some trick of the light meant that the glass reflected the image with near-perfect quality: a pair of salmon chinos were discarded in a heap on the lounger opposite. Michail brought the screen as close to his nose as possible to double-check. It was undeniable. They were Teddy Menkopf's – hardly noticeable unless you were looking closely – precisely next to where Alek had been sitting.

His fingers beginning to tingle, Michail checked the date of the post. It was two days before Teddy's body had been found. Michail flicked back to the still image again. There was, of course, a possibility that Alek also had a pair of salmon chinos. Although, this was unlikely. Michail had noted that he favoured a muted colour palette when it came to clothing. There was also the possibility that Teddy had left his clothes by the pool by accident, before Alek and Innes had arrived. Michail frowned and watched the video again, this time bringing the speaker close to his ear.

'...there's a bit of a party going on...' There! Michail

rewound and heard it again. Two splashes which sounded like people jumping into the pool consecutively could be heard in the background. One. Two. There were two additional people at Alek's party. Was one of them Teddy? It was probable. Teddy had been the only other guest at the hotel. Why would Alek have lied about not spending time with him, about avoiding him? If these were Teddy's trousers, then it seemed that not only had Alek spent some time with him, but that they had been relatively close, sitting right next to each other. Michail sighed and leaned against the bench. The intoxicating pull of exhaustion simmered through his bones, heavy in the heat. He closed his eyes and let the warm breeze gently graze his face.

'Sleeping on the job?'

His eyes flew open at the unexpected voice. Before him stood Maria, two large folders in her arms. She laughed when he sat up straight, almost dropping his phone.

'Sorry, I didn't mean to startle you—'

'No. No, I was immersed in the details of the case, but I remain alert, always.'

She set the folders down before stretching her arms above her head. 'They're heavy.' She yawned and bobbed her head towards him. '*Baba* said that his passport's been returned to him. I suppose that means you've started looking into serious suspects?' A shadow passed over her face. 'I heard about Alek.'

He nodded; of course, everyone had heard about Alek. 'It is understandable that you feel angry,' he said, standing to help her carry the folders. 'But it's imperative that we exhaust every line of inquiry. However, yes, your father is no longer a suspect.'

'Have you worked out who stole his key card?'

'Of course, I cannot go into the details of the case with you. Do you have any theories?'

She laughed and Michail could not help but notice the soft

crinkles that appeared at the corners of her eyes. 'I'll take that as a no, then?'

He placed one of the folders beneath his arm. 'Is your father at the desk today? You're visiting him?'

'No.' She exhaled softly as she grabbed the second folder. 'These are for Lily. She's obsessed with showcasing local artists. Thinks it looks good for the hotel, the brand. It's actually not a bad initiative. Better than the NFT rubbish she's splayed across the walls.'

'Ah yes, the NFTs. I have them in my room. They're quite an interesting concept, even though I find the style to be aesthetically unpleasing. Apparently, the images projected on the screens are symbols, or rather, phantom representations of the real artwork, which is a series of numbers, a code. The theory – if not the output – is like the symbology employed in ancient archaic art. For example, the way that human figures are presented as an amalgamation of symmetry and geometry creates an ideal form, something not real, but not meaning to be. If one thinks about it, the NFTs mirror Plato's Theory of the Forms – there is one unseeable, untouchable beauty, only mimicked by the physical iterations.'

He took a deep breath, pleased to have someone with whom he could share his artistic musings. There was quite a long pause. He waited patiently for Maria to formulate her response. He'd explored some moderately serious philosophical ideas, so it was reasonable for her to need a bit of time.

'That's an interesting take, actually. I've never thought about them in that way, but you're right. The four characteristics of Plato's forms are that they are eternal, unchanging, unmoving, and indivisible. The objects in our world are merely imperfect shadows of them. I suppose it's the same with NFT codes... as unique cryptographic tokens, they cannot be replicated but real-world images can represent them. I like that.'

'Yes!' An electric surge of excitement that Michail had not experienced in a long time flared through his guts. 'That's precisely it! I have been formulating my theory over the past two days – in between finding the perpetrator of the murders, of course – and you have summarised it expertly. Thank you!'

'You're welcome,' she replied, and he nodded, satisfied that they had both understood each other.

They walked up the path to the hotel. 'So, these are your paintings?'

'Prints mainly, but yes. I always wanted to be an artist, but... well, it's not exactly an easy way to make money, is it?'

'I have heard the income is unpredictable, yes.'

'So, I make art in my spare time, when I can. My job isn't so dissimilar anyway, it's creative at least.'

'You work in advertising?' Michail remembered Sofia relaying their conversation from yesterday.

'That's right.' Maria set her folder in the middle of the lobby, which was now filled with various boxes of sound equipment and other party-related paraphernalia. 'We've actually done a bit for the Balcombe House Group, which means I know that Lily's championing of local art is less of a good deed and more of a marketing ploy. The grassroots, small artisanal movement, is huge right now. She knows what she's talking about.'

'I see.' Michail folded his arms as a constable arrived through the main door of the lobby.

'Sergeant Mikras?'

'Yes? Ah, the phone?'

The constable nodded nervously. For the first time, Michail experienced the dizzying realisation that he was now a well-known, if not well-respected, member of the Hellenic Police

Force. He had worn the same nervous, excited expression when he had first approached Sofia just over a year ago. Michail took Alek's phone and placed it in his pocket. 'Thank you very much, Constable, this is most useful indeed.'

The man's cheeks glowed a deep shade of red before he gave Michail a brisk nod and hurried back from the way he came. Michail felt the weight of the phone's package in his hands: inside this plastic casing could well be a momentous clue. There was no time to delay.

'Ms Barlas, it has been wonderful speaking with you, but now I must continue with my duties.'

Her eyes widened but her lips curled into a kind smile. 'Don't let me keep you.'

He turned to leave but before he could disappear along the corridor, she called after him. 'Um, Sergeant Mikras... Michail, isn't it? I wondered... I mean, now that *Baba* is no longer on your hit list... would you want to go for a drink?'

Note

Katerina nibbled on the corner of her nail, wincing as she tasted blood. Swearing aloud, she placed her hand beneath the table, where it would be safe from anxiety-induced gnawing. She took a long sip of coffee and stared at the pool's surface. She tried to imagine what would have been happening off-camera from the video Michail had forwarded to her. She was sitting on Alek's lounger, the table upon which the cocktail glass would have been within reach. The second lounger, next to her, was where the missing chinos had been placed.

'Katerina, you're early!' Michail strode from the far side of the pool, waving at her slightly robotically.

'You're right about the trousers,' she said. 'If Alek didn't like Teddy, as he kept mentioning, then why did they sit right next to where his stuff was? There's plenty of space here. Even if Teddy had joined him, Alek could have moved.'

'Indeed. He also said that the day of Teddy's murder was the first time the two of them had been by the pool at the same time. And why was he swimming with him? The booking records confirm there were no visitors at the hotel on that day. It seems that Alek downplayed his relationship with Teddy.'

'Hmmm.' Katerina stood up and rolled back and forth on the balls of her feet. 'Sofia's chasing Domenico Bonarelli. If there is something going on, then Innes will have warned him by now, but I'd still like to speak with him. Innes doesn't know that we suspect she and Alek were close with Teddy... perhaps Domenico might shed some light on the relationship?'

'Possibly, possibly.' Michail scratched his head.

'Something on your mind?'

He looked at her, as if surprised that she had asked him the question, and opened his mouth. Then, as if he had changed his mind, he pressed his lips together and shook his head. 'No, Katerina, not at all. I am eager to get to the harbour though. You saw the email from Yiorgos?'

'Yes.' She heard the defensiveness in her own voice. 'If forensics' estimate about the bullet entry is right then we should have a good idea about where to start looking.'

'Good.' He was still wearing an expression that she couldn't quite read. She thought about double-checking that he was all right, but decided it was best to leave him to it.

'Oh!' She began to lead the way around the back entrance towards the road. 'The local police have finally loaned us a car. Better late than never, eh? Are you driving or me?'

She had meant the question to be casual, but as they approached the vehicle, the sight stopped them both in their tracks. It was a standard police issue, with all the usual marks and bumps. It wasn't the car that made them pause. It was the fact they hadn't been in a car together since last summer, since the long investigation which had snaked all over Athens. Now she thought about it properly, she realised the significance of climbing back into a vehicle with him: it was a symbol, an emblem of their partnership.

He cleared his throat. 'I am happy for you to drive, Katerina.

In fact, I would like to think about how to hack Alek's mobile device on the way.'

'They couldn't get into it?' She opened the driver's door and jumped in.

'No, it's more difficult than it used to be with these newer models, apparently. There is a passcode, but we only have three attempts before the phone locks. Alek seemed like the type of person to have something meaningful, significant to him.'

She pulled out of the driveway into full view of the shimmering sea. 'What makes you say that?'

'I have conducted a thorough assessment of his character, which, thanks to his incessant social media posting, has proved quite fruitful. According to various online psychological tests and research, Alek would have been considered a high-functioning narcissist. His influencer lifestyle befits this personality trait, as does his obsession with creating a specific narrative about his life. Narcissists also have a tendency for souvenirs and egocentric sentimentality. Based on this conclusion, I think it's safe to assume that his password is something that would have been significant or meaningful to him, rather than a random assortment of numbers, which is, of course, optimal in terms of security.'

Katerina blew through her teeth. 'A narcissistic influencer, what a surprise!'

'Yes,' Michail replied. 'According to research, it is a common trait among the profession.'

Katerina turned the corner along the winding coastal path and slammed on her brakes as a group of people stepped out onto the road without warning. 'Jesus! Sorry!' She looked at Michail, who was clutching Alek's phone, his eyes narrowed.

'Picketers,' he said, studying them as they blocked the whole width of the road. 'Interesting...'

Without explanation, he jumped out of the car and Katerina

watched him march up to a woman at the front of the group who was sporting a T-shirt that read: SAY NO TO SATURNALIA! Katerina scanned the signs quickly. All of them showed some message or other about closing Saturn House or putting a stop to the festival. Most of the protestors wore the same determined, yet friendly expression. This was something they thought was worth taking a stand against, but she could tell that they conducted themselves peacefully. She pulled the car over by the shrubbery and followed Michail's lead.

'I see...' Michail had his notebook out and was writing as he spoke. 'And the main complaints? If you could be as specific as possible, that would be excellent.'

'Where to start!' The woman let out an exasperated squeal. 'Well, firstly we can no longer use the beach... *our* beach! I have no idea how they managed to buy the land, but they did. You used to be able to walk all the way down–'

'Anything else?' Michail interrupted, still writing away.

'Yes, oh yes. The music! The parties they throw, constantly! Every night some weeks, pumping, trembling music coming from the place!'

'Have you complained to the police?' Michail asked. 'If it's throughout the night, then they are transgressing the noise curfew.'

'Of course we have,' the woman replied. 'Do you think anyone has bothered to enforce it? I think they sent someone around once, but the music had stopped by the time he arrived, so...'

'I understand.' Michail nodded. 'Is that all?'

'That Saturnalia! The awful event! I wouldn't mind so much if it brought local businesses income, but it's an all-inclusive ticketed event. They block the harbour with their yachts and spoil the stars with their bright lights. It's not the sort of people we want visiting Aegina – we don't want to become the next Mykonos – and now, well, you'll probably know, they've brought the most horrific crimes to our island. Nobody can stop talking about that terrible, terrible scene at the harbour. I have never heard of anything like it.'

'END SATURNALIA! END SATURN HOUSE! END SATURNALIA! END SATURN HOUSE!' The group began to chant in unison and the woman nodded at Michail, who seemed satisfied with what he'd learned.

'Thank you for speaking with me,' he said. 'Now, please remove yourself from the road. We are on important investigative business.'

Katerina almost laughed at the look on the woman's face but was pleased that she ushered her fellow protestors to the roadside. Once they were back in the car, Michail stared at his notes, biting his lip, and twitching his fingers at the corners of his notebook. 'What do you think?'

'About the picketers?'

'Correct.'

She had the distinct impression that he was expecting a very specific answer. As she started the ignition, she held a hand up to the protestors as she continued up the hill towards the town. The turquoise water lapped close by the roadside here, as if urging her to follow Michail's train of thought.

'They're annoyed...' she began.

'Yes.' She heard him shift next to her impatiently.

'Um, well, they don't like the parties. Who would, I suppose? Those things are only fun if you're in the thick of them–'

'Very true. Revellers rarely understand the nuisance that they're causing; it's all relative.'

'So...'

Michail placed his book on the dashboard, his fingers

drumming rhythmically. 'Her description indicated that the parties were loud. *Trembling* is the word she used.'

'I guess that crowd can get pretty wild.'

'I don't doubt that at all. But...' He shifted again and Katerina glanced over at him. He placed his fingers against his temples. What was bothering him? She hadn't noticed anything out of the ordinary. Nothing the woman said had been suspicious; anyone would be bothered by such a racket, especially in such a small place–

'Where's the music coming from?' She almost shouted the question as they passed the small harbour on the edge of town, finally understanding his point. The boats bobbed gently in the water, as if nodding for her to continue. 'Lily's panicking about the music being loud enough. I overheard her shouting at some poor man about the sound needing to be loud enough to appease the festival guests, but...'

'By the sounds of it, the hotel already has a satisfactory sound system. Almost too satisfactory.' Michail looked out of his window, his head dipping in concentration as they crawled past the various tavernas at the main harbour waterfront.

'That woman could have been exaggerating,' suggested Katerina, as she pulled over. 'People like to complain, cause a fuss.'

'It's possible,' Michail said. 'But Saturn House only has twenty bedrooms.'

'Yes, that's weird.' Katerina climbed out of the car and took in the assortment of baby-blue and white chairs spread over the decking. The pergola framed the vista of glittering blue sea. Were it not for the police tape and the black stain of blood, it would have been pretty. 'It's for rich people, but not necessarily party animals. It doesn't make sense that they'd be throwing huge parties every night, at least, not ones loud enough to bother the locals.'

Michail placed his hands on his hips and turned his back on the decking to look up at the building behind them. 'Another archaic warrior clue,' he muttered.

Katerina stood next to him, following his gaze up to the numerous shuttered windows. 'Archaic warrior clue?'

'Yes. Smiling at us, confident and calm, like it knows it's pretending.'

'Seems like it's normal on the surface but something's a bit off?'

'Precisely,' Michail said. 'We just need to understand what the smiles are hiding, Katerina.'

'Sorry, I'm not following.'

Sofia paced around the pool, her phone pressed against her ear. She hadn't expected Domenico to be an easy man to get hold of. After six messages left with an assistant, who at no point had reacted with the level of gravitas that would have been appropriate when hearing the words *Hellenic Police Force* and *double murder inquiry*, she had finally managed to get through to the man himself. She had also expected a certain arrogance, slipperiness, all the qualities she assumed went along with being a white male millionaire. What she had not expected was the sickening dose of charm offensive that oozed, sweet and horrible, from the receiver.

'I apologise, *Sofia*, for confusing you–'

'No,' she replied bluntly. 'I'm not confused. What I'm not following is why you are refusing to aid a serious murder investigation that has happened in your hotel's–'

'One of the bodies was simply found on our beach, am I right? As far as I understand, there is no evidence to indicate that any foul play happened on the premises. As for Alek, well, that tragedy happened miles away from Marathon.'

'A ten-minute drive–'

'Well beyond the boundaries of Saturn House. If there was anything that I thought I could do to help, believe me, I'd be on my way to Aegina as we speak.'

'Your phone conversation with Innes–'

'She must be devastated.'

'Yes.' Sofia took a deep breath. 'Do you remember anything else about what you discussed?'

'Oh...' The pause felt deliberate and forced. 'The usual things. Innes is a good friend – she and Alek were together for about... well, now... it would be around five years. Of course, I asked about Alek's well-being, as he'd been ill.'

Sofia gritted her teeth. She had interviewed enough people to know when they were toying with her; he'd left that last nugget right until the very end, almost like he knew that she was trying to corroborate Innes's story. It was likely, then, that the two of them had spoken.

'Ill? How so?'

'Oh, you know... under the weather by the sounds of it. It wasn't a big deal. But I do remember asking after him.'

Sofia slumped down onto a lounger and stretched out her legs, wiping her forehead with the back of her hand. 'I'd appreciate it if you could come to answer some questions,' she repeated. 'We can do it in Athens if it's easier–'

'I'm afraid that won't work. Like I said, I have business in London. The fine art division of my company is hosting an event here. Leaving would be out of the question. I am, as you say it, a hands-on sort of person.'

'The Hellenic authorities are requesting that you–'

'I mean no offence by this, Sofia, but I checked with my lawyers, and you have no legal mandate nor power at present.

I've answered your questions, surely, that should be enough? I assume that you're enjoying the accommodation?'

'It's a little slick for my tastes,' she replied, clicking her tongue against the roof of her mouth. 'But we appreciate the gesture, of course.'

There was a brief pause, before he replied. 'Anything I can do to help. These are terrible things. I often find that people unveil themselves in times such as these.'

She opened her mouth to respond that these *people unveiling themselves* were the very reason why she wanted to speak to him in person, but he hung up. She swore softly, listening to the harsh consonants drift melodious into the greenery.

The fish vendor in the peach-coloured building across the street watched them approach with small, suspicious twitches of his moustache. Michail placed his badge on the plastic counter. He felt his nostrils flare involuntarily at the strong aquatic aroma.

'We need to inspect the building.'

The man's nostrils flared, giving the impression that he was sniffing Michail. His eyes moved from side to side. 'It's already been searched, the space upstairs.' He gestured to the police tape pulled across a door in the back of the shop. 'Back for more?'

'Correct.' Michail tapped an impatient finger on the badge. 'I believe there are two floors above?'

'Two, yes. I don't own them, though. I live in the back, here.' He pointed to the back of the shop. 'And there's a terrace at the top,' the man added gruffly. He squinted at Michail. 'You're investigating the shooting?'

Normally, Michail would have reminded him that he was

not at liberty to discuss police business. However, based on where the premises were, this man had likely watched everything from the shooting to the grisly clean-up in gruesome detail. 'That's right. Do you know who owns the floors above you?' He flipped through his notes. 'The initial forensics said it was your landlord?'

The man shrugged, his eyes drifting away from Michail's face and out to sea. 'Same people that collect my rent, that's all I know.'

'No one lives up there?'

He shook his head and steadily brought his gaze back to Michail's face. His eyes seemed wetter than they had before, as if afflicted by the sea salt. 'They were rooms for tourists. The place used to be called Hotel Plaza. Now it's just for spiders.'

'Do you have the key?' Michail asked. The man blinked at him twice before, finally, nodding and disappearing along the narrow corridor.

'Do you think this might be it?' Katerina whispered, her eyes scanning the ceiling. 'The sniper was here?'

'Impossible to say for certain,' Michail replied from the corner of his mouth. 'But it's in the perfect position. They could have easily missed something in the first search, given the amount of ground they had to cover. Deserted, locked, outside access... it fits the profile.'

The man reappeared with a key in his hand. A large wooden keyring in the shape of a fish was attached to it, with Hotel Plaza engraved in its belly. 'There you go,' he said, handing it over. 'It still works. I sometimes use the stairs to store supply boxes. Not sure about the rooms, though.'

'When was the last time you went up?' Michail asked.

The man shook his head, as if Michail had said something truly distasteful. 'It's not my property. I never go up the stairs. I shouldn't even store my things there.'

'Of course,' said Michail, gripping the key in his fist. 'We won't be long.'

The lock gave a satisfying click as the door swung open. Crouching under the police tape, the smell of fish was replaced with a thick mouthful of damp, rotting wood. Katerina closed the door behind them and peered up into the dimly lit stairway. 'It stinks in here.'

'I suspect a dead rodent or bird.'

There were two doors leading off the first landing. 'Rooms one and two,' Katerina read. 'Slightly different vibe than Saturn House.' She tried the first handle and the door swung open easily, its hinges squealing as if exhaling in relief. 'Ugh.'

Placing his arm over his face, Michail followed Katerina in. The shutters were closed, but a couple of rotten slats meant that slivers of sunlight cut through the thick air and illuminated the filth. A swollen covering of dust spread atop every surface. Mould grew in the centre of the bare mattress in a circular festering pit. Michail looked up and saw its source: a greenish-brown hole gaped in the ceiling, the damp relic of an old leak. Katerina moved to the window and crouched down, pushing open the shutters to get a better view. The extra light made the mess seem even worse. Michail kept his arm pressed tightly against his mouth.

'Yes, we're too low here,' Katerina said. 'Forensics said that the shooter needed to have been at least eight metres above street level. This isn't that high.'

'Let's try upstairs. The rooms all overlook the decking next door.' Michail backed out of the room and closed the door behind them, breathing a sigh of relief to be out of the sour air. The stairway leading to the next floor was even more narrow and flimsy. The wood seemed to bend and squelch in the heat as they climbed.

'Careful!' The second landing was almost completely dark,

lit only by the soft fuzz of light from beneath the bedroom doors. Michail fumbled in his pocket for his torch and switched it on. A low grunt escaped his mouth. Dark-brown stains trickled down the walls all the way to the floorboards. The smell was almost unbearable.

'Whoever the owner is needs to do some serious repairs.' Katerina choked softly.

They pushed open the door to room three and entered an identical-looking bedroom. Katerina made straight for the window and peered out of the dusty glass. She nodded to Michail. 'It's about right, I think. We should give forensics a call. They should sweep the place again and the room next door.'

'Absolutely.' Michail trailed his eyes along the floorboards, attempting to picture the killer stalking their way silently through the shadows, their footsteps light, their knees bent and soft, positioning themselves by the window, watching the decking from above. The thought made him nauseous. 'These rooms are easily broken into; anyone could have accessed them.'

'I suppose it's unlikely anyone professional enough to use a sniper would leave any clues for us to find.' Katerina smiled, heading past him for the door.

At first, the sound didn't make any sense at all. It was a panicked pounding, growing louder and louder from nowhere in particular. Michail hadn't yet worked out what was happening when Katerina was flung through the air, her limbs suddenly loose and lifeless, her head snapping back like something had driven into her. Every breath, every minute sound swelled, slow and impossible, in Michail's ears. The crack as Katerina hit the wall, the papery exhale as she slid to the floor. The sound, again, this time moving away from them. Pummelling. Escaping.

'Stop!' The word came from his mouth as if independent of thought. 'Police! Stop!'

He charged forwards towards the corridor, reflex setting his legs into motion. Then he registered Katerina crumpled in the corner, blood pouring down her face, eyes closed. He heard a clatter of footsteps above him – someone was on the terrace. The noises grew louder between his ears. The footsteps. The creak of the floorboards. The insects in the walls. The drip of Katerina's blood as it fell through the cracks. The slowing of her breath. The damp, shallow contraction of her lungs. The decision was clear: he could not leave her. Keeping his eye on the door, he threw himself next to her, wrapping her head in his jacket.

'Katerina! Katerina?'

The dusty air seemed to freeze, hardened by his cries. She didn't move. He couldn't identify the rise of her chest. Impossible. The thought was as clear as anything he had ever thought. Impossible. 'Katerina!'

The air shifted. Her eyes opened. 'Michail, go…'

He seemed rooted to the spot, unable to make any sort of a decision. 'Go,' she repeated. 'I'll be fine.'

He blinked at her for a couple of seconds, before tearing himself away. Bolting up the next set of stairs towards the light, he hurled himself through the narrow doorway when he spotted the figure – dressed from head to toe in black – on the far side of the roof. 'Stop where you are!'

For a moment, it looked like the figure might surrender. They held their hands above their head and appeared to stand very still, as if giving themselves up. Then, as if stepping off a kerb, they strode forwards into the thin air and disappeared.

'No!' Michail lurched forwards, knowing that he would be too late. His momentum took him to the building's edge, and he held his breath, bracing himself for the sight below. He blinked. Then again. The yawning sensation of stupidity rising at the back of his neck. A fire escape ran down the back of the building into the winding streets of the old town: the figure had merely jumped over the wall. Grabbing his radio, he scanned the area, trying desperately to see the direction in which they'd run. 'Officer down! Officer down and injured at the harbourside. The attacker is heading south-east towards the centre of the old town, possibly still wearing all black – backup required. Backup required!'

As he tore back down the stairs to Katerina, his brain seemed to implode into a thousand images, all of Katerina, flickering: smiling, crying, screaming, bleeding. His throat grew thick and his chest tight. She was where he had left her, limp and unmoving. He knelt at her side and cupped her head onto his lap, applying more pressure on her head wound. He wanted to speak to her, to reassure her in hushed tones, to speak to that element of the subconscious that knows – always knows – when things are going well or not. However, the words, as he suspected they would, failed him.

'She'll be fine. It's just a couple of stitches.' Sofia pushed the glass of water she'd ordered for Michail across the plastic tabletop. She looked over his shoulder at forensics going in and out of the building: hopefully they'd come up with something. Michail hadn't yet spoken short of a detailed, detached breakdown about what had happened inside. 'You should have some water,' she said. 'It's hot.'

He slowly brought the glass to his lips and took a determined sip. She leaned back in her chair and rolled her shoulders backwards, releasing the tension in her spine. 'You did the right thing,' she offered. 'You had to follow them.'

'I didn't catch them, though.'

She nodded, pressing her lips together; there was no

denying that this was a huge disappointment. 'How is it now? With Katerina? Are you... are you working things out?'

He looked at the rim of his glass and tilted his head to one side. The expression he wore reminded her of a child's: lost and helpless, yet with that innocent resolution, determination. She took a quick, long sip of her coffee.

'She is working very diligently,' he said without looking up. 'She is better at investigating now than before.'

'I've noticed that.' Sofia folded her arms and closed her eyes for a moment. 'It's obvious she's putting the effort in. That's something.'

Michail tapped the side of his glass as if deep in thought, then pushed it carefully to one side. He raised his eyes nervously to meet hers. 'Did you know?'

Sofia raised an eyebrow at him. She should have been ready for the question – he was always going to have asked her. Integrity and honesty were values that he held deep, possibly deeper than anyone else she knew. He would want the truth. She slid her chair back and stood, walking to the edge of the deck. It was as if these restaurants were made for conversations like these; the hot breeze, the open sea, impatient yet still – the landscape was prepared for weighty words. Shaking her head, she slipped her stilettos off and sat on the edge of the deck, dipping her feet into the sea. She let a relieved groan escape her throat. Looking back at Michail, she chuckled at the expression on his face. 'If you want to do this now, then I'm afraid you'll need to take me shoeless.'

After what looked like a short internal battle, he followed her lead, folding his trousers to his knees in neat, regular folds. He settled next to her and lowered his own feet into the water. She let him luxuriate for a while, feel the enormity of the sea at his feet. Keeping her eyes on the horizon, she began, 'We can only do what we think at the time, Michail. It isn't always a question of what's right and wrong.' She felt him tense next to her. 'Really, it isn't. Sometimes it's about what's better or worse, what's kind and cruel,' she exhaled, 'what's understanding and what's not.'

'The Hellenic Police Force is built on trust and honesty. We fought the corruption, we put things right. How can I live with it if I... if I am no longer honest? I lied, Sofia. You knew it. You expected it, didn't you?'

Tiny silver fish appeared beneath their feet, twisting and darting in their tight-knit mass. 'You see that shoal of fish? They're moving together, aren't they? They're swimming as one, protecting each other, moving in the same direction, just like they've learned.'

'Yes. This is a school, though, not a shoal. They are all the same species, you see,' Michail pointed out.

'I see. But they are moving in the same direction?'

'Correct.'

'But look, are they turning in precisely the same way? See the ones in the front, they need to twist more, at a greater angle than those at the back? And the ones in the middle, well, they need to keep the group together, they barely need to change direction at all.'

'You are referring to relative motion–'

'Yes, yes I am, Michail. My point is there are lots of ways to work towards the right direction, to work towards good. Sometimes, you just need to twist a little more than you think.'

'A satisfactory metaphor,' Michail said. She glanced at him out of her peripheral vision and spotted the corner of his mouth twitch.

'And you didn't lie,' she continued. 'You twisted the truth, ever so slightly. Katerina was manipulated; she was physically and mentally abused. Her mistake was choosing the wrong man. You said what you needed to keep her out of prison and keep a good officer in the force. She *didn't* have anything to do with The Awakening. That was all Theo. She was a victim and she proved herself on that very night, like I said at the time.'

'You... you think that I did the right thing?'

'I think that if this conversation is ever repeated to anyone, then I'll deny every word of it. But, yes, here and now, I think you made the right call. If you'd said anything else, then there is absolutely no chance that she'd be back with us. And, between you and me, I quite like her.'

He drew soft circles with his feet in the water, watching the fish dart away into the depths. 'I've lied about another thing.'

'Oh?' Sofia drew her knees to her chest, enjoying the cooling effect of the droplets drying in the breeze.

'Yes. I have told Katerina that everything is fine between us, but it is not. I've done what you said. I've pretended to be her friend again. I have pretended that everything is fine. The problem is that I am afraid it's a lie. Even though I've successfully buried all my unhelpful feelings, I realised... when I thought that she was... I realised that perhaps I should have addressed them with her. And I thought for a moment that I wouldn't ever get the chance. That the syphon would be blocked forever. Without opening it, I am not sure that I'll ever know whether I can... whether *we* can be what we were.'

Sofia pushed herself up to standing. 'I'm afraid that I'm not the best person to give personal advice. When it comes to matters of the heart, I'm somewhat lacking myself. I suppose all I can say is that time heals, although not always as much as we might hope.' She folded her arms. 'But I didn't tell you to pretend or block anything. I'm not sure where you got that from.'

'I distinctly remember you ordering me to ensure the harmonious working relationship—'

She sighed. 'Not at the expense of yourself, Michail. I was

just trying to help. Clearly, you must take things at your own pace.'

He looked like his thoughts had subsumed him, which was a relief: she had run out of life advice. Before she suggested heading back to the hotel, a forensic worker called her name.

'Yes? Please tell me you've got something?'

The woman grinned as she approached. 'We've got something, Major.'

'Tell me.'

'Great call about ordering a second look. Despite the state of it in there, it's swept up; clearly a professional job, so we're unlikely to find DNA. However.' She held up an evidence bag. 'We found this under a gap in the flooring. It would've been easy to miss in a clean-up–'

Sofia peered at the bag. 'An English tenner?'

'Yes, but also–' The woman held out another evidence bag, this time with a receipt in it. 'Wrapped around the note, so it could easily have fallen out whenever whoever was in there pulled something out of their pocket.'

Sofia grabbed the bag and studied the small piece of paper. 'A Post-it?' She twisted the bag in front of her face. 'Wait, it's embossed with the Balcombe House logo – *Mia cara, La vita svelata è la via migliore, come sempre* – anyone speak Italian?'

Michail was already on his phone finding the translation. '*My darling, the unveiled life is the best way, like always.*'

She shook her head; it was a small leap, although not an entirely ridiculous one. 'That word, *unveiled*, when I spoke to Domenico earlier today, he said something similar: people unveil themselves. I thought it was an odd turn of phrase.'

'Obviously, it's his hotel group. I conducted a thorough search of the reception and administrative offices at Saturn House – there is no supply of Post-its with this letterhead. I think it safe to assume, coupled with the English money, that this has come from Balcombe House itself, in London.'

She looked at Michail. 'What's a note from Balcombe House from Domenico Bonarelli, doing here?' She stamped her foot without remembering that she didn't have her heels on. This was a brilliant, yet frustrating find. 'And who the hell is "*my darling*"? This isn't anywhere near enough to call him in, you know. It's circumstantial: anyone could have stayed at Balcombe House – they're not responsible for every guest's action.' She swore loudly, causing the rest of the forensic team to look up. Speaking mainly to herself, she fingered the note. 'We need to find a way to meet with him. I can't put this down to coincidence.'

'Excellent decision,' replied Michail, already running to the edge of the decking to retrieve his shoes.

Unveiled

Katerina resisted the urge to finger the stitches that pulled taut across her forehead, despite how much they itched. All three of them stared at Alek's phone which sat, quietly tormenting them, on the table on Michail's terrace. Michail paced in front of the board, pen in one hand, the other tapping gently at the side of his thigh. She'd noticed him avoiding eye contact with her since she'd got back from the hospital. Perhaps he was disappointed that she'd allowed herself to be pushed over, letting the mystery assailant escape the Hotel Plaza? She hadn't seen the force coming until it was too late, until her head had slammed against the wall. She remembered how she'd insisted that Michail leave her. It was like the words had been ready-made, hiding beneath her tongue, waiting to float out and surrender. *Leave me. I'm not worth it. Not worth anything.* And he had listened to her; he'd left her in a pool of blood. She'd been glad.

Clearing her throat, she winced as she accidentally moved her eyebrows – the painkillers were wearing off. The music that Sofia had insisted they play to drown out their low voices engulfed her skull with an unbearable, rhythmic friction.

'Two weeks? How can it take so long?' Fatigue made her voice sound tinny, as if she was listening to someone else speak. She was glad that they'd been forced to hold the meeting outside. The air, although muggy, was keeping her awake.

'Something to do with new regulations about data protection. They *say* they're moving as fast as they can, but I think it's safe to assume that we're not at the top of any social media platform's priority list,' Sofia whispered. 'They're co-operating in the eyes of the law. The fastest way to see Alek's private messages is to guess his password.'

Michail placed his hands on his hips and scrunched up his face, deep in thought. 'I've studied his public videos and I can't think of anything that gives us any clues. Innes is sure that she doesn't know?'

Sofia shrugged. 'Apparently not. She's not giving much away, although she has agreed to stay put for a few days. I'd like to rule her out of being the owner of the note before she leaves the country. She's the only person who has a personal relationship with Domenico that we know of, plus her bank records prove she's been in London on numerous occasions – staying at Balcombe House – over the last year. We're waiting on a call for the prints – if hers match, then we'll arrest her.'

'Let's not forget Lily Woodstow.' Michail tapped his pen against the name on the board. 'She has a relationship with Domenico.'

'In a professional capacity,' Sofia replied. 'And she hasn't left Aegina, let alone Greece, for over two years. She's annoying as they come, but I'm not sure she's dangerous.'

Michail glanced around the terrace, his shoulders tense, and beckoned them to move even closer to him. Dutifully, they huddled around, and he began, 'I think it unwise for us to remain here any longer, Major Sampson. With Domenico and

Innes as unofficial suspects, this is a compromising location from which to conduct our investigation.'

Katerina nodded. 'He's right. Anyone could be listening and we don't know what they've got rigged in our rooms.' The thought of being monitored made her shudder, even in the warm night.

'We're sweeping the rooms regularly and we have people on patrol,' Sofia said reassuringly.

'But I agree the time has come to move – we have somewhere ready. Remember, we don't know who's watching, what they know and what they don't. I suggest we make it known that we need more space for our work – I don't want anyone here thinking we suspect them. We must act naturally, but pack tonight.'

The song of the *tzitzikas* seemed to rise to a crescendo as the three of them stood in silence on the terrace. Unable to shake the feeling that they were huddling, helpless, in the centre of a lions' pit, Katerina walked to the balcony and rested her weight on her hands, letting her head roll backwards to look at the sky. '8 1 726,' she muttered, to nobody in particular.

'What was that?' Sofia asked; Katerina could hear the concern in her voice: they'd been watching her like she was going mad. She exhaled, forcing herself to string her thoughts together clearly.

'Innes's password to her phone: 8 1 726. We didn't ask her about it – not that she'd have given us a straight answer – but doesn't it seem odd to you?'

'How so?' Sofia motioned to Michail to write the numbers on the board.

'Well, first of all, people usually have a four-digit password, because they use the same number combination for their bank cards–'

'An extremely insecure approach,' Michail added. 'But it's true, the majority of people favour a four-digit code.'

'It's really rare for someone to have five digits, six digits sometimes, but five isn't popular.' She exhaled, trying to think it through. 'I wonder what those numbers mean to her?'

'They could be random?' suggested Sofia.

'Unlikely,' said Michail, beginning to pace back and forth again, although even more quickly than before. 'An astounding amount of people do not take the pertinent security advice to choose numbers at random. Usually, passwords hold a personal significance.'

'That's what I mean.' Katerina approached the board and stared at the figures. 'It's not her birthday, it doesn't spell anything sensible when transposed to letters... so what is it?'

Sofia sighed and shrugged. 'I feel like we're stumbling at random clue after random clue, here. Did either of you have any thoughts about Domenico? The *unveiled* comment?'

As if a spring had unwound somewhere inside of him, Michail's back straightened and he whipped a fresh piece of paper over the board. 'Unveiled,' he began, writing the word in large capitals. 'A brief etymological explanation will be useful, here; the meaning is more symbolic in Greek, of course – αποκαλύπτω[1]. In any case, as Sofia correctly pointed out, it was an odd turn of phrase for Domenico to use, and he has used it twice: once when speaking English to Sofia on the telephone, and once when writing in Italian on his hotel's Post-it, we can reasonably assume.'

He took a deep breath and began to write on the board again. 'The word originated directly from the Latin verb *velare*, meaning "to cover, or to veil". Therefore, the adjective *velatus* means "covered".' He listed the words on the board, his hand almost shaking with excitement. 'Add the prefix "in", or "un" for

English, "s" for the Italian *s-velato* and we arrive at the Latin *invelatus*: unveiled.'

Katerina glanced at Sofia, who seemed just as confused as she was. 'Um, so it's from Latin? I mean, aren't a lot of words derived from Latin? Especially Italian and English ones?'

'Correct, Katerina. Italian, in fact, borrows seventy-five per cent of its words directly from Latin. English sits a little lower, at sixty per cent.' He stepped back from the board, nodding with deep satisfaction.

'Michail, if you could get to the point.' Sofia pushed her hands out in front of her, flexing her fingers.

'Certainly. The fact that the word is derived from Latin is inconsequential on its own. However, I found it useful to put it into context.' He checked over his shoulder and lowered his voice to a barely audible murmur. Katerina scraped her chair closer to him. 'Where are we staying?'

Sofia rolled her eyes and replied, drily, 'Saturn House.'

'Precisely!' He wrote the name of the hotel on the board. 'It bothered me that the hotel group had chosen to use the Roman name, Saturn, over the Greek name, Kronos. We are in Greece: the oversight has the potential to misguide many tourists about correct mythological terminology–'

Sofia cleared her throat.

'–at first, I thought that it was careless ignorance. However, the "unveiled" reference set me on an etymological examination–'

'An etymological examination? Michail, please tell me this isn't an excuse to reinstate the Myth Buster Unit?' Sofia groaned, placing her head in her hands.

'On the contrary, this is a very serious line of inquiry.' Michail turned his back to them as he wrote more on the board. When he stepped away, Katerina saw that he had written three distinct points. 'Firstly,' he whispered, 'we are staying in Saturn

House. An unusual naming convention, as I've already explained. Secondly, when I researched the word *"invelatus"* and "Saturn" together, as paired terms, I came up with only one reference: texts relating to the Roman festival of the Saturnalia, for which the sacrificial rites were carried out by an *unveiled* priest. This was unusual for the Romans, since they favoured sacrifices to be made *capite velato*–'

'Michail...' Sofia's voice was low with warning.

'–that's *with the head covered* by a robe, for example,' continued Michail.

Sofia stood in a quick, sharp movement, causing her chair to topple behind her. 'Michail!' she hissed, her arms crossed tightly across her midriff. 'You cannot be serious. *This* cannot be serious. I explicitly told you that we were not entertaining any myths. We're not a joke, Michail! We can't solve every crime by looking at *stories.*'

Katerina held her breath as Sofia continued to rail at him, her anger managing to ring through the air despite the quiet volume of her voice. 'You are wasting time here. We have two dead, we have Athens clawing at our backs, demanding a breakthrough, we've let a sniper and whomever that was today get away from us... what am I supposed to tell my seniors? That we only look at myths now? That we don't do crimes that aren't based around myths? That we're no longer the Special Violent Crime Unit, but instead have decided to focus our attention exclusively on *Myth Busting*?'

Katerina looked to the sky. The stars seemed to sag heavily above them. Her stitches throbbed as if feeding off the tension in the air and she lifted her head to offer Michail some support; he had only been trying to help. She could see his logical, if misguided, train of thought: if he had solved last summer's murders by looking to mythology and history, then why not now? Surprisingly, Michail's expression was perfectly serene.

Sofia's barrage didn't seem to have bothered him in the slightest.

Sofia stalked to the balcony and hung her head over it. 'Michail–' she began, without turning to face them.

'I understand, Major Sampson. You are right to question my methods if you think them unhelpful. However, with your permission I would like to explain my final point?'

'The "T"?' Katerina looked back at the board and frowned. 'The "T" on Teddy's necklace? And Tatiana's?'

'Exactly.' Michail smiled in the way that Katerina knew meant he had connected a few, almost impossible, dots. 'Except, we were mistaken,' he said, pulling his phone from his pocket. He held up the image of Teddy's necklace and then swiped to the photograph of Irene's daughter. 'We noted that it was strange how both Teddy and Tatiana were wearing the same "T"-shaped necklace, we assumed, to stand for the initial of their first name. Unbelievable, really, that both "T"s had the same volute lettering, with the flick, just here, ticking down in the same way, almost resembling a Greek η or an English h, rather than a T.'

Katerina stared at the image of the necklace and then back at the board. 'Oh... oh my God, wait...' She grabbed her phone and scrolled through Alek's feed. 'Here! Here – a post from a couple of years ago. Yes... that's it!' She read the caption aloud. '*Sometimes, a commander is the only thing that'll get you to where you want to be. That's the role of the taskmaster of the zodiac. Saturn commands us to get to work and to work hard. Discipline and responsibility are important to this planet, if you want to conquer the world, then take Saturn's lead.* Uh, the hashtags: *#MasculineEnergy #ZodiacTeachings #SelfImprovement.* But look at the image! It's the same as the necklaces. They're not initials, they're the sickle, Saturn's symbol!'

'That's right.' Michail counted the fingers on his hand as he listed the main points. 'Saturn House, references to the Saturnalia, Saturn's zodiac glyph.'

'I don't believe this,' Sofia breathed. 'So, what are we saying? That both Teddy and Tatiana belonged to some Saturn cult?'

'The evidence is insufficient for that assumption,' Michail said. 'Although, we need to speak to Tatiana–'

'Yes!' Katerina looked at her phone again and then at the sheet of paper Michail was halfway through rolling up. 'I knew it!' She pushed herself from her chair, swaying slightly at the pain across her head. 'I just searched "Saturn astrology numbers" and listen to this: *Saturn is the lord of number 8. In numerology, the ruling planet of the number 8 is Saturn, and therefore people who are born on the 8th, 17th, and 26th have special blessings from Saturn.*' She took a short, excited breath. 'That's Innes's password – 81726. That's what it means! She's in on this, well, whatever this Saturn business is about too... oh, there's more... *The number 8 is the most influential in numerology, holding great importance and the masculine, dominant energy of its lord, Saturn.*' She glanced at Alek's phone. 'I bet–'

'8888?' Sofia suggested, clicking her tongue as she thought it through. 'Egotistical, full of toxic masculinity, striving for power, popularity, teaching about discipline, overly simplistic... I wouldn't be surprised at all.'

Katerina, her hands trembling slightly, reached for Alek's phone and held her thumbs over the keyboard. 'Are you sure?' She looked nervously up at her colleagues. There were only so many guesses they'd have before blocking the phone.

'No,' Sofia replied softly. 'But I'll back you.'

Katerina gritted her teeth as she tapped the number into the keys. She closed her eyes as she entered the last digit and waited for Sofia's reaction.

'There you go.'

The phone loaded into Alek's homescreen. A cool energy trickled down Katerina's spine; for the first time in a long while, she realised that she was excited, that the possibilities of tomorrow glowed a little brighter.

A buzzing sounded from Sofia's handbag. 'Forensics, about the prints.' She walked to the plunge pool at the end of the terrace to take the call, leaving Katerina and Michail alone. Katerina shrugged, attempting to throw him a smile. 'I suppose that's tonight taken care of,' she said, nodding at the phone.

If the prospect of spending the night working with her made him uncomfortable, then he wasn't given the chance to respond. Sofia strode back towards them as sirens echoed in the mid-distance. 'It's a match,' she said. 'If Innes isn't our sniper, then I want to know what she was doing in room three at the Hotel Plaza.'

---

1. *Apocalypse*

Speakers

'So sad to see you go,' Lily cooed. Despite the late hour, she was wide awake, dressed in a tightly fitted transparent golden kimono, sipping a tall, icy orange drink and seemed to be labouring under the entirely unnecessary misconception that she was required to make conversation with him. 'And, obviously, so tragic we didn't meet under better circumstances.'

'It is unlikely we would have met at all were it not for the murders,' Michail replied. 'But thank you for your hospitality.'

'Are you travelling to Athens tonight? I think the last boat has—'

'Arrangements have been made,' he cut in, wishing that Katerina would hurry up packing. He added for good measure, remembering Sofia's instructions, 'We require more space to conduct our duties to the best of our abilities.'

The marble floor reflected the moonlight shining through the tall glass doors. He stared at it unblinkingly, before his gaze drifted to the sculpture of the god Saturn to the left of the entrance. A strange detail stood out to him, one he had missed before. 'Saturn's sickle.' He nodded in its direction. 'It appears to be discoloured.'

Lily looked momentarily surprised before following his gaze. 'Ah, our Saturn! The namesake of the hotel! Yes, a funny little tradition we have! Our guests really lean into it, you know? They rub the top of his stick for good luck. Health, wealth and happiness, that sort of thing!'

'I see.' Unsure about how to reply without being rude about the completely illogical practice, he stood in silence, feeling the weight of Alek's phone in his pocket beckoning him to investigate his private messages.

'Unbelievable news about Innes,' Lily said with a great sigh. 'I never, ever would have thought she'd be capable of something–'

'We must have woken you up,' he interrupted, attempting to steer the conversation away from the case. 'I apologise for that.'

'Oh! Oh no, actually, I was beavering away on the business, you know, I work into the night a lot of the time.'

'Ah, your pistachio venture?'

'That's right. I was hoping to gain a bit of brand awareness at the Saturnalia. It's the perfect setting, don't you think? The sea, the pool, the actual trees within touching distance... it could be a huge boost.'

He shook his head in amazement. 'You expect the party to go ahead? Even now?'

Lily seemed genuinely shocked by the question. Her eyebrows shot upwards as she replied, 'It's one of the most exclusive events in the world. People – people so important that you can't even imagine – have been looking forward to it for months. They're sad about Alek, and Teddy, but this is their chance to let go. Imagine never being able to do that. We provide a safe environment for them. Away from the fans, the press. They can be themselves with people just like them. It's a haven for them. They don't want to give that up.'

'People just like them?'

'Money and power,' she replied simply, looking at her lilac nails. 'You know, most people don't understand what it means to be a person like that, at the top, the very top, of the food chain. *When you have everything, then nothing looms large.* That's what Domenico once said to me. Imagine that! Imagine feeling like you've completed life, bagged the dream, won the game with no more levels to overcome? With only *nothingness* to fear?' She laughed, a hint of bitterness deflecting off the sharp surfaces of the foyer.

'Do you aspire to be a... a fearer-of-nothing?' Michail asked.

She rolled her shoulders back at the question and shook her head, looking at her feet. 'No. No – I work with them; I make things happen for them. I'm happy enough with that. Look at where it gets me!' She whirled on the spot, her glass tilting dangerously as she gestured to the space around her. She resembled a sycamore seed caught in a flitting spin, dancing under the current of the pleasant, yet unyielding wild. He was not sure how to reply, so settled on nodding politely.

Lily hiccoughed as she stopped turning, which signalled to Michail that this was likely not her first alcoholic beverage of the night. After another sip, she lowered her voice and spoke in a more serious tone. 'I want to give them the best party of their lives, do you understand? That's my job. And they thank me for it. Everything is going to be perfect!'

'Did you manage to sort out the sound systems? My colleague mentioned that you were concerned about them not being up to scratch.' Michail watched her closely as she digested the question. He detected a slight droop of the mouth, as if her brain was desperately trying to inform her over-plumped lips.

'Yes, thank you for asking,' she said, widening her eyes at him. 'The speakers should work brilliantly.'

'I'm glad to hear that. I was going to suggest that your

existing speakers might do the job. The locals say that they can hear your music most clearly.'

Again, her face behaved like a listless mask, her lips slowly bending into a grateful smile, but a little too delayed, a little too confused. 'Existing speakers?'

'Yes, Saturn House's parties are quite legendary. You must have been told about the noise complaints?'

'Oh!' Her head snapped up as the lift doors opened to reveal Katerina. 'Oh! Yes... silly me... I must have forgotten about those spare speakers, how stupid.'

Katerina took in the scene and caught Michail's eye before giving him a tiny nod. 'I'll load up the car,' she said. 'Ms Woodstow, would you mind helping me? Michail, remember that I left my earrings by the pool? Could you fetch them?'

'Certainly,' Michail replied, already halfway to the door. 'I won't be long!'

Glancing behind him to check that Katerina had Lily under control, he swiftly headed past the pool area to the hotel boundaries. It was difficult to know what he was searching for, but he was certain that Lily was hiding something. The noise pollution issue made no sense. Where was the music coming from? Why would Lily act so suspiciously when asked about the music? It was difficult to believe that she, a self-confessed workaholic, would simply 'forget' about a sound system. He edged around the pool area and shone his torch into the bushes, checking over his shoulder. Nothing out of the ordinary.

Quickening his pace, he jogged down the path and through the gate that led to the beach. The night sky bled blue over the sand and the sea seemed to breathe at regular intervals, rolling gently in its inky dreams. The circular torchlight moved steadily along the corner of the wall, where the sand was slightly higher. Everything looked normal. He let out a low, frustrated sigh. *Archaic warrior clues. Pretending to be something they weren't.*

What was the pretence, here? What was he hoping to uncover? Lily, inebriated and harmless as she seemed, could easily mention to Domenico that the police had been snooping about the hotel at night. If he was going to find something, he had to find it quickly.

He placed his hand against the wall. Here was the boundary, the liminal space between the everythings and the nothings, as Lily had put it. He traced his way back up towards the pool area, his hand gently grazing the brushed concrete. Built to keep those who didn't understand out. Built to keep those who did understand together. Built to maintain the impression of power and wealth and influence. The impression...

A jolt ignited at the bottom of his belly. A wall built to give an impression...

He took three long, quick strides back and shone the torch along the wall again. It didn't fit. The wall was concrete, a cheap alternative to the rest of the stonework that adorned the rest of the hotel. An inconsistent choice. A soft breeze licked the dry leaves in the trees hanging over the wall. He cocked his head to one side and stared. The branches pointed towards the beach in a highly irregular sequence. Without delay, he catapulted himself as high as he could against the wall so that he could hoist himself up. Pushing with his legs, he managed to roll and position himself on the top. Here, he saw what he had suspected: the trunks of the trees were bent and misshapen in the same way, as if growing around something that had been placed beneath the ground. He swung his legs around and gripped on to the most stable-looking branch to lower himself onto the other side.

'Officer Mikras? Is everything all right? Can I help with anything? The earrings might have been picked up...' Lily's voice carried from the other side of the wall.

He didn't have much time. Placing the torch between his teeth, he pushed his hands into the undergrowth, wincing as his thumb caught something sharp.

'Sergeant Mikras?'

He continued to dig, focusing only on the movement of his hands, until he felt something hard and inorganic. He nodded. This made perfect sense. It explained the concrete. Built into the external side of the wall were numerous, powerful-looking speakers, facing out towards the village. Cables had been wedged beneath the tree roots, causing them to grow at odd angles. There was no doubt that this sound system had been set up to make a lot of noise... projecting away from the hotel.

'Sergeant Mikras!'

Michail took a quick photo of the speakers and covered them up as quietly as possible, before creeping into the darkness along the side of the hotel.

The new accommodation was a nice break from the aching luxury of Saturn House. The house was on the edge of Aegina town, overlooking the roadside beach that would be lined with parasols in the daytime. A balcony stretched along the front of the building, adjoining Katerina and Michail's rooms. At night, the view of the sea was a smoky fusion of blues and greys. The moon's reflection seemed to shatter in long shards across the water.

Katerina looked back at Michail, whose head was bowed in deep concentration over Alek's phone. 'You're sure there's nothing? Not even a meetup message?'

'I am afraid not.' Michail continued to scroll. 'There is no evidence whatsoever of a pre-existing connection between Alek and Teddy. There are not even many messages between

Domenico and Alek – just what you'd expect: instructions about what to post about the Saturnalia party, general niceties, nothing out of the ordinary. Same with his exchanges with Innes.'

'The ones from Lily aren't exactly illuminating, either,' Katerina said. The initial elation at hacking into the phone had begun to sink rapidly.

'She certainly values his opinion,' Michail said. 'Most of her messages are about which type of pistachio variety he prefers. Small, yellow, green, fresh. Just research for her business.'

Katerina let out an irritated yelp and kicked her feet into the air, throwing her body weight against the deckchair. 'There must be something!' she groaned. 'There must be something, anything, that points us in the direction of why someone would want to kill him. Have you checked his drafts again? Scheduled posts?'

'Like you have already noted, he has many draft posts stored across various platforms. Nothing looks particularly unusual...' His voice trailed off into a low, thoughtful hum.

'What is it?'

He didn't reply, instead, he jumped up from his seat and paced along the length of the balcony.

'Michail–'

'Yes. Yes, Katerina, listen to this caption: *Sometimes you need to question yourself. Question who you are, what you stand for, and, most importantly, who pulls your strings. No good being a master if you're a master of fools. No good being healthy on the outside if there's sickness inside. Be true to yourself. Don't be swayed or persuaded. Live your truth. Be your truth. Reveal the secrets you hate. Otherwise, you'll end up hating yourself. #FaceYourDemons #ComingClean #Revelations.*'

'More astrological, self-help mumbo-jumbo.' Katerina

sighed. 'He created that draft the day before he was killed, didn't he? It's the last one?'

'Correct.' Michail nodded. 'About both the timing of the draft and the mumbo-jumbo, as you say... but...'

'But...'

'It's not necessarily clear, not yet, but suppose it means what I think it means? It throws Alek's last draft into a new perspective completely.'

Katerina joined him on her feet and held out her hand. 'Let me see.' She read the caption again, which was accompanied by a photograph of Alek in swimming trunks on a small yacht in front of a picturesque cave. 'You're looking at the "sickness" reference? I spotted that too, it reminded me of what I heard Innes saying, but he's just talking about, well, it's just a ridiculous self-improvement mantra.'

'Unless, of course, that's not what it is at all.' Michail's face almost trembled with anticipation. 'We have assumed that, like the rest of his posts, this draft was intended for Alek's social media followers, correct?'

'Yes, that's right.'

'But what if it wasn't? What if, just like the sound system in Saturn House's walls, it was intended for someone else?'

Katerina studied the caption again. Her eyes stung with tiredness, but she forced herself to try and understand what Michail was getting at. 'Sickness... the sickness inside. Innes said, "He's sick". It's the same terminology. It's weird.' Her eyes flew to meet Michail's as the thought entered her mind. 'The symbol of Saturn—'

'Is a sickle,' Michail interrupted. 'I believe that neither Innes nor Alek were referring to an illness at all; I think that the term "sick" is a reference to Saturn's sickle, the symbol on Teddy's necklace and the namesake of the hotel. When Innes was speaking to Domenico, I'd be willing to guess that she was telling him that someone, most likely Teddy, was "sick", to put it another way: he was in the sickle group, the group that is appearing increasingly to have ties to Saturn House.'

'So what does this have to do with Alek's murder?'

'Inconclusive, yet again.' Michail shook his head, seeming visibly irritated. 'Although, the draft refers to some sort of a revelation or telling of the truth.'

'You think he was killed because he was threatening to reveal a secret about Saturn House?' It was the most solid theory that they'd reached so far. 'We should tell Sofia straight away. She'll be questioning Innes right now.'

He promptly typed a message on his phone, awaited Sofia's response, then slumped back onto his chair.

They sat listening to the restless chorus of the night for a while. Darkness sounded so different here than it did in the city. Over the past year, Katerina had spent what seemed like countless sleepless nights on her mama's balcony, wishing that with each car backfiring, each hacking of phlegm, each bottle breaking, each alarm shrieking that she would be cut out of the soundscape, flattened, made irrelevant. She had imagined, gripping her long-turned-cold cup of coffee, that if she sat on that narrow balcony for long enough, night after night, then the city and its voices would submerge her, beginning at her feet, bathing her calves, then her knees, lap at her waist, and rise to her neck until she could breathe a final relieved sigh and disappear into nothingness.

It seemed impossible that she was now on another balcony with Michail, the city's fitful outbursts replaced by the gentle stirring of insects. She heard a preparatory intake of breath and waited for Michail to make a comment, most likely about their tasks for tomorrow morning, however, he let his chest fall without a word. A memory, febrile and sudden, of the sensation of his body beneath hers, his hands around her waist, his lips close and warm, flickered behind her eyelids. She clenched her fists, willing herself to push it from her mind. Whatever spark or affection they might have had for each other had died when he discovered who she was, what she had done. She had broken whatever might have been. She sighed and realised that her eyes were wet. She covered her face, pretending that she was feeling her stitches and stood to leave. 'It's late. I'll... head to bed.'

'How does your head feel? Are you sure that you are not experiencing concussion? The doctor said to remain vigilant.'

Stupidly, she shook her head in response, and winced, a sharp hiss escaping from her mouth. 'I'm fine–'

Michail jumped up from his chair and turned her towards him, placing a hand on each side of her arm. 'We should check your pupils.'

She noticed his eyes widened as her tears fell, although he didn't say anything as he shone his torch into each eye. 'Michail, honestly, I'm fine.'

He gave her a quick nod and lowered the torch, his other hand dropping, it seemed without much thought, to the curve of her hip. She couldn't bring herself to tear her eyes away from his. An old sensation of reassurance and comfort seeped through her tired limbs. It was as if, for a moment, they pretended that nothing had changed. That nothing had broken. She wasn't thinking – she was sure about that – as she leant forwards towards his face, feeling the soft caress of his breath.

He drew himself away from her, almost flinching.

'Oh... I...' Her thoughts seemed to implode, flipping this way and that, rising and falling in gushing waves of embarrassment. 'Michail, I'm sorry.'

He backed away from her and frantically began tidying up his things.

Her mouth hung open, groping for some words that might help her explain herself. 'I... Michail, look, I should never–'

'No.' He snapped his laptop closed with such force that his hands shook. His face was flushed and tense. He looked to his feet, his shoulders rising to his ears and falling. 'No, you shouldn't.'

'I just... it's so difficult. Being here, alone with you. There are so many feelings, memories spinning about in my head, then you were there, and I thought...'

He held himself very still and spoke to his feet, his hands clenched, as if he was in pain. 'Your thoughts were incorrect.'

She would have taken being shoved against a brick wall ten times over this. She didn't bother to wipe the tears away from her cheeks. 'Incorrect?'

'I am sorry, Katerina, but I do not think that you can possibly understand. You were my friend, perhaps more. But none of it was real. And now, it is more difficult than you can imagine.'

'I get it.' Her voice was very small beneath the weight of her tears. 'I do. You didn't need to pretend that everything was okay, Michail. You don't need to spare my feelings. Nothing anyone says could make me feel less awful, believe me—'

For a moment, his face softened, but then, as if remembering himself, he nodded, his expression hardening. 'There's no requirement for me to consider your feelings; understood.'

'Okay then.' She turned so that he couldn't see her face and hurried into her bedroom, closing the door gently behind her. Only then did she allow the torrent that had been building in her chest to release. The force of emotion brought her to a foetal position as she lowered herself onto her bed, biting down on a clenched fist to muffle the sound of her tears.

Vi

Sleep evaded Michail. He had closed his eyes in defiance to the noise of his brain for a restless number of hours, before creeping downstairs to the kitchen, Aegina books in hand, to make some coffee. He fingered an intricately painted cup as he waited for the coffee to simmer. It was a scene of the harbour, brought to life with innocent blues and pinks and whites: a tourist's rose-tinted dream. He stirred the liquid in rapid, regular beats, his thoughts turning to Maria. She had suggested a meeting early that evening at the entrance to the archaeology museum. Assuming that he and Katerina succeeded in completing their workload for the day, and no unexpected events occurred, he was confident that he would make it. He took a swift gulp of his drink, feeling heat rush to his face as he relived, yet again, what had happened on the balcony last night. It was true that he – they had both – been sleep-deprived, as well as mentally drained. That was the logical explanation of how they had found themselves so close. He shut his eyes and shook his head, attempting to blur the memory of it. The curve of her hip, the soft brush of her hair as she leaned forward. Unacceptable. The possibility could never be entertained again. He had done the right thing, he was certain, by being clear with Katerina about his feelings. Although, he hadn't experienced the same relief as he had when syphoning his other wax-feelings. Instead, once the words had spilled from his mouth, he had only felt empty, and awkward, and very alone. Obviously, these were not the desired outcomes.

Beyond the small square kitchen window, the sun's early hues began to ripple along the sea. A cat trotted along the empty road, its tail high and alert, meowing a greeting to the new day. The creature made him long for Athens, the sounds of it, the habits of it. He missed the comforting ways of the city, its organic timetable that slid easily, yet reliably, day to day.

The beach was empty apart from a solitary figure in the middle distance. Suddenly, the prospect of fresh sea air upon his face seemed extremely appealing. He refilled his cup and slipped out of the house, crossed the road, and settled his toes into the cool sand. It wasn't quite the same as the peace that architecture brought him: human achievements, the culmination of rationality and imagination that stood the test of time, steeped in history and story and logic, would forever soothe him; however, as he stepped closer to the edge of the water, his eyes set on the horizon as it glowed in technicolour, he conceded that the natural world had something to offer. The glimmering expanse was untouched, uncultivated. It was a restive canvas upon which humans had built ideas and machines, myths and ships. It was the beginning.

'It is the right house, then.'

The voice was familiar, although he couldn't place it. He turned to face its source. 'You're from the protest? The right house?'

The woman to whom he had spoken grinned, apparently pleased with herself, and gestured to the space next to him, as if asking permission to stand next to him on the sand. He nodded. 'This beach is still public.'

She chuckled and moved to watch the remainder of the dawn with him. 'The boy who clears the beach beds away said he'd seen police cars outside this house. I'm glad it was you.'

'You were looking for me?'

'Yes.'

'You could have gone to the police station. They would have either helped you themselves or, if necessary, put you in touch with me.'

She grumbled something indistinguishable and puckered her lips, sending shoots of deep wrinkles to sprout along the side of her face. 'You're not from here, which means you're not afraid.'

'Afraid?'

She shrugged and hugged her arms around her front, her chin drooping slightly as if weighed down by thought. 'Rich, powerful people often line their path with fear, don't you think?'

Unsure how to reply to this, he gave a sharp nod. 'More often than not, I suspect.'

She sighed; a deep, volcanic sound. 'The police are good, good people, good at their jobs. I know most of them personally. That's how I know they're scared. They don't think we should protest; they say it's dangerous.'

'Do you know what they're scared of?' Michail watched her as she nodded in a slow movement, like she had thought about this moment for a long while.

'You're used to violence, aren't you? The shooting at the harbour, it wouldn't have come as a surprise to you?'

Michail opened his mouth to contradict, but then corrected himself. She was right: he hadn't been as appalled as he would have been a year ago.

'It's true,' she said. 'But it shattered most people here. We're not accustomed to things like that. It's all anyone can talk about... the man on the beach too.'

'Any community would find these things difficult,' Michail replied. 'But I'm not sure I understand why you think that the police are scared—'

'It's not the first time that...' she said. 'Things have happened before.'

Michail felt his face tense with confusion. 'What things?'

She waved a hand in the air and gave a low laugh. 'Do you mind?' Without waiting for him to reply, she produced a packet of cigarettes from a pocket in her skirt and lit one. She blew a long and heavy puff of smoke towards the sea and then turned her eyes to him.

'Nothing as bad as the shooting,' she said. 'Nothing criminal, I suppose... well...'

'It would be helpful if you could be as clear as possible,' pressed Michail, wishing that he'd brought his notebook outside.

Her eyes moved from side to side as if she was calculating a tricky sum. 'The hotel's been here for about ten years,' she said. 'Nobody particularly liked it – Aegina's not a luxury resort destination – but, you know, no one made a fuss. They bought the land, fair's fair. There weren't any problems at the beginning, everything seemed fine. Then, a girl in her late teens got... er... spotted by one of the guests.'

'Spotted? Could you be specific about what you mean by that?'

She blew another smoke-cloud before she continued, closing her eyes as the last of the whitish-grey vapour left her lips. 'Spotted... uh, scouted? She was beautiful, you know? She was told that she'd do some modelling, perhaps be introduced to movie producers. She was excited.'

'I see.'

'So, she went on these trips. I heard that she always came back with some expensive watch, or money, or a designer handbag. Other girls started to idolise her, you see, on social media. She was living the high life, a dream life to some, I suppose. The girls here – the younger ones, still at school – they followed her on social media. She was always posting pictures of herself on yachts, private jets, in fancy restaurants. I think they hoped that the same might happen to them, they'd be swept off their feet for their good looks in the same way... but then she stopped posting. We haven't heard from her since.'

'Apologies, Ms...' Michail realised that he hadn't asked the woman her name.

'Virginia Tzamargias.' She gazed at him unblinkingly, then held out her hand. 'Vi.'

'Ms Tzamargias,' he repeated, shaking her hand. 'Do you mean to say that she's missing? Was there a report filed?'

'Oh, no, no.' Vi shook her head, dropping the cigarette and stamping it over with sand. 'No, no. Her mother insists that she's alive and well. She said that she had spoken to her, that she had decided to live abroad, in Los Angeles, I think.'

'You didn't believe her?'

Vi held her breath, her eyes trailing the sea's surface. 'I didn't. No, I don't. Her mother cleaned my house at the time and... something changed in her. She used to be a joyful person, always smiling, content. Something changed. Also, Tatiana stopped posting on social media. My granddaughter told me. She used to post pictures of herself all the time and then... nothing. I... I don't know what happened.'

'Tatiana?' Michail's head jerked up. 'You said that her name was Tatiana, the girl?'

'Tatiana Kanatas,' she said, nodding. 'Yes, she would have been nineteen at the time.'

Michail's eyebrows shot high up his forehead. 'Your cleaner, that was Irene Kanatas, Tatiana's mother?'

'Yes, that's right.' Vi seemed pleased with his interest. 'Like I said, she insisted that everything was fine. There was no reason to worry about Tatiana. Most people assumed she'd met some man and moved away for good.' A tremor of suspicion vibrated through her voice.

'You didn't think that, though?'

'I didn't think much of it at all, to tell you the truth. It wasn't until about a year later when the rumours started at the *Lykeio*. At first, I thought it was just my granddaughter being fantastical. You know the type of things they watch these days, hmm? All that drama, all that darkness pouring into their young minds. *That* should be illegal, if you ask me.'

'What did she say, your granddaughter?'

'Look, none of this is confirmed, which is why I came to find you, that's what I think the police are frightened about. What if they missed the rumours? And now... I don't know!' She threw her hands up to the sky, her face colouring with embarrassment. 'It might be nothing, it truly might be nothing. But it's been buzzing about my head.'

'Please, Ms Tzamargias, any detail you could give would prove most useful. Sometimes we don't realise what we're looking at until we see it in its full context.'

'Eloquent. Yes, I suppose you're right.' She looked over her shoulder as if to check that nobody was listening. 'Talk to the headmistress at the *Lykeio*, she'll have more details, I'm sure. All I know is that there were rumours of a cohort of girls, all in their late teens, who worked at Saturn House. I think they were waitressing or... look, some of them used to recruit others from their year group. It seems fine, you know, like a good way for the girls to earn some money but...' She took a deep breath and furrowed her brow. 'The girls my granddaughter named all left the island for some reason or other, at least, they're not here anymore. They, well, my granddaughter mentioned the word "brainwashed" for what it's worth. It might be nothing, like I say, but with what's been happening to guests at the hotel, it came to my mind. I wanted someone to know. Someone who wasn't local.'

Michail finally comprehended her meaning. It was likely that some of the girls would be family members of the Aegina Police Department. 'I think I understand. You don't want to cause undue stress and worry with unfounded suggestions? You think that the police are scared that these deaths might have something to do with... with their daughters, who were connected to Saturn House? How?'

She shook her head, biting her lip, her eyes narrowing. 'Who knows? It's a mess, isn't it? A jagged mass spinning about my thoughts, and I can't make out the shapes! I hope to God that it's nothing. I pray that you find the killer and we can be done with this whole matter!'

Undoubtedly, the police should have told them about these rumours, although, with no records, arrests, evidence or even a straight story, he wasn't sure how they would have presented the information, nor if it would even have occurred to them that it was related. He cleared his throat. 'I'll need a list of the girls' names, if your granddaughter can remember them. Ideally, if she's still in contact with any of them, I'd like their details too. You said that Tatiana stopped posting photographs? Has anyone heard from her since she went away at all? Apart from Irene?'

Vi shook her head again. 'I don't think so. Like I say, speak to the headmistress, Lena Gimosoulis. She's been at the *Lykeio* for fifteen years and she seems to really care about the students. If anything untoward was reported to her, she'll have notes.'

'It would have been good if she'd reported any of this to the police,' Michail murmured, turning to see Sofia waving for him to return to the house.

'Like you say,' Vi replied. 'Sometimes you don't know what you're looking at until it's in its full context.'

'Very true.'

Sofia slid her coffee cup towards Michail for him to pour her another. 'Jesus, I hadn't realised how on edge I'd been at the hotel. I feel like we can talk properly here.'

Michail looked ragged, with dark half-moons beneath his eyes. However, he was dressed and ready in his usual meticulous manner, perhaps even more meticulous than usual. The tension between him and Katerina had not escaped Sofia's notice, although she had little interest in involving herself and had news.

'Innes is giving us nothing. She knows her rights, clearly, and offered no comment in response to all my questions. I can't see her budging. We can hold her for a bit longer but then it's up to the *anakritis* to decide whether she can be kept in pre-trial detention. I'm not sure how a fingerprint on a note is going to hold up. Still, we've got her in the country for a while, at least.'

'Do you think she could really be the sniper?' Katerina asked, looking almost as haggard as Michail.

Sofia shrugged. 'Stranger things and all that, but we've done all we can on that front. In my mind, there are a few urgent outstanding items that need to be addressed today. Firstly, do we have any leads on the whereabouts of Iraklis's key card, Teddy's clothing and Teddy's phone? Anything at all?' She hadn't meant to sound so condescending; a blush rushed to Michail's cheeks and Katerina looked at her hands, which were white at the knuckles.

'I'll take that as a no.' She had to fight not to roll her eyes. 'It's safe to assume that they're not on the hotel premises, as they've been thoroughly searched. Chances of finding them are slim, however, *if* somebody's holding on to them then they're currently our best chance of cracking this.'

'I don't think we should assume that the items have been discarded. The perpetrator may be feeling watched, and additionally, the sniper has already proven themselves sloppy,' Michail said.

'Good. Right, now about Tatiana – it's not every day that a clue practically knocks on your front door. You both need to talk to Irene again. What's she hiding, if anything? Where's Tatiana and why hasn't she reported her as a missing person if she is, in fact, missing? Find out as much as you can about this "modelling" job of hers. It sounds dodgy to me, *plus* she's been photographed wearing one of those Saturn necklaces, whatever that means.'

'It'd be worth visiting the *Lykeio* too,' Katerina added. 'See if this headmistress has anything to add about the schoolgirls.'

'Excellent. Michail, you said this Virginia woman would send you the names?'

'Yes... not yet...' Michail checked his phone again. 'She knows we're waiting for them.'

'Okay. Now there's the issue of Domenico.' She eyed them both, still undecided about who she wanted to take with her. 'The powers that be agree we have no grounds to bring him in from overseas, but I still want to speak to him in person. So, we'll go to him. This actually gives us an opportunity to observe him discreetly.'

'Where will this observation take place?' Michail asked, looking ready to spring into action.

'London. We're in talks with the police over there, but without anything solid, it's unlikely they'll work with us on this in any meaningful capacity. I'm drawing a blank there, to be honest.' She breathed, trying not to let the annoyance at her old colleagues ring too loudly in her voice. 'So, we'll have no jurisdiction. The purpose of the trip is largely informational. Do either of you want to volunteer to come with me? Yiorgos will come back from Athens to help whoever stays behind. We won't be long, just a night. My...' She cleared her throat, irritated at the heat crawling up her chest. 'My ex-husband still lives in London. He's an investigative journalist, specialising in organised crime – especially, well, rich white men. I've asked him to have a dig around the Balcombe House Group. You never know, he might turn something up.'

She tried not to notice the widening of both of her colleagues' eyes. She had never discussed her ex, nor her life in London with anyone at work. The phone call she had made to him last night had been strained at first. That was to be expected. She could handle awkwardness. It was the gentle trickle towards old, never forgotten in-jokes and habits that she detested. She would have preferred it if the conversation had remained wooden. But that cruel alchemy happened when their voices entwined, bringing shape to memories that had lost their colour and form, dropping breadcrumb after breadcrumb back in time to a world she could barely believe used to exist.

'Pete, hi.'

'*Sofia, it's good to hear your voice.*'

She had wanted to hang up. It couldn't have been good for him. How could her voice be good for him? He was still doing this then. Still offering pretence and lies in the face of discomfort, never wanting to have a proper discussion, to seize the heart of things. It had always irritated her. She dealt in facts. Thrived on bluntness. He thought feelings and situations could be manipulated with words, that if you thought something with enough conviction, ignored it hard enough, then all would be fine. Even when the worst thing, the thing that chews at parents' brains in the middle of sleepless nights, the thing that they are too afraid to fear, even when it happened, Pete had held her and whispered empty aphorisms into her wet shoulder like they could help. They couldn't. Yet, here he was, years later, beginning his new life, doing the same thing.

She had looked out of her window at the sea, imagining the miles that stretched between them.

'I'm coming to London, tomorrow. It's part of an investigation. I... are you busy?'

'No... no.' His voice dripped with reluctance.

'Is she there? Your... um...?'

'Lillian? No. She's asleep. It's the middle of the night. I'm in the kitchen.'

'Still in Archway?'

'That's right, but we sold the flat. I'm moving up in the world... we're in a townhouse.'

'Fancy.'

'Always.' He laughed, a quiet shrug of a sound. 'So, an investigation you said?'

'Yes. It's complex...'

'Most are.'

'Yes. I need you to look into something for me. You're still working?'

'For my sins...' She listened to a rustling sound and then the click of a pen. 'Go on.'

She rolled her shoulders back, steadying her gaze between Michail and Katerina. 'So, come on, which one of you wants to join me? I think it's best that we have two heads on the ground. Don't worry.' She rolled her eyes. 'Pete's civil and a professional, as am I.'

Katerina bit her lip then said, rather pointedly, 'I think I'd like to get away for a bit, Sofia.' In response, Michail looked at the ground, shifting his weight awkwardly from side to side.

The mood between the two of them had grown even stranger. Sofia narrowed her eyes and pointed first at Michail, then Katerina. 'Is there anything that you need to tell me? Something's going on.'

'No,' replied Katerina.

'Absolutely not,' snapped Michail.

Sofia sighed and rubbed her temples. It was too early for this. 'Right, well, Katerina it is. Michail, you'll be working with Yiorgos this afternoon. I trust you have everything under control–'

'Oh, I'm sure Sergeant Mikras has everything under control,' Katerina interrupted, turning her face up to Michail, her eyes blazing. He stepped backwards, edging towards the kitchen counter.

'Yes, like I said–' Sofia rested her hands on the table, almost dizzy with confusion.

'I mean, he calls the shots, doesn't he? Does whatever he wants. He makes you think one thing, then changes his mind last minute, making you seem like you're deranged, like you're just a desperate–'

'Katerina.' Sofia said her name very quietly. This was beginning to sound like a soap opera. 'Officer Galanis, check yourself.'

Katerina placed her hands over her mouth, as if she couldn't believe what had just come out of it. Then, her lips trembling, she stood. 'Sorry,' she said. 'I'll be outside, ready to go.'

Sofia watched her leave before resting her eyes on Michail.

'Care to tell me what all that was about?' He visibly squirmed on the spot. 'Michail!'

At that, he straightened himself up, a colour deepening in

his cheeks. 'I understand completely. Katerina and I... we had a small incident last night–'

'An incident?' She was honestly incredulous. 'Michail, we are in the middle of a murder investigation in case it escaped your notice. I cannot allow my team to be *overwhelmed* with distractions. You said that Katerina was doing well, that she clearly wanted to prove herself. What happened?'

'I believe I also said that personally–' he began quietly.

'We aren't here to work on our personal lives!' she exploded, almost spilling her coffee over her shirt. 'We are here to solve crimes.' Her voice had lowered to something resembling a hiss. 'Tell me the truth, because I'm beginning to question this – can you two work together? May I remind you, at this point, that it is *because of you* that you are still partners? This...' she waved her arm about in the space around her head, 'is a direct consequence of your decision? Have you changed your mind? Is it too difficult, after all?'

He hung his head, the tension in his shoulders palpable. Then, he raised his eyes and replied. 'It is not too difficult. We can manage, I am certain.'

'And there won't be any more incidents, whatever that means?'

'No. No. I will ensure that no more incidents occur.' His cheeks were now glowing. 'I agree that it was most unprofessional–'

'You don't need to tell me.' She cut him off, holding her hand up as a signal for him to be quiet. He was sensible enough to stop talking. She nodded and let the silence settle for a few moments. 'Good,' she said, taking a deep breath.

Thought Nugget

Katerina heard the cat meowing before she'd pulled over. The pots were as she remembered them, placed at various positions around the front garden, according to no particular pattern nor plan. She liked that. The randomness. Chaos felt like a good distraction at the moment.

She and Michail said nothing in the car. Normally, she would have felt obliged to try and lift his spirits, alleviate his obvious discomfort, but, this morning, she was happy to let him stew. After she had expunged what had felt like every last drop of energy from crying last night, her anguish had metamorphosed into a cool anger. She had *not* imagined his hand on her hip. She wasn't completely insane. Nor had she imagined his easy demeanour with her over the past couple of days. If truth and trust were such important tenets to him, then maybe he ought to start living by them. As her mama had said, she could only apologise so many times.

Once to God, once to herself, and once to the people affected.

She didn't deserve this to be easy, that was true. But she couldn't take the torment. It was too much.

'Hey, kitty.' She jumped out from the car as the cat trotted towards them, its mouth open, its tongue lolling in stress. 'What's wrong? What's the matter?'

The cat rubbed its cheeks against her hand, a deep purr rumbling from its throat. She stroked its cheek with her thumb, and it pressed up closer to her, its purr growing more intense. 'Hey, what is it? Are you hungry? Been locked out?'

The cat meowed a long, mournful sound. Michail joined her, crouching by her side. 'The cat seemed happy last time we visited,' he whispered.

She nodded, eyeing the house as a sickening unease spasmed deep in her belly. 'Something doesn't feel right,' she said. 'Look at the plants.' She gestured to the pink flowers on either side of the door. Unlike their previous visit, they were beginning to wither. Nobody had watered them.

'Do you hear that?' As she uttered the words, a rigid apprehension settled in her chest. It was a buzzing sound. The soft, frenzied sound of tiny wings drawn to early decay. She breathed in, then placed a hand over her mouth. The cat meowed again, this time more gently, as if it understood what she was thinking.

'There's a smell,' she said, pushing herself to stand. Michail gave a slow, grim nod. For a moment, neither of them moved as if they could make whatever horror lay behind the stone walls of the cottage disappear. A warm breeze whipped around the hills, about the trees and through the open windows of the house; the smell intensified. Sweet and raw and terrible. She groaned and wrapped an elbow around her face. Michail tapped her on the shoulder, indicating that he would walk around the back of the house. She nodded, readying her right arm by her side just in case. The cat followed at her heels, padding with an impatient urgency. The buzzing grew louder with each step, as if warning her not to go any further. The front door was left slightly ajar. She flattened herself against the wall and pushed it open in one quick swing.

'Mrs Kanatas?'

Even with her mouth covered, the smell penetrated her taste-buds. Nausea rolled through her entire body as she scanned the small, dim space, swallowing quickly to try and wash away the acrid taste. At first, she thought that a large cut of meat lay arranged and ready to be prepared on the small kitchen counter. She swayed slightly as blood rushed to her brain, imploring it to catch up with her eyes.

'The area is secure and clear.' Michail entered through the opposite door, bathing the kitchen worktop in a swathe of sunlight.

It wasn't an animal waiting to be prepared. She had known it; she had known it but had not wanted to see it. The cat made a soft growl, pushing back onto its hind legs, writhing at the sight of its owner, the smell, the horror. Irene Kanatas's body hung over the counter like a discarded fish, her eyes rolled back, as if in one final prayer. There had been a struggle – that was immediately apparent – smashed jars and cups littered the floor. Bruises inked their way up the woman's thin arms; green and yellow and purple. She had been held down, by the looks of it. Her wrists faced upwards, a sordid supplication, two wide gashes severing the flesh between her hands and her forearms. This is where the flies gathered, tumbling and writhing inside the wounds like one rampant black organism.

Katerina turned her back to the body and forced herself to remain composed. They were too late. They hadn't seen this coming, hadn't seen the danger. Had they let this slip through the cracks? Had they been too focused on what now seemed like childish petulant issues? And this was the price. A woman dead. She hung her head. 'I'll call it in.'

With that, she scooped up the cat and returned to the car.

Holding its furry panicked body on her lap, she looked straight ahead at the dusty road and blinked as one, then two, then more tears trailed uselessly down her cheeks.

Michail waited for Yiorgos at the harbour, breathing deeply in and then releasing the air in a manner that should have brought him a sense of calm. Instead, with every inhalation, a new manifestation of Irene Kanatas, left to rot for the flies, loomed large in his mind. He blinked as he remembered Katerina's rage; his head tilted to one side as if her voice had left a bitter residual upon his skin.

Stroking the cat's head, keeping her voice low, she had spoken to the windscreen. 'We haven't been concentrating, Michail. Whatever this is between us – trust, lust, hate, I don't know – we need to work it out. This, *this* is on us. We've been so busy focusing on our *working relationship*. I've been so busy trying to prove myself to you, instead... instead of...'

'Instead of solving the case. Instead of saving people. Saving Irene.' The realisation had come like a churning torrent, the weight of it physically forcing his head backwards onto the headrest. He felt his hands tremble. She was right; he had been remiss. He had been unfocused and entitled. He had been so busy worrying about himself that he had missed something. Something that would have led them to Irene. Something that would have prevented this.

'Maybe this won't work.' Katerina had spoken very clearly. 'We're not a team. We're not effective. It's dangerous.'

'We are not professionally proficient.'

'No. If you don't trust me, Michail, then we can't be. I'll talk to Sofia in London, ask for a transfer. We're flying this afternoon. You won't need to put up with me for much longer.'

Michail had wanted to reply, but his throat had grown tight and constricted. The shame of having done anything less than the best job possible, of the minutes and hours wasted thinking about Katerina and not the case, had been tightening about his chest since that morning. Her suggestion was sensible. He should feel relieved. Yet, again, he was empty; there was no wax to syphon at all, just a meaningless space filled with things he wanted to say but couldn't.

'Michail.' Yiorgos approached him having disembarked from the ferry; his face sterner than usual. 'Another body, Jesus, this island's turning into a bloodbath.'

'There are similarities between the first victim and this one.' Michail gestured to where their car was parked. 'The most salient, of course, being the severed wrists.'

'We're assuming it's the same killer?' Yiorgos asked, pulling out a cigarette. 'That would make sense, given the nature of the mutilations.'

'It would seem that way, although like everything in this case, things aren't always what they appear, just like the archaic smile.'

Yiorgos squinted at him over the car roof before getting in. 'In plain speech if you can manage it, Michail.'

'Teddy's cause of death was drowning; his wrists were cut after he died. It's been confirmed that Irene died from blood loss. The wrist wounds killed her.'

As they headed towards the *Lykeio*, Yiorgos opened his window to smoke, which rendered the air conditioning completely ineffective. Still, it was important they maintained a harmonious working relationship. As painful as he and Katerina's reintroduction had been, he could, at least, take some learned lessons from the disaster. Therefore, he decided not to comment.

'An inconsistent killer,' Yiorgos grunted. 'How considerate of them.'

'On the contrary, I would usually consider inconsistencies as an investigator's bane–'

'I know, Michail, I–'

'–however, in this case, I think you might be correct. The key differences in these murders might provide us with the answers we're looking for.'

'Answers like?'

Michail pulled into the car park. 'Unconfirmed for now,' he replied. 'However, I would like to request time after this meeting for some deep thought. There was something about Irene's wrists–'

'They were cut?'

Michail detected an edge of sarcasm. His hands tightened around the steering wheel. 'Yes, obviously. But there was something else. A thought nugget.'

'A thought nugget?'

'Correct. I require some time to think it through.'

Yiorgos sighed and shook his head. 'Whatever you want. Right–' he eyed the school building, a low-set amalgamation of concrete and glass. It was the type of architecture that seemed simultaneously designed to be inconspicuous and brassy – the more you looked at it, the more it revealed: more windows, more jagged edges, '–I read your notes. This headmistress, do we have any reason to be suspicious of her?'

'It is most efficient to be suspicious of everyone initially,' Michail replied, inspecting his phone as it vibrated. Vi had sent him the list of names as promised. Unfortunately, it was too late for them to conduct any research before their meeting, but this would prove most useful. He scrolled down the list. 'There are five names here.'

'Five? What, you mean five young women have gone

missing and nobody has thought to tell anyone?' Yiorgos blew through his nostrils. 'What the hell are they thinking?'

'I agree that it's unusual,' Michail said, his eyes resting on one name in particular. 'But remember, they're not missing. Our source said that they'd just moved away with limited contact. Of course, that needs to be confirmed.'

'Seen something interesting?'

'Perhaps,' Michail replied. 'One of the names here is Eleni Barlas, the same name as the desk manager at Saturn House. Vi's included a note next to it: *obviously, the school will have all the information.* I don't know what she's referring to. I wonder if she's a member of our Barlas family?'

Yiorgos shrugged. 'Could be. Let's see what this woman knows, then.'

'Certainly,' said Michail, wondering if Maria might know anything too, and, indeed, whether a date was the appropriate time to bring it up.

Michail knew that he was no longer a teenager, that he was now a respected member of the Special Violent Crime Squad, and that corridors filled with children and teachers did not pose any sort of a threat. However, as he followed the secretary down the seemingly never-ending tunnel of excited chatter, elated screeches and back-hand murmurs, the noises rumbled through his bones reminding him of his own unhappy experience in the education system. He breathed in through his nose and out again, as his counsellor had prescribed him to do in these sorts of situations, but it didn't work. The smell of school corridors, it seemed, were untouched by time and place: it was as if he was seventeen all over again. There could be little worse.

'Michail?' Yiorgos turned to face him, a deep frown etched across his face.

'Right behind you–'

Yiorgos slowed to walk next to him. 'All okay? You're humming loudly.'

'There is nothing to be concerned about, Yiorgos. It is merely a coping mechanism as I am sure I have explained to you before, often occurring when I am placed in situations of high stress.' He didn't mention that the compulsion had all but disappeared until a few days ago.

Yiorgos looked up and down the corridor. 'High stress?'

'Correct. My schooling was not the happy time that people often look back on fondly.'

'Ah,' Yiorgos said. 'I can imagine.'

Michail opened his mouth to explain that he highly suspected that Yiorgos could *not* imagine, when the secretary stopped outside a large white door punctuated by a long strip of glass.

'Mrs Gimosoulis is expecting you both–' She knocked, five sharp raps, then nodded, smiling through the glass, before disappearing back down the corridor. The door opened to reveal a small, wiry woman who, at first, conveyed the demeanour of a chirpy, frightened sparrow.

'Officers, please come in.' Lena Gimosoulis stood to one side, shaking their hands one by one. Her handshake, in contrast to her appearance, was firm, almost forceful. 'And take a seat. I'm afraid we only have fifteen minutes or so – I have a few meetings in the diary.'

'I am sure that we will be efficient,' Michail replied. Lena nodded and took her place behind the desk. 'We are here to ask about some students who would have attended your institution about seven years ago.'

'Oh?' Her hand flitted to her face and removed her glasses.

Then, in stark contrast to the way her hands fluttered on the desktop, she stared unflinchingly into Michail's eyes. 'I had assumed you were here about the murders?'

'We are investigating several lines of inquiry,' he replied, before placing his phone on the table so that she could read the names. 'I was hoping that you would tell us whether these names mean anything significant to you?'

She brought the screen very close to her nose, replacing her glasses with the same jittery movement, and peered at the screen, her lips pursed. 'They were students, like you say.' With one hand, she typed a few quick words onto her keyboard. '2017, all of them. I remember them well, of course.'

'They were friends with each other?'

Her eyes ran up and down the list of names. 'The group of them, yes, they were friends.'

She handed Michail the phone, her thin lips pressing into a mound that resembled a small sharp beak. 'I'm not sure what they have to do with anything,' she said, barely moving her mouth. 'Did you have specific questions?'

'Are you still in touch with any of these students?' Michail asked, watching her face very carefully. He didn't have the impression she was lying. However, the way she formed her words suggested she was taking great care over them.

'In touch?'

'It's a small place.' Yiorgos folded his arms, drawing her gaze to him. 'Did any of these students end up settling or maybe working locally?'

'No.' She shook her head, a little too vehemently. 'No. They... well, they all left Aegina. It's not uncommon, of course, we're so close to Athens, people come and go. Others move away entirely. But this whole group left. I don't hear much about them, if anything.'

'Is that commonplace?' Yiorgos pressed. 'For a whole group

of friends to leave their hometown? Where I'm from, some of us moved to the city, others abroad, but there are always a couple who stay put, at home.'

Lena observed Yiorgos for a second, and, again, her wide eyes seemed avian to Michail, as if she were watching a squirming worm in the ground. The muscles in her neck shuddered in a tiny convulsion before she responded. 'May I ask how this is relevant to your investigation?'

'Can you think of anything unusual about this group?' Yiorgos leant back in his chair, unfolding his arms. 'Anything that sticks in your mind from their time at school?'

She exhaled through taut lips and placed her hands gently on the top of the desk. Her eyes flicked between the two of them as she spoke. 'Plenty. It's an occupational hazard, educating children. You remember the wins, the good things – they're sweet, sit on the tongue easily.' She scanned the group of names again and gave an affirmative nod. 'They were diligent girls, all of them. Studious, yes, but also outgoing. Most of them were ambitious–'

'Would you describe them as popular?' Yiorgos asked.

She acted as if the question had caught her off-guard, her eyebrows flying to the top of her forehead. That was strange. It wasn't an unreasonable line of inquiry, given what they were discussing. Eventually, Lena nodded, although it was as if she was pressing her neck through treacle. 'Yes. They were popular. You mean with boys?'

'Not particularly.' Michail noticed that Yiorgos's voice thickened; he must have been pleased with how this was going. Indeed, he had deftly led Lena to the topic whilst making it seem she had willingly offered the information. 'Why? Do you remember anything strange about their romantic lives?'

Lena pushed the keyboard away from her as if it was some incriminating object. Her eyes seemed beady, alert – she no longer resembled a sparrow, Michail surmised, but an eagle. An inner beating stealth seemed to emanate from her every tiny movement. She surveyed them, her head very still apart from a wisp of hair blown wayward by the air conditioning. 'They were young – younger than they imagined. It's always the case, at that age, isn't it? You're almost done with your schooling, on the brink of adulthood, so mature and in charge of your own decisions... at least that's how you feel. I often think it's the most vulnerable age. So secretive, so sure of themselves and yet, well, they're still children, really. Intellectually, no, but emotionally, tactically, they are still young.'

Michail was unable to take his eyes off Lena. As she spoke, it seemed like a dark memory wavered across her face in a series of involuntary, almost imperceptible twitches. Intentional or not, he suspected her mind's eye had seized an uneasy image. 'You said that this group of young women were secretive. What makes you say that?'

She stared at Michail, and, for a moment, he was convinced that she was about to scold him for asking the question. However, she instead tutted, a soft guttural sound, and turned her screen to face him. At first, he thought he was looking at a photograph of Maria. The girl in the photograph had the same heart-shaped face, the same slightly pinched lips, the deepened groove between her top lip and her nose. However, the girl in the photograph had a longer, narrower nose and her face was arranged in an expression he couldn't imagine Maria wearing. She was pouting, her eyes almost mocking the camera, her cheeks pushed into sharp angles. 'Eleni Barlas,' Michail said, now certain that this must be Maria's sister.

'Yes.' Lena appeared to gulp before continuing. 'She had a presence, a shining one. It's unusual for students to be so popular yet also genuine. She wasn't mean. She wasn't a bully.

She was just...' Her mouth convulsed as she searched for the word. 'Just a nice girl. That's all.'

There was something odd about the way she spoke about Eleni. Michail had heard people speak in the same tone before; the slight drop in volume, the small tightening of the throat which placed a mournful strain upon the vocal cords. 'You're speaking like she is dead.'

Lena started at the word, retreating into the fold of her chair. 'Yes. Yes. I'm sorry, I assumed–'

'Eleni Barlas died?' He wondered why Maria hadn't mentioned this, then realised that there would have been no logical reason for her to. Neither he nor anyone else had thought to ask about the wider Barlas family.

'Why, yes. I thought... I thought that's why you were asking me about all this. It was the saddest thing that's ever happened in my entire career. I'll never forget. The screams...' Her jittery behaviour was beginning to make sense.

'Apologies for interrupting you, but she died here at school?'

Lena pressed her hands to her lips and closed her eyes, as if banishing unwanted images from her mind. Then, her eyelids twitched before fluttering open, revealing a newly steeled focus. 'Yes. In the toilets. Her friends found her–' She turned the computer screen to face her and recounted the names, each syllable seeming to solidify around her lips until they were pressed together with what looked like a painful force. 'Evia, Dimitra, Georgia, Konstandina. They shouldn't have seen what they did. No one should, but at that age...'

Michail flipped open his notepad without taking his eyes off Lena's face. 'It would be most useful if you could recount what happened, to the best of your memory.'

Lena blinked at him, her eyes losing their focus. 'I already told the police everything at the time. I don't see how this relates to the deaths on the island. This was years ago–'

'You might be correct. The events could, of course, be unrelated. However, as I said, it's useful for us to follow every thread – sometimes things reveal themselves in the most unexpected of ways.'

Lena folded her arms delicately as if cradling a broken wing. 'I remember thinking that the skies looked so angry that morning. The drive to work felt unsettled, the whole way. There was a persistent breeze, the clouds rolled. I often think, well, blue skies lift the spirits, don't they? Perhaps if...' She shook her head, as if annoyed at herself. 'It was before lessons began. Students often turn up early to catch up with their friends, hang around. They caught the bus together most days, all of them. I was in reception when I heard the... the screams.'

She raised her eyebrows in a sad sort of way. 'I'd never heard this kind of sound before. I say scream, but it was more of a cry, a wail. Almost inhuman, like some terrible visitation. Four voices, lifting and thrashing through the corridor.'

'Eleni's friends?' Michail confirmed. 'That's who you heard?'

'Everyone heard, it was impossible not to. I ran, along with other staff, to where the voices were coming from. The bathrooms... Georgia was holding the door ajar... and... inside... they were there. I saw the blood on the floor, spilling out from under the cubicle. It was on their shoes, smeared up their legs. I...' She shook her head and turned away from them. 'I thought at first that someone must have been giving birth. Stupid, isn't it? That's where my mind went.'

'It's not an entirely unreasonable assumption.'

'No.' She sighed, a wispy, high-pitched sound. 'No. But you can already guess that it wasn't the case. I shouted for someone to call an ambulance, but it was too late. She – Eleni – was already dead. She'd gone to the bathroom, messaged her friends. By the time they'd seen it and gone to find her... that's how it ended. She'd taken her own life, here, where she was supposed to be kept safe. You can speak to the local police, they'll have all the details, exactly as I've said.'

'We will, thank you.' Michail fingered his notepad. 'Do you mind me asking, in what manner did Eleni take her life? You mentioned that there was a lot of blood.'

'She cut her wrists.' Her voice wavered but she continued. 'Apparently, this sort of thing can be a cry for help, which would explain why she texted her friends. Perhaps she was asking to be heard and it went horribly wrong. I don't know.'

'I see.' Michail straightened his back, feeling his senses sharpen. He looked down at his notepad and frowned. 'You mentioned something about keeping secrets earlier? You said that girls that age are secretive?'

'The message to her friends. The police put it down to Eleni's state of mind, which, of course, I can understand, especially since none of her friends claimed to know what she meant–'

'What she meant?'

'I wrote it down, I don't know why. The girls waited in my office before speaking to the police and they showed me the text. I thought, well, I don't know. Here...' She turned her screen to face them again; this time it displayed a short paragraph.

By the time you see this I'll be gone and peaceful. I'm so sorry. You're all so strong. You can all keep smiling. I can't. It's like an infection, like a disease. It's inside my head. Every time I close my eyes it's there. The images. The movements. I can hear the sounds. This is the only way. An escape. I love you all.

Michail stared at the screen. It was quite possibly the saddest thing he had ever read. A teenager's final desperate thoughts preserved on a stale, stagnant screen. It felt wrong for them to be reading them at all.

'Her friends didn't know what this infection was?'

'No.' Lena shook her head. 'They were beside themselves, as you might imagine, but they were clever girls. None of them could explain what Eleni meant. I have no idea whether they were telling the truth or not.'

'But you thought it was something to do with a boy?' Yiorgos asked, his voice taking a dogged tone.

Lena waited a moment before answering. 'When I first read it, yes, I thought that she must have got herself in trouble. The infection, disease, I thought it could have something to do with a boy. I... the truth is that I don't know.'

'And then all of them left?' Yiorgos stood, apparently deciding that the meeting had come to an end.

'Yes, more or less. It was their final year and they all moved away. I can understand, to tell you the truth. This island will remind them of the worst thing in their lives. I'd want to get as far away as I could and never look back.'

She stood, signalling that she had said everything she could, and showed them to the door. 'If I can be of any further use...'

'You have been most helpful,' Michail replied, eyeing the corridor, which, following a bell, had begun to fill up with students. 'We will be in touch if required.'

Michail kept his eyes straight ahead of him as they walked through the school, past reception and through the car park. As soon as the car doors were firmly closed, he said, 'I don't believe that this is a coincidence.'

Yiorgos, inexplicably, gave a low laugh as they pulled out onto the road. 'Of course you don't. You mean the method of suicide?'

'First, Teddy, then Irene, and now Eleni.'

'But not Alek. And it's a common method for suicide, unfortunately. Especially amongst teenage girls.'

'Yet we have been directed, through a series of leads, to learn about how Eleni Barlas killed herself. It would be irresponsible to assume that she is entirely unconnected to the investigation at hand.'

'I'm more interested in the reasons behind her suicide. That text sets alarm bells ringing. As well as her friends all leaving. What if they were running away from something? Something other than Eleni's death, I mean?'

'It's possible.' Michail squeezed his eyes shut momentarily. 'You remember the thought nugget I mentioned earlier?'

'How could I forget?'

'Would you object to a trip to the Temple of Aphaia? I have an idea forming and believe that it will be best guided in that location.'

'At the temple?'

'Yes, precisely.'

Intentions

The flight had been turbulent, which Sofia had hated. However, it had given them time to get through the burgeoning paperwork that had been building up over the past few days. Katerina had spent much of the flight stooped awkwardly over her laptop, making notes about the Irene Kanatas scene. Now, in Sofia's hotel room, they ran through the plan for that evening.

'We'll need to work quickly – two days is all I could get authorised, which is understandable. Remember, we're not here officially in the capacity of the Hellenic Police. We're just looking for anything and everything we can get on Domenico that will help aid the investigation in Aegina. He'll know that we've left Saturn House, so, assuming he's not entirely idiotic, he'll have an idea that we suspect something.'

'But he doesn't know we're attending tonight?'

'No. Pete's put aliases down on the guest list. He's attending on a press pass, and so are we. To be honest, he's probably better at this undercover thing than we are. Investigative journalists do this sort of thing all the time.'

'We need to assume that Domenico knows what we look

like.'

'Yes.' Sofia smiled and reapplied her lipstick. 'That will be a good indication as to how high on alert he is. If he's got people on the lookout for us – here, in London – then he's scared. In any case, our job is to gather as much information as we can about the man, whether he knows who he's talking to or not. All we have on him is a phone call to Innes and an odd turn of phrase. It's hardly incriminating stuff. I'd be interested in listening to the conversations surrounding him: what's his character, who is close to him, what are they saying?'

'Got it.' Katerina tugged at her dress. They'd had a short window of time to pick up formal wear at the airport. Sofia had opted for a backless black number, whilst Katerina had chosen a flowing cut of emerald silk. She looked beautiful and not nearly as fragile as that morning. It was as if a new confidence, a thread of assertion, had been pulled through her, making her stand taller than she had before. This was a good sign. 'Are we acting like we know Pete?'

Sofia paused momentarily, her arms lifted above her head as she fixed her hair, at the sound of his name on Katerina's lips. 'No reason for you to. If Domenico notices us, let him draw his own conclusions. I'm sure he's doing his own digging, but no need to hand anything to him on a plate.'

'He's not as clever as he thinks.'

'They never are.'

Sofia observed herself in the mirror. She looked old. There was no escaping it. The fine lines around her eyes had multiplied and her cheekbones, which had always been a source of private pride, now seemed to sag, lifeless and tired. Pete would have aged too, of course, but that vain, unrealistic voice that berated herself for drinking, smoking, generally living, was persistent. Still, there was nothing that could be done now.

Katerina answered the call for the taxis and they made their way to the front of the hotel. Sofia smiled and thanked the doorman, revving herself into character.

'Where to?' The taxi driver looked in his mirror, wearing a beaming grin for what must have seemed like two women dressed to the nines for a night out on the town.

'National Portrait Gallery,' Sofia replied.

'Big event going on there. Taken a few people past it. Important night?'

'I hope so.'

———

Michail stood between the tall shadows of the columns in the afternoon light. The air had deadened and the humidity draped across his face like an invisible veil. He was pleased that Yiorgos had chosen to remain in the air-conditioned car; this was precisely the solitude that he needed to think properly. He retrieved his book from his rucksack and conducted a slow walk around the temple. Here, as he had shown Katerina, would have been the archaic portrayal of the battle scene at Troy: the expression of the warrior pinched and smiling, an inaccurate, highly stylised depiction of the subject matter. He scratched his head and looked at the severed entablature where the pediment would have once been. Now, it was only the blue sky that looked down at him. However, with his book, he pieced together the marble in his mind's eye, scooping the stones up and to the positions into which they would once have commanded. He nodded. It was clear. The smiling warrior greeted him, pulled his mind through the centuries and the stories and the wars and the intentions and imaginations of those who had created him. *The intentions.*

Michail snapped his head back towards his book, jogging to the other side of the temple, where the early classical depiction of the same scene would have stood. He did the same here: he re-amalgamated the pediment, limb by limb, figure by figure, until he could see in the blank sky what was depicted in the photographs on the pages. Here, the scene was more natural. The warrior's head was turned, the expression was less of a jarring smile and – as much as the sculptor could have managed at the time – more like a painful grimace. The *intent* was naturalism. The intent was real life, real pain.

An excited hum seemed to rise up above his ears. The *tzitzikas'* chorus. It was as if they knew that he was on the precipice of a breakthrough. He walked, this time more slowly, allowing his thoughts to converge and solidify, back to the archaic side. Here, there would have been no hint of real life. Here, the intent was symbolism. It was representation – a figurative structure, a geometric approach intended to spur thought, to nod in the direction of the thing, yet act as an artistic statement. *The intentions.*

He stepped back. And then again. His eyes moved rapidly between his book and the temple. It made sense. It made perfect sense. The answers were so often found in the hidden voices of the past.

'Michail!' Yiorgos's voice cut through his thoughts, but it didn't matter. He had an answer, an explanation. 'What are you doing?'

Michail ran back towards the car. 'Teddy's wrists. There was something about them that didn't ring true–'

'Yes, he died of drowning, not blood loss.'

'Yes, yes, but the way that the wounds were executed. I couldn't put my finger on it, but, luckily, the Temple of Aphaia has come through for us.'

'The temple has come through–'

'Correct.'

'Okay, so care to explain how the temple has anything to do

with the case?'

'Nothing. Everything. I just didn't see it before. Unfortunately, it took another set of wrist wounds for me to come to my conclusion.'

'You mean Irene Kanatas?'

'Precisely. Her wrist wounds were not meticulous. Obviously, she did not inflict the wounds upon herself, but they were not executed in the same way as Teddy's. They were more natural. The cuts on Teddy's wrists were perfect; too perfect, like the archaic, symbolic dying warrior. Equal angles, the same length, the same diameter, which means the same steady pressure was applied for the duration of each cut.'

'So, what are you saying? We have different perpetrators?'

'Almost certainly.' Michail nodded quickly. 'But also, and more significantly, different intentions. Think of what a symbol *is*, in particular, why a symbol exists. It is the medium through which an idea is transferred. The archaic sculpture is a symbolic representation of a dying man. Teddy's wounds are the same.'

'Well, we already knew that they weren't real, as in, Teddy didn't do them.'

'Of course not, that would be completely illogical.' Michail gestured into the air with both hands, as if sculpting an invisible scene before him. 'But their perfection, the cuts' *meticulous* execution tells us something particular and revealing about the mindset of our murderer. The incisions were done in such a way that they suggest a *meaning* behind the wounds. I think that they are symbolic.'

'So we're looking for a murderer for whom slit wrists might mean more than just slit wrists?'

Michail's mind was whirring. 'We're looking for a murderer who might want to use this type of wound as a message. Perhaps someone who has been traumatised by the sight of it. Perhaps someone who was driven from their hometown due to it.'

Michail was pleasantly surprised to see that Yiorgos was nodding, slowly, not entirely convincingly, but nodding all the same. 'One of Eleni's friends. Lena described the screams. I'd say that this type of wound left a deep impact on those girls. It would be difficult to forget something like that.'

'I agree.'

'Still, it's a stretch. But, to be honest, all we've got. So what next? We try and find these friends? How?'

'Helpfully, I have a meeting tonight with Eleni's older sister. I am sure that she will be able to help.'

'A meeting?'

'Affirmative.'

Sofia shivered as she climbed out of the cab. By London standards, this was a pleasant summer evening; clearly, the blistering Greek summers had altered her tolerance. Her eyes fell upon his face with an almost comic immediacy.

She had prepared herself as best as she could. However, the reality of seeing him in person, of knowing that only a short space of thin air separated him from her, made the back of her neck prickle.

Pete waved from a short queue filled with well-dressed people spilling out from the tall glass doors of the entrance. He was thinner than she remembered. His eyes, which had always twinkled with a simmering, unyielding optimism, remained the same, although they were accentuated by new crinkles around his eyes. For a second, she wanted to run. It was a stupid thought, one grounded in pure instinct. An animal desire to dart between the tightly packed traffic snaking past the pub on the corner, to scurry down the steps of St Giles and hide in the crypt there until she was sure that he was gone. That she wouldn't need to see him again.

Instead, she made her way through the crowd, breathing in the soft scent of perfume and the undercurrent of the day's sweat, towards him. 'Quite the turnout.'

'The Balcombe House Group funded the renovations, as "*ardent patrons of the arts*",' he read from a programme. 'Tonight is a "*celebration of Domenico's generosity, unwavering dedication to the gallery and continued sponsorship*". Apparently a lot of people want to thank him.'

Pete smiled, then looked impatiently as the queue crept forward. At the entrance were two heavy-set security guards dressed in black, flanking two women who were checking names off. 'You look great,' he said, without turning towards her.

'Doubtful,' she replied, scanning the people ahead of them. 'Anything you think we should know?'

'Nothing I haven't already told you. It's a classic: there's something going on. I'm just not sure what yet.'

'I know how you feel,' she breathed, taking a step forward.

'Look–' A car pulled up to the front of the gallery. She hadn't been watching, but Katerina would by now have taken her place in the queue. The door opened and a small round of applause sounded as Domenico appeared. He played humble extremely well, tilting his head forwards as if embarrassed. As he made his way up the steps, one of the two women who had been checking names practically fell over trying to greet him. He steadied her by offering an arm and made some sort of joke as she flushed, giggling through the humiliation.

'We know he's here, at least,' Sofia murmured.

Just before he entered the building, he stopped suddenly, pushing the woman gently forwards ahead of him, and beckoned a security guard to his side. After Domenico had whispered something in his ear, the security guard nodded and jogged down the steps. Sofia strained to see where he was headed as Domenico entered the building. She was about to turn to see where Katerina was in the queue, when a warm weight pressed up behind her. Before she could turn around, a strong force wrapped about her right wrist – a man's hand. 'Everything's fine.'

Pete had his back to her, although she knew him well enough to gauge that he was aware of what was happening. Good. He was clever enough to know not to interfere and to listen as carefully as possible. She cleared her throat and twisted up to see the face that was nuzzled against her cheek. It was the security guard to whom Domenico had whispered. 'Good to know.'

'If you'll follow me.' He released her wrist with enough roughness to indicate force without harming her. She met his eyes to show that she understood: if she did as she was asked, then this didn't need to escalate. The security guard stepped to one side and gestured for her to walk along the queue and up the steps.

'This way.'

The man tugged on her arm and led her past a table laden with champagne flutes and down a vast stone staircase. From memory, she thought this was the way to the cloakrooms. Her chest tightened as she descended. The walls were thick here and it didn't look as if these cloakrooms were being used for the event. Nobody would hear a commotion.

She'd been right: the stairs opened into a large room filled with tall lockers. A low electric hum vibrated gently through the cooler air – a sound one only hears in empty, isolated spaces. As they moved forwards, sections of the strip lighting beamed into action with each footstep. Her spine tingled as if physically warning her not to edge deeper into the building. Still, she was here for a reason. She was about to ask where she was being taken, when she heard a door open from behind the lockers. The security guard's grip tightened on her arm and she tensed, readying herself to fight. She listened to the door close and waited as quick footsteps approached.

'Sofia Sampson. An unexpected pleasure.'

Domenico approached from the shadows, nodding for her to be released. He looked smug, like a child who had outwitted a parent. There was a nervous energy to him that didn't come across in photographs. His stance looked forced, like he didn't know where to place his limbs, although he held his head with a stiff arrogance.

'I wish I could say the same about your hospitality,' she replied, rubbing her wrist.

'What can I say? Perhaps if I'd been informed of your attendance I could have arranged a better welcome.'

She forced the sides of her mouth to twitch. It was a good idea to play his game. She could already tell that this was a man who liked being appreciated. 'I'm flattered that you recognised me.' She watched his face carefully.

'Of course.' He shrugged, again giving the impression that he had done something of which to be immensely proud. 'You're an accomplished woman, Sofia, with a public image. It wasn't difficult to find the face behind the voice on the phone.'

'Well, as a detective, I'm impressed that you managed to spot me in the queue so quickly.'

He chuckled, as if he was impressed by his own abilities. 'I saw you as soon as my car pulled in. Like I say, you're not difficult to spot. And I have an eye for exceptional women.'

Good. He didn't know that Katerina was here, nor, she suspected, who she was. She stepped forwards, making sure to keep her gaze steady. 'You've gone to the trouble of the theatrics, care to tell me why we're down here?' Her voice reflected back at her, muted and almost muffled against the cream stone walls.

'I thought you wanted to talk.'

'Seems like you do too.' She cocked her head to one side, trying to gauge how serious of a situation she was in. Surely, he wouldn't be so audacious as to try anything here in the gallery building? It's what she was counting on. And it's why Pete would likely not be coming to her rescue. She hoped she was right.

He laughed at this, a full-bellied sound which rebounded off the surface of the lockers and flooded her ear canals. She resisted the urge to run. This was all a show, she was sure. That was enough to reassure her. He wanted to display his power, nothing more, for the moment. 'Surprising to see you here, that's all,' he said. 'I'm intrigued to know what you think you have to say to me. It must be important to have come all this way.'

'I'm from London originally and was visiting anyway,' she lied. 'But you're right, as I said on the phone, I'd like to talk. There are a few things I need clearing up–'

'I've told you everything I know.' The energy that seemed to be continuously coursing through his limbs flared; he flinched. She had irritated him.

'Yes, I'm grateful for that. However, I have a couple more questions, if you have time?'

He looked over her shoulder and she braced herself for being manhandled again. Instead, she listened to the security guard jogging up the stairs, leaving her alone with Domenico. He turned his back to her. 'Follow me, then. There's a conference room here. We can talk.'

She hesitated: following a man like Domenico further into the building seemed counterintuitive, but she wanted to read him. Already, she had a far better impression of him than she had gathered over the phone. At this stage, anything, any weakness in his character, any slight hesitation, could help her. He held a glass door open to a square stale meeting room and she settled into a leather swivel chair, resting her elbows on the table. 'I'll cut to the chase, I know you're a busy man.'

He nodded, his chin resting in his hands, his eyes drinking her in. She made sure to hold his gaze.

'You'll have heard that Innes was arrested?'

'Terrible news,' he said, biting his lip. 'You think she had something to do with Alek's death?'

'His murder?' she clarified. 'We have sufficient evidence linking her to the shooting. Does this seem within character to you?' She finished the sentence with a sharp inflection, hoping to jolt him into giving, if not an honest, then at least an unplanned response.

'I am afraid that I'm not familiar enough with her character to make a judgement call,' he said. The tips of his fingers pressed against his cheeks, making his face appear stretched and ghoulish.

'You are friends? Enough to exchange phone conversations, for example?'

'You and I have exchanged phone conversations,' he said, far too suggestively for her liking. 'Would you count me as a friend?'

She ignored him, purposefully diving into the next question to catch him off-guard. 'Does the word "unveil" mean anything to you?'

There it was. If nothing else, she had gained something from this trip. A flicker in the eye – she was practised enough to know when an errant thought passed through someone's brain. 'Unveil' meant something to him, she was sure. 'Domenico?'

'The word doesn't ring a bell. But I am Italian–'

'*Svelatare*, then?'

He shook his head, although she noticed the colour rising steadily up his cheeks. She smiled. 'Never mind, it was a long shot anyway.'

There was a short pause in which she detected something that felt strangely close to a mutual understanding. Then, he broke her gaze with a quick sigh. 'I won't pretend to understand the complexities of a police investigation.' He chuckled, revealing his front teeth to her. He looked lupine, like he wanted to taste her.

'No, no need for that.' She froze, a thorny instinct beginning to prickle beneath her skin. She was also well-practised at identifying individuals with whom it was a bad idea to spend much time alone. He was smooth, sophisticated, good-looking in a wealthy sort of way – but he had that quality; it bristled through his every manicured movement. That intangible sense of being above everything. Of the rules being mere toys. People like this were the most dangerous types. They saw everything as a game. She stood, pulling her shoulders back, forcing the movement to seem relaxed.

'Oh–' She began walking to the door, silently hoping that he didn't stop her. He followed her lead. 'A silly thing really...'

Thankfully, he held the door open for her. 'Yes?'

'We found some odd speakers on the hotel grounds, by the wall that leads to the beach. You wouldn't know anything about those?'

'Odd how? You mean they're unsafe? I don't really have a handle on the details of the place – Lily is best placed to help you there.'

'Not unsafe, no. They're hidden in the walls. Facing the wrong way, away from the hotel.'

He walked beside her, and she watched his jaw tighten, then slacken, as if he was forcing himself to remain relaxed. He pouted, giving a shrug. 'You can never find decent workmen – I'll ask Lily to look into it. You're concerned about noise complaints?'

'Should I be?'

He stopped, that jolt of nervous energy reverberating through his profile. 'If there is a problem with the speakers, I can arrange for them to be fixed.'

'Good.' She met his eyes, which glinted almost yellow beneath the halogen light. 'It's just that they're built into the wall itself, cemented in. I imagine it will be a big job. Unbelievable that someone would make that sort of mistake, isn't it? And that no one would notice?'

His eyes traced her face, as if he was trying to piece her expression together. She gave him nothing, keeping her lips narrow and straight, her eyes placid and amicable.

'I'd say just as unbelievable as you happening to be in London this week.'

Her nerves betrayed her; she glanced towards the stairs that lay at the end of the long corridor of lockers.

'Do I make you anxious, Sofia?'

She filled her lungs and faced him again, ignoring the sensation of her heart pumping more quickly, more urgently, sounding the alarm. 'Not anxious, no. I don't think you'd be stupid enough to hurt me down here. You make me suspicious, though.'

His lips curled upwards in a satisfied grin. 'Suspicion is just another word for ignorance.'

She raised her eyes to the ceiling. The gallery would be filling up with guests sipping champagne and chattering happily. She hoped that Katerina would continue as planned. 'You'll be missed upstairs. Maybe I'll see you at the Saturnalia.'

His grin turned into a baring of teeth. 'Oh, I doubt that. It's a highly exclusive event. Unless the police have good reason, I'd ask that you don't interfere.'

She nodded and began to walk towards the exit, forcing herself to maintain a reasonable pace. 'You'd better get those speakers seen to, then.'

Screensaver

'*Baba* never talks about it. He finds it too painful.' Maria clasped her hands behind her knees. An unopened bottle of wine was propped up in the sand, along with two plastic wine cups. The beach by the Temple of Apollo was mostly empty, apart from the meowing cats in the dunes. 'He would have mentioned it if he'd thought he was supposed to, though. It's not like you asked him, is it?'

Her voice had an edge to it, which Michail suspected had a lot to do with the direction their conversation had taken. It was likely that she had not expected him to open with the topic of her sister's suicide. Hopefully, given the urgency of the investigation, she would understand.

'That's correct. The most pressing fact to establish was your father's whereabouts on the night of Teddy's murder. Once he had confirmed his alibi, there was no logical reason to ask him further questions.'

She squinted at him. He couldn't help but notice how her eyelashes grazed the top of her cheekbones. She almost moved like a sculpture; the tiny hairs seemed to rest as heavy as marble on her flesh when she blinked. 'Then why are you asking me?

Or did I misunderstand? I thought we were meeting socially. I didn't realise that I should prepare for questioning.'

'No, no.' He slid his hands beneath the fine sand, clenching his fists tight and full of the grainy substance. It was cooler beneath the surface. 'I agree that it is, on the one hand, unfortunate timing. However, on the other, it is quite fortunate. I need your help in tracking down Eleni's friends, if you would be willing to help? A personal contact will be the most efficient way.'

She shook her head and sighed, before retrieving a corkscrew from her bag and opening the wine. 'You think this will help find the murderer? I know you can't tell me much more, but you think it will help?'

'The circumstances of Eleni's death have raised a few questions–'

She gulped, the wine almost spurting from her mouth. 'Eleni killed herself years ago, Michail. Please, unless you're certain that this is useful, don't rake all this up for *Baba*. He doesn't need to go through it all again. She killed herself. That's it.' Her voice cracked at the end of the sentence and she took another long sip of wine, before sighing. 'I can try and contact some of the girls. Maybe Georgia? She used to post a lot. I think I'm still following her.'

'Apparently the friendship group is not the easiest to contact.'

She gritted her teeth. 'Like I said, I'll try. Just don't mention it to *Baba* if you can help it, okay?'

It felt very important not to cause more upset than necessary. The death of a loved one was like an incurable, flimsy scar. You could live with it most days. You could avert your darkest thoughts and memories. Sometimes it would itch, which was natural for any healing wound. But it could also break all too easily, spill and ooze with the black liquid that it kept locked up and tidy. Michail spoke very carefully and quietly. 'It is incomprehensible, I know.'

'What?' She looked at him, her eyes slightly damp, somehow larger than before.

'Loss. It is impossible to understand it. In fact, the mind is not built to comprehend death, nor longing. Humans are not built for it. If we were, then memories would be malleable. We would be able to pick and choose. Instead, they run free with the ability to bring joy, of course, but also torment.'

She gave a long, low exhale and the sound of her breath mingled with the lapping of the evening sea. 'It's not just memories that I can't control.' She laughed. 'First dates can also bring up the past just as unexpectedly.'

'Ah.' She made a very pertinent point. 'I'm afraid I have a few more questions.'

'All right.' She held the bottle up to him and began to pour him a cup. 'No point letting it go to waste.'

He accepted the wine and bowed his head forwards, scanning his notebook which was now grainy from the sand. 'You'd already moved to Athens when Eleni died. The Aegina police treated her death as a straightforward suicide. Did you speak to her in the lead-up to her death?'

'She was younger than me. Especially at that age – I'd finished with my studies, moved away. I saw her very much as a baby sister.'

'There was no change in her behaviour? Nothing that suggested she was unhappy?'

She stared blankly at the sea for a few moments, before pushing up to her feet. 'Mind if we walk up to the temple? The view of the sky is brilliant from there in the evening.' She looked down at him and smiled. 'Don't worry, we can keep talking. Although, hopefully we can move on to another topic in a bit.'

His wine clasped in one hand, he followed her up the

dunes and to the dusty road that led to the archaeological site's entrance. He thought about hurrying to catch her up, however, as he followed her, a quiet descended over his limbs, a calm. It was nice being led, being told where to go. It was safe, secure.

As she approached the entrance, he called, 'It's past closing hours.'

'We used to hang out up there all the time as kids. There's no gate or anything. No one minds.'

He frowned but managed to fight the urge to refuse, as well as explain to her why rules were put in place for a reason and, if everybody ignored them, then the very fabric of society as they knew it would collapse. Without warning, Maria rounded back and rested her head on his shoulder. Her hair smelled almost salty with a hint of something citrus. 'Don't look so worried! Come on, surely even police officers bend the rules once in a while?'

He was about to explain that she was unfortunately correct and that plenty of officers took a sloppy view of society's laws, which was why it was important that he took a strict stance on the matter. Then he remembered how he had not only bent the rules, but completely disregarded them when he had lied about Katerina. What right did he have to pass judgement on others? He had none. No right at all. But he could begin to make amends within himself, to restore balance. He stopped sharp in his tracks. The solitary remaining column of the Temple of Apollo reached lonely into the sky, a few metres up the slope from where they stood. It had lasted millennia, retaining its strength and integrity throughout war and weather and unprecedented change. As the rest of the temple had crumbled around it, as its god had ceased to be worshipped, it stood tall. Quiet and reliable.

'Michail, are you okay?'

'Yes.' He nodded, a sharp, decisive movement. 'Yes, if you don't mind, Maria, I would like to stop here.'

'Here?' She pouted. 'But we can't see the view from here.'

'That is true. I...' That empty sensation, like a hand groping uselessly through his brain, surfaced. He wanted to explain how this tiny transgression, this slight, innocuous bending of the law, seemed now like a gargantuan step in the wrong direction. The beginning of a slippery slope. He wanted to put into words how, since last summer, he had felt like a broken version of himself and that, despite him fastidiously following the various tips from his counsellor, he had been unsuccessful in regaining his former assuredness. His former sense of who he was. He blew out useless air through his lips. 'I have a strong preference not to trespass the Temple of Apollo.'

Maria looked like she was about to laugh, but she didn't. Instead, she tilted her head to one side and traced his face with gentle eyes. 'I understand.'

'Thank you–'

'But you would be neglecting your duty if you refused to intervene having seen someone drinking on the temple grounds, who had broken in after opening hours.'

'Of course, I–'

Before he understood what she meant, a stream of laughter escaped her lips and she dashed under the wooden barrier, taking a sharp left up the path that led towards the top of the hill, leaving a cloud of dust in her wake. In the place of words, he let out a deep groan and ducked under the barrier himself. Quickening his pace, he meandered through the low excavations, the remnants of the Helladic settlements, the Mycenaean constructs now reduced to their foundations; in times gone by this Acropolis would have been a bustling fusion of various temples and tombs, theatrical structures, and an aqueduct. Now, as he wound up the short hill, it felt homogenised, bathed in beige, muted and sad. Maria sat at the top of the steps leading up to the column. She was leaning on her hands, her face tilted up to the orange clouds. Against the lava sky, she appeared like a grey statue.

She smiled without opening her eyes as he approached. 'Am I in trouble?'

He sighed, exhausted. 'I will make an exception this once, considering the fact that I still have a few important questions.' The lilt in his own voice surprised him: he sounded as if he was joking. It was an odd sensation. He felt ungrounded, like he was barefoot on unfamiliar land. It was a complete diversion from the security he had felt following her only moments before – she flitted between emotions easily. He realised he didn't hate it, far from irritating him, her unpredictability seemed organic, natural. He nodded at the column. 'The *entasis* is more obvious when there is only one column standing.'

'*Entasis?*'

'Yes. The thickening of the column at the bottom. It's narrower at the top.' He twisted, gesturing to the width around the base. 'The ancients applied the geometrical philosophy to their temples. This is a part of it – the thickening isn't regular, you see. It curves, but never wider than the base. When looked at in the whole, the temple seems built upon straight lines. However, the lines are all curved in reality. But on its own, the illusion is broken.'

'You sound disappointed.'

He raised his eyebrows. 'Not disappointed, no. Just observant of the facts.'

'Got it.' Her smile remained although her expression carried a hint of unhappiness. 'You asked about Eleni's behaviour in the lead-up?'

'That's right.' Michail took a seat next to her on the bottom of the column. She had been correct: the view from here was magical. The sea glimmered and shimmied and rolled in an unimaginable technicolour mirage. It was as if it imitated Maria. If it weren't for the half-dipped sun, it would have been impossible to tell where the water began and the skies ended. 'Was there anything unusual?'

She shifted, seeming like she hadn't heard the question. Twice she smiled, the movement setting tiny crinkles at the side of her eyes, before her face slackened, snapping back. Finally, a solitary tear curved over her cheek and dripped onto her lap. 'You don't think that these things are strange at the time, do you? It's always retrospective, when it's too late. The thing is, Eleni was always popular with boys – she was beautiful and she had this manner about her, like she was constantly thinking of something mischievous, something that she wouldn't say. It made people want to be around her.' Michail remembered the photograph that he had seen at the *Lykeio*. It was as Maria explained: that knowing glint had come across even in the picture.

'She got serious with this guy. I never met him, don't even know his name. She talked about him all the time but just called him "my man". It was weird. He was a frequent guest at the hotel–' Her eyes darkened at this. 'She was working as a hostess there. It was good money and seemed glamorous in a way.'

This confirmed what Vi had said that morning. 'Was your father also working as the desk manager at that time?'

'No. He only started afterwards. He has to be there, for Eleni. That's what he says.'

'He has to?'

Maria wiped a second tear from her face. 'I think he means that he feels close to her there. When she died, she was spending most evenings on shifts, most weekends. She worked with her friends. I don't know, he can hardly hang around at the *Lykeio*, can he? So, he took a job there.'

It made some sort of logical sense. Michail could not imagine what the death of a child felt like. 'This boyfriend?'

'I don't know much about him. He was rich, obviously. She had all these new handbags and he paid for their dinners at the hotel when she wasn't working. It wasn't a long-term thing; this was probably only over the span of six weeks or so. That's why I found it so strange, the way she spoke about him. I wouldn't call it obsessed, but maybe like she was in awe? She started saying odd things to me, stuff she'd never usually say.'

'Do you remember what?'

'This wasn't anything that she would have ever said before, but that she was happy to "submit" to this man. The more she thought about it, the more she could see how – *although it was nothing against women as a whole* – that civilisation was declining due to the mainstream's agenda to force women out of their "natural state". She said that women had been duped into thinking they needed to be independent, earn money. Really, they should serve the *stronger sex*.'

This sounded like familiar extremist, misogynistic rhetoric. 'Did she follow Alek Knox on social media? Do you think she had met him before? Perhaps at the hotel?'

Maria shook her head. 'You know, it crossed my mind too. It's similar sort of stuff, isn't it? And she was in the right age group – he said that he only dated women in their late teens so that he could... what was it he used to say? Oh, "guide" them. But no, I'm sure it wasn't him. I checked: you can see on his feed that he was in Bali for that whole period.'

'Perhaps a fan of his, then,' Michail suggested.

'Whoever it was, my best guess is that he broke it off with her and she...' She looked at her lap. 'If she had just spoken to me about it. I could have helped her. Told her it wasn't love... but anyway.' The sun had almost disappeared and its last reddish fingers stretched out across the water towards the temple. Maria glanced up at it, her eyes shining. 'This is my favourite part.'

He wasn't sure how or when it had happened, but Michail was suddenly very aware of her thigh pressing against his as they watched the view. An intricate tapestry of unplaceable colours dancing upon the sea's surface teased their onlookers.

'This island is complex,' Michail said. 'I don't just mean the case: its history, its mythology, its architecture. Things weave in one direction then veer off in another. It is difficult to anchor anything here without it flipping and twisting.'

Maria laughed. 'More complex than Athens?'

'Yes.' He clasped his hands on his lap. 'It's steeped in disguise. The nymph Aegina herself is said to have been stolen from her parents by Zeus in the guise of a flame, giving the island its name. This is where Zeus turned ants into Myrmidons. The mythology of Athens is rooted in order overcoming chaos. Here, it's rooted in change, flux, tricks.'

'You sound like you hate it.'

He looked at her, genuinely amazed. 'Hate it? No! I am fascinated by it, Maria. There is always value in stories, no matter what their themes. They are the voices of the past, the web of collective consciousness and morals and imagination that hold us together as human. I just wish that I could work out the story behind the case – it's true to its location, every time I think I have it, it spirals in another direction out of my grasp.'

'It's just so crazy, all of it.' She took a long sip of wine before facing him, her neck elongated, her shoulders drawn back. From here, he could smell the sweet alcohol on her breath. 'Do you really think Eleni has anything to do with this?'

Her eyes were wide with fear. He understood; dragging up the past, the buried pain, would be unbearable. He could understand her wanting to avoid it. 'I'm not sure.' It was an insufficient answer, but truthful, at least. Maria sighed and rested her head against his shoulder. He surprised himself by not flinching from her. In fact, the presence of her breath against his neck had a calming effect, releasing a tension deep between his shoulder blades. They sat without speaking for a long while, Michail willed the song of the *tzitzikas* to engulf his thoughts like a probing mist, to connect the dots that he was unable to connect, to see those innocuous details that lay hidden in the forgotten crevices of his mind.

It happened very naturally. Her lips found their way to his. Her body twisted to face him, the curvature of her pressing against him. Somewhere inside of him erupted a deep comfort, a stability that he had not felt in a long while. Her mouth worked against his as if with an intimate knowledge; she stroked the back of his head and he pressed more urgently towards her, a low moan escaping his lips. When the kiss was finished, he opened his eyes. Maria's forehead was resting against his, her own eyes blinking drowsily back at him. 'Sorry, I–'

'There is no need for an apology.'

This made her laugh, and he joined in with her, realising this was the first time in over a year that he had thought of anything other than work. She topped up his wine and nestled next to him, watching the blue darkness begin to roll out into the horizon. 'I wish I had my sketchbook with me, this would make a good print, hang on...' She rifled about in her bag. 'I'll take a photo.'

He saw her screensaver when he glanced down as she opened her phone. He almost averted his eyes out of respect: the image was of her and Eleni, two sisters in a moment of happiness before tragedy struck. They were posing on Maria's motorbike, heads thrown back in laughter. 'Maria, wait–'

'Oh yes, that's her.' She bit her lip as she blinked at the photograph. 'It's one of my favourites. I keep meaning to do something with it, frame it maybe or something. The composition is good, I think.'

'On her lower leg, is that a tattoo?' Just above Eleni's trainers was what looked like a new tattoo, still covered with a protective transparent film.

'Oh God, that...' Maria nodded, zooming in on the image. 'Another symptom of the mystery boyfriend. They got matching tattoos. After only a few weeks. I remember being relieved that she hadn't got his name printed on her or anything like that–'

The cross at the top, the way that it curved about at the bottom, forming a sharp scythe-like shape. 'Did she say what it was?'

Maria frowned. 'No. Why? Is it relevant?'

Michail bit his tongue inside of his mouth. He could trust Maria, he felt that with every molecule, but he could not share details of the ongoing case, no matter how much he wanted to. When he had unravelled everything, she would be given some peace. 'No. Most likely not. It's just an interesting pattern, that's all.'

Masks

Katerina forced herself to breathe steadily. Sofia had left, walking past without throwing her so much as a glance, which meant she was avoiding looking at her... which must mean she was expected to carry on as planned – alone. She caught a glimpse of who she assumed was Sofia's ex-husband, buried deep in a crowd gathered around a painting she couldn't see. Taking a glass of champagne, she circled back towards the main entrance hall, in which an a cappella group were now performing, their voices competing with the rising chatter.

Scanning the tall room, she searched for Domenico. It was no use: there were too many people, all packed into tight groups, heads bobbing up and down to the rhythm of chuckles and anecdotes. She took a quick nip of champagne, which had already grown warm, and walked up the marble staircase behind her, gliding past those descending it as discreetly as she could. The staircase opened into an emptier gallery, filled with what looked like a series of human heads. She stepped forwards, checking behind her. The voices echoed from the main gallery downstairs, giving the impression that the strange mask-sculptures were whispering as she edged through the long room.

A couple emerged from the other side of the gallery and, although she knew it was stupid, she felt relief. They stopped to observe a particularly grotesque piece: it looked like a larger-than-life man's head, filled with–

'Blood, real blood,' the man, whose hand dangled around the woman's waist, said. Katerina didn't realise that he was speaking to her until the silence became awkward.

'Blood?'

'Yes. Marc Quinn's *Self*. Been here for years, before the renovation. It's his blood inside. Needs to be refrigerated, obviously.'

'I... I see...' It was difficult to be impressed, given the information card was right in front of him.

The man eyed her through the glass case. 'Press, are you? What publication? Let me guess... women's rag, is it? *Glamour*, no, *Stylist*? I'm right, aren't I? You've got the look.'

The young woman next to him giggled, her full lips forming a perfect heart of a smile. Katerina had a hairbreadth of a moment to react appropriately; the woman was wearing a sickle necklace. It dangled, catching the dim lights as if it was simultaneously meant to be seen and unseen. Katerina felt the tiny muscles around her eyes tense in reflex before she forced her face to relax, sliding her stare back to the man. 'And you are?'

He stood straighter at the question. It seemed like he was the sort of man who wasn't used to having his questions left unanswered, nor turned onto him. Katerina took another sip of her champagne, waiting patiently for his response.

'A friend of the guest of honour, himself.' He spoke slowly, like he thought he was saying something unbelievably impressive. He'd also expertly avoided giving his name. She kept her face impassive, clocking in her peripheral vision that another couple had entered the gallery from the same direction.

'The guest of honour?'

This caused the man to laugh; he smoothed down his hair, which was peppered with just the right amount of silver hairs, cut in a way that was stylishly unkempt. 'You really haven't done your research, have you? You know, I wonder what they pay your type for, nowadays.'

Katerina managed to squeeze out a reciprocal chuckle through gritted teeth. 'Oh, you've caught me!' She shrugged, pretending to have the grace to be embarrassed.

He cocked his head to one side, his lips settling in a pout. 'Go on then, where are you from? I'm struggling to place your accent.'

'Cyprus,' she said smoothly. 'I moved here a few years ago.' She paused, tracing her nail across the lip of the warm champagne flute. Whoever the woman on his arm was, she clearly didn't have a problem with him blatantly ignoring her. That was odd. 'So, help me out here. The guest of honour...?' Hopefully her steer back towards Domenico was subtle enough.

'Domenico Bonarelli.' He said the name with a deep relish. 'He paid for most of this – the building's unrecognisable, actually, assuming you haven't visited before. Donated almost thirty million. Mind you, he doesn't shout about it. He's honoured the artists, no time for ego.'

Katerina raised an eyebrow as if she was enthralled to be speaking to the friend of such a man, but didn't want to come across too desperate. The way he spoke about Domenico was weird, almost like he was reciting a script.

'Ha!' The man laughed, making her jump. The woman next to him seemed to have gone into some sort of blank trance. She stared at the gruesome blood head with dull eyes, as if she wasn't hearing any of the conversation happening next to her. 'You're thinking I might introduce you?' the man continued, sniggering. 'Quite the scoop for the editor, wouldn't that be? Bet it would make your career. Well, little *madame*, you've got a lot to learn about the world, clearly. You don't just–'

'We all have a lot to learn about the world.'

The voice came from behind her, the warm words caressed her back, making the hairs on her arms stand on end. A fresh glass of champagne slipped into her hand, the old one whisked away.

'Domenico, we were just talking about–'

Domenico appeared at her side, raising his glass to clink against hers. 'You're in luck. He's right, I don't normally give individual press interviews.'

Katerina followed his lead in taking a swift sip of the cool, bubbly liquid, watching his face. There was no sense that he suspected she was anyone other than an eager journalist wanting to gain an edge. Sofia would have warned her had her cover been blown. His gaze flickered, for less than a second, to the woman who was still staring at the head, before focusing back on her. She blinked slowly as though she was surprised to find that she had eyelids at all. Her partner's arm around her waist increasingly gave Katerina the impression of someone propping up a rag doll.

'Is she all right?' Katerina frowned at the woman. 'Are you okay?'

'Fine.' The man blew heavily through his teeth, spurting tiny droplets of spittle onto the glass container. 'Too much champagne, as usual. Most women can't handle their drink. I'll leave you to it.'

With that, the woman leaned into the man, almost fully supported by his weight. There was a tightening in Katerina's chest: every fibre of her wanted to follow them as the woman stumbled at his side, a hazy smile lolling across her face, further into the museum. She couldn't track them. That would be suspicious. Why would an arts journalist suddenly have an interest in a random drunk woman when Domenico Bonarelli, the big scoop himself, stood before her? Her heart clenching into a tight ball, she noted the direction they'd gone and resumed her conversation with Domenico, her mind racing to come up with a plan to end it as soon as possible.

'Impressive.' She gestured to the gallery. 'Your friend was telling me you're the man behind this renovation. You must love art very much to have used your personal funds.'

'Ah yes, very much. It's the expression of the soul, is it not? I curated this space. Do you like it?'

She turned to survey the long display of the different moulded faces, all eerily still and absent compared to the small groups who had finally begun to filter through into the gallery. 'It's interesting. The heads–'

'Masks.' He corrected her with a short, sharp breath. 'The theme is masks. Masks from different people, from different places and times. The human mask that we all wear.'

She nodded, turning to face him. 'It's a conversation starter.'

'Tell me...' His eyes flicked to her press lanyard. 'Isabella, what's your mask? Your daily disguise?'

An electric jolt of paranoia reverberated through her abdomen. 'I don't know what you mean.'

'Your disguise.' He stepped forwards so that his chest was almost touching hers. She began to step back but he, very tenderly, pushed a strand of hair behind her ear. 'What are your deepest secrets, Isabella? How do you hide them in the light of day?'

'I... I don't have any–'

'We all do.' He whispered the words into her ear, and she shuddered in revulsion, her breath quickening in panic. 'You can interview me later. My hotel isn't far from here... show me who you are without the mask...' She had never been more relieved to be the object of a misogynistic pervert's attention: he was just trying to get her to go home with him.

'I have all I need, thank you.' She stepped back, bumping into the group of people behind her. Anger flashed in his eyes – that cold, flinted frustration at not getting the prize. Not getting what he wanted. She had seen that look before, many times. She would not bend to its will ever again. 'Thank you for your time.'

Without waiting for him to reply, she hurried away, hoping that the girl with the necklace hadn't been dragged too far. Domenico didn't follow her – that was good. Her cover was safe, for now. She darted between the bodies in the next gallery, this one filled with photographs of beautiful and powerful women, most of whom she recognised. The clink of glasses and rising chatter grated upon her skin; they were so unaware, so blind to the type of man who had funded the night.

'Jesus, she was wasted.' A woman giggled under her breath with her head close to her friend's. Katerina snapped her head in their direction, just in time to see the fire exit door closing behind them. She launched herself as best she could through the crowd, trying not to draw attention to herself, and slipped behind the door. Here, the air was a lot cooler. She pressed herself against the wall, removed her stilettos, and listened to the footsteps spiralling below. The staircase was wide and white and stark: if anyone came this way, she would be spotted immediately.

'What happened?' Katerina froze at the sound of a woman's voice. She didn't speak with an English accent. She crept around the corner, struggling to get a view. Her fingers trembled as she pressed record on her phone, hoping their voices would carry. Crouching beneath the railing, she couldn't risk going further – she'd be in plain sight. A voice recording would have to do.

'Keeps happening, doesn't it? Give them an inch. She's

hammered, you take her.' There was a shuffle and what sounded like the legs of a chair scraping along the floor.

'Did you hurt her?' The woman spoke again. It was difficult to tell, but she sounded Greek.

'Hurt her? She should be grateful for having access to a party like this. Not to mention the dinners paid for, the clothes, the bags. Instead, she decides to get off her face on whatever she managed to get her hands on.'

There was a pause before the woman replied, 'Her pupils look okay. She'll just need to sleep it off. Where's next?'

'Where else? Saturn House, obviously. Jesus. I don't know why he lets you get involved. Slow out the gate, aren't you?'

'She has bruises on her legs.' The woman spoke in a tone that Katerina couldn't quite place. There was a thread of accusation, but also an awful acceptance.

'They'll heal, don't worry about it.' The chair scraped again and there was a soft groan. The sound travelled up the stairs and wrapped itself about Katerina's neck like soft, airy fingers. It was so tired; so resigned. It was hurt.

'She can't go back up. She'll draw attention. I'll take care of her.'

The man muttered something under his breath and Katerina jumped into action, throwing herself in long strides up the stairs and back through the fire exit. She slipped behind a waiter offering canapés just in time; five seconds later, the man emerged from the exit. He shook his head, a snarl spreading across his face, before snatching a glass from a tray, downing the whole thing and storming back towards the main hall. The waiter stared at her, alarmed, but then decided to offer her a canapé.

'No, thank you,' she breathed before diving back through the fire exit and hurtling down the stairs. The two women remained on the bottom floor, one seated, one standing.

Katerina gripped the bannister, her mouth falling open in shock. The woman who was standing, one hand on the seated girl's wilted spine, was Tatiana Kanatas.

'The party's upstairs, nothing down here.' Tatiana pulled the girl to her feet, rolling her eyes towards Katerina as if embarrassed by her drunk friend. Katerina caught a glimpse of the bruises on the girl's legs before her dress fell over them.

'Where are you taking her?' Katerina lowered herself onto the next step, a thunderous pressure building within the inside of her skull: she could not lose her. The air between them twitched, slippery and unsettled, like they could slide away through the door with one misjudged word. But she would not let that happen. She would tread carefully.

'Home.' Tatiana's face sharpened, her eyes narrowing as Katerina moved closer. 'Not that it's got anything to do with you.'

Katerina stopped moving. It took all the discipline she had not to lunge for the girl. The bruises, that awful man: clearly, something was deeply wrong. But it was more than that. She found it amazing that neither of the women before her could hear the deafening beat of her heart, singing not with fear but with recognition. It recognised the imprint of purple bruises, cruelly delicate and vaporous, as if they knew they had to be discreet. It knew the awkward twist of the neck – anything to avoid eye contact. It knew the mask that Tatiana wore: the one that said how fine everything was. How normal everything was. These women had everything to do with her.

'Tatiana. Tatiana Kanatas?' The name sounded clear on the concrete walls.

It was like lighting a match and watching it die in a gust of wind. Tatiana's face glowed for a warm moment as it caught her name, then quivered, her eyes deadening as she stared at Katerina. 'I don't know who that is. You're mistaken.'

Katerina shook her head, taking the final step so that she now stood at the same level as Tatiana. 'It's okay. I'm not going to do anything. I just need to ask you some questions. I want to help–'

'We don't need help.' She gripped the girl's face in her hands and, using her thumbs, wiped the black smears from under her eyes.

Katerina didn't want to do it here, but it seemed the only way to get her attention. 'Your mother was killed. I'm sorry, Tatiana. I don't know how much you know, but we think it's related to the murders on Aegina. That man earlier – he mentioned Saturn House? Anything you know, anything at all could help us. Please... it could help us find who killed your mother.'

The news hit, as it always did, like a physical blow. Tatiana's arms dropped to her side, and she backed away from the girl, her legs collapsing as her spine found support against the wall. Her body shook, her head jerked from side to side in small, helpless movements. 'No. No, no. You don't know that. You don't know what you're talking about. You're lying. Lying!'

Her eyes blazed as she fired the accusation with such force that her saliva travelled through the air, reaching Katerina in a horrible, desperate spray. The girl had sunk back onto the chair, her head hanging between her knees. Katerina knelt and placed her hands on the side of Tatiana's arms. She didn't pull away. 'I'm so sorry, Tatiana. I... I can't imagine how awful this must be for you. I just need some answers. I'm a part of the investigation with the Hellenic Police. I need to know who you're working for, who that man is. Anything you can tell me about Domenico–'

She thought that Tatiana was going to strike her, but instead she placed a hand over her mouth at the mention of Domenico's name. 'Not here.'

Katerina nodded, evidently convincingly enough for Tatiana to drop her hand.

'We'll need to take her. Come on.' She pushed herself up from the floor and helped the girl to her feet. 'She'll walk if we help her.'

Katerina hurriedly slipped back into her stilettos and helped Tatiana support the girl through the door. Outside, the air had a faint acidity, the familiar mixture of urine and stale alcohol that lingered in most city alleys. The girl's fingers clung to the back of Katerina's dress as she lolloped, sleepily, in between them. 'Will you take her home? I can come with you.'

Tatiana answered quickly as if she had already prepared for this question. 'She can come with me later to sleep it off, but not now. There's a pub just here.'

They drew surprisingly little attention crossing the road; the after-work crowd had spilled out of the offices and either marched past them with their heads down and eyes averted, or gathered in large, gregarious groups outside the various bars and restaurants.

'It's always like this when it's warm.'

Katerina nodded towards the pub doors. 'Here? Can we go inside?'

Tatiana didn't reply but held the door open with one foot so they could enter. The pub was packed wall to wall with people waiting to be served at the small bar. There was nowhere to sit, let alone talk. Tatiana didn't stop – she took most of the girl's weight and dragged her, pushed against the far wall, towards the back of the room.

'Wait–'

Katerina pushed her own way through the crowd. They

were so intent on their conversations, roaring and squealing with laughter, arms around their friends' shoulders, that they barely noticed her. She slid out of the mass of bodies into a small, cool vestibule.

'Up here.' Tatiana stood halfway up a narrow wooden staircase. 'A bit of help?'

The girl swung dangerously in Tatiana's arms; her lips now parted in a dazed smile. Katerina hurried up to steady her. 'What's she taken? Are you sure she's safe?'

Tatiana gave a small barbed laugh. 'The drugs are the least of her worries. Come on. It's always quiet up here, especially when everyone's outside.'

She was right: the room at the top of the pub was completely empty. They took a table by the window, and settled the girl onto a chair, who immediately rested her forehead on the sticky, grainy wood. Tatiana eyed the street below, before her eyes closed for a few seconds. The sound of people drinking seemed like it was miles away. The evening light, tinged with grey, fell upon her face like a sad, oily veil.

'Again, I'm so sorry...' Katerina began.

'You're sure about it?' Her eyes flew open. Tatiana seemed to steel herself. Her jawline was clenched and tight. She was ready for a fight with the facts.

'Yes.'

'And you think it was...' She lowered her voice. 'You think it was him, Domenico?'

'Do you?'

Tatiana stared at her and, for a moment, Katerina was sure that she was about to say something explosive. Then, the fire behind her eyes died and she shrugged, her lips pressed together. 'He's been in Rome and now here. Not Aegina.'

'Tatiana...' There was no delicate way of putting this. 'Your mother, Irene. I found her body. Please believe me

209

when I tell you that whoever did this needs to be brought to justice.'

Her composure faltered as visible cracks of pain erupted at the corners of her eyes. Tatiana clasped her hands tightly together, as if in prayer, and looked at the table. Katerina reached to comfort her, but she flinched, her shoulders trembling. 'Tell me.'

'We believe she was attacked in her home. Her wrists were slit. Her murderer likely held her down. She was strong, clearly strong enough to do her cleaning job, but she was small. A younger person would have overpowered her–'

A low, animal yelp escaped from Tatiana's throat. She bore her knuckles into the tabletop in a horrible rhythm; the sound of her bones grated against the hard surface.

'If you're protecting anyone–' That awful feeling of having worn this skin before, or having been trapped between the terror of truth and lie caught her breath. What would she have needed to hear to turn on Theo? Surely, surely the death of her mother would have been enough. The thought burned, acidic, at the back of her throat.

'You think I have the power to protect?' Tatiana looked up, tears erupting from her eyes. 'You think that I'm anyone? I stayed away to keep her safe. She was supposed to be safe. To be looked after.'

'Keep her safe? From who? Domenico?'

Tatiana's eyes darted from one corner of the room to the other.

'Are you frightened he can hear you? Do you work for him?'

'A lot of people work for him.' She bit her lip. Although her eyes were locked on Katerina's, it was like she wasn't really looking at her at all. The slumped girl next to them let out a soft snore. The sound was so innocent, so out of place. Tatiana shook her head. 'He's rich. Powerful. I'd stay away from him. He has people everywhere. You don't know–'

'Then tell me.' She slid her hands over the table towards Tatiana. 'Just tell me, I can help you.'

Whatever thought had been sitting behind Tatiana's eyes seemed to find a resolve. She sniffed, a horrible wet sound, and wiped a tear from her cheek. She closed her eyes for a moment and when she opened them, they were filled with a hard certainty. 'I need to go. I shouldn't have spoken to you. Just leave it, okay? Stop whatever you're doing. I mean it.'

Katerina almost flinched at the change in her demeanour. 'But your mother...'

'She's dead.' The word struck the air like a whip. 'She's been put out of her misery. That's all any of us can hope for.'

The bitterness in her voice was painful. 'Tatiana, I don't understand.'

She stood abruptly and prodded the girl, who had begun to stir. 'You'll let us leave? You won't cause any trouble?'

'Earlier, you said there were bruises on her legs.' Katerina gestured to the girl. 'Has someone hurt her? Is she being trafficked? Is that what happened to you?' There was no time to be delicate about it.

'She's off her face, she fell.' Tatiana blew through her teeth with an air of impatience. The girl raised her face from the table and started to giggle. 'Come on, get up. We're going.'

A hundred questions raced through Katerina's mind. Her time was running out: neither she nor Sofia had any jurisdiction. They shouldn't even have been in London. As much as she wanted to intervene, she was helpless. What she needed was information. 'You asked that man earlier about where was next and he said Saturn House. What does that mean?'

'Oh my God.' Tatiana's voice changed; a low, sarcastic drawl seeped into her words. 'You might have heard about it? A small, low-key gathering at the hotel? You know, just the world's richest and most powerful celebrating the end of the summer.'

'The Saturnalia?' Katerina frowned and looked at the girl. 'You're going to the Saturnalia?'

The girl's eyes widened and she spoke for the first time. 'Oh? Am I, Tat? Seriously? The Saturnalia? I didn't know...' Her accent sounded English and, as much as Katerina could make out, very well-spoken.

'Let's go.' Tatiana stepped to one side to allow the girl to lead the way. She was clever – it meant that Katerina couldn't ask her friend any more questions. She folded her arms as she watched the two women descend the stairs into the buzz below, a familiar feeling of dread gurgling in her stomach. Just before they disappeared, she grabbed a napkin from a table and hurried after them.

'Wait!' She grabbed Tatiana's shoulder, fumbling about in her bag for a pen. 'Wait.' She quickly wrote down her number and reached past Tatiana, forcing it into the girl's hand. 'Call me if you need anything, help, anything at all.'

'Thanks so much.' More sarcasm rolled through Tatiana's every syllable. It was as if she had forgotten the horrific news about her mother. Katerina watched them leave with a sinking heart.

Boyfriend

Michail sat across from Lily on one of the marble tables nestled in the shrubbery around the corner from the pool. If Saturn House's preparations had felt fraught yesterday, then they had accelerated today. This corner was the only quiet spot they could find.

Lily typed at an impressive speed on her laptop, her orange-red lips pressed together in determined concentration. 'Sorry, sorry...' she mumbled, holding a finger up to him, presumably as a sign that she was going as quickly as she could.

Michail studied her: once again she was oblivious to the severity of the situation at hand. The call from London last night had been simultaneously revelatory and confusing. The fact that Tatiana Kanatas was in London, seemingly working in some capacity for Domenico, was interesting to say the least. The suspicion about trafficking was damning, especially given the narrative surrounding Eleni and her mystery boyfriend. It was also possible that Alek had been planning to reveal a related scandal before he was killed. The Saturnalia, Domenico, Irene, Eleni, Alek, Teddy – all roads led to Saturn House. At present, the question was precisely what and how much Lily knew. So far, she had hidden nothing from the police: she'd even given them the video of her being attacked by Irene. It was possible that Domenico had purposefully employed her for her lack of meticulousness and observational skills, which meant that she was treading, unaware, in dangerous waters.

'Ms Woodstow, it's imperative that I have your full concentration for this conversation.'

She responded with a high-pitched humming noise, before hitting the keyboard with two final elaborate taps. 'Gosh, I'm busy...'

'Yes. I must admit that I was not aware of how much work party planning entails.'

The comment seemed to please her. She sat back in the chair, a grin erupting over her face. 'Well, it's not just that; being a businesswoman eats up quite a chunk of time!'

'Ah, yes.' He stared at her laptop and waited for her to close it to ensure her full concentration. 'I wanted to speak with you about two former employees here at Saturn House.'

'Oh God. Is this about Irene? Oh...' She shook her head slowly, her eyes wide and watery. 'I'm still in shock. We didn't see eye to eye, as you know. But... who... who on earth would do that to an old woman? Makes me feel sick.'

The news of Irene's death had spread through the community with virulent force. The police had been forced to release some details, including that they were treating it as a murder, to quell rumours and hysteria.

'A natural reaction. However, I'm here to ask about her daughter, Tatiana Kanatas, and Eleni Barlas. Do you remember them?'

Lily squinted, as if deep in thought. 'Erm, yes, yes, you know I do. We're talking years ago now. They were hostesses?'

'Correct. What did this role encompass?'

'Oh, well, you haven't seen the hotel in full swing, since

we've been closed to guests. Normally, when the restaurants and bars are running, we have hostesses. They'll serve drinks, work poolside to check on guests and fetch them anything they need. That sort of thing.'

'Are they typically young women?'

Lily, who had been fiddling with a leaf between her thumb and forefinger, stopped. She met his gaze, her eyes widening. 'What do you mean?'

'The hostesses,' he repeated. 'Are they female and young?'

Although her smile didn't falter, she tilted her head to one side, as if weighing up how she might answer the question very carefully. 'I suppose so, yes. It's a social job. I worked in a similar industry myself when I was young in London. It's not seedy or anything. It's just good, well-paid fun.'

He remembered the expensive handbags that Maria had mentioned Eleni had received. 'How well-paid, specifically?'

She laughed at that. 'Specifically? Well, that depends on a lot of things. Like most high-end bar staff, a good chunk of money comes from tips.'

'I see. Were you ever aware of Eleni Barlas receiving such tips? Or even gifts?'

Lily considered the question for a moment, plucking another leaf from the branch. 'Yes... yes, actually. She was really beautiful... and fun. I think she probably got a lot of gifts from the single male guests. Why do you ask?'

'Do you remember any guest in particular with whom she had a close relationship? He would most likely have stayed at the hotel for quite a period of time.'

She shrugged. 'We get a few guests staying for long periods to work on projects or escape the English drizzle. If they're still a member, I'll have those records. I can check?'

'That would be most useful. Is it possible to do it now?'

She reached for her laptop. 'Sure. Do you have a year? Dates?'

He nodded, opening his notepad. 'Five years ago. Between March and June. Please search for any guest who stayed longer than two weeks or visited regularly within that period.'

She bit her lip in concentration, as he moved to get a look at the screen. 'It's searching. It'll take a few minutes to load. You're welcome to wait.' She pushed the laptop to one side.

'Thank you, I will. It will be a good opportunity for you to tell me about Tatiana Kanatas.'

He detected a slight twitch in her face as he mentioned the name; perhaps it was understandable. The name 'Kanatas' would no doubt remind her of her last meeting with Irene. He continued, 'She was a hostess too? At around the same time?'

'That's right. She was a little older, but she worked here. Same sort of stuff.'

He asked the next question very casually. 'Any idea where she is now?'

He watched her digest the question, poised to detect any hint of deception. The furrowing of the brow, the flick of the eyes, the flush of the cheeks. No such signs occurred. She pouted, shaking her head. 'No, sorry. I know that she left home abruptly. That's it, I'm afraid. I tried not to have that much to do with Irene.'

He folded his arms as a soft breeze danced through the trees surrounding them. For a moment, the bristling of the leaves provided a gentle distraction to the backdrop of drilling and hammering. Lily sighed, and rested her chin on her hands.

'You still don't understand how on earth the Saturnalia is going ahead? You find it callous?'

It was an unusually direct question. 'I understand it, Ms Woodstow. However, I don't agree with it. I've been unfortunate enough to learn that the path to money and power is more often than not laid with blunt, ruthless force. I wouldn't expect the "haves", as you called them, to possess the sensitivity required to cancel their party.'

An odd look came over her face. 'It's just a party.'

'That depends on your perspective.'

'Perhaps you're right.' She smiled and looked at the trees, apparently ready to change the subject. 'It's set to be a great pistachio harvest this year.'

Michail turned to see where she was looking. The trees surrounding them were all olive, not pistachio. He frowned, confused. 'Do you keep pistachio trees somewhere in the grounds?'

She looked momentarily confused, as if she didn't understand the question, when the laptop beeped. 'Ah!' She glanced at the screen. 'Success... oh... well, that's a coincidence...' She turned the screen to face him.

The database had provided only three names, all male. Only one name could be mistaken for a coincidence: Teddy Menkopf.

Next Best Thing

Sofia folded her arms tightly as Pete placed the soft toy on the grave. Grave. It was a disastrous word. She never said it aloud, because she knew that it would lodge, sticky and painful, at the back of her throat. He'd chosen a giraffe. It sat at an odd angle against the black-flecked marble. The sky was tinged with purples and pinks and yellows and reds, like a giant child's finger painting. It was too early even for the birds to have reached their full song. Only the distant trundle from the train track at the bottom of the hill was audible above the silence. And Pete's breathing: always steady, but shallow, as if he thought that, by limiting the air he breathed, he might be able to numb himself. To feel less.

'I only have an hour. It's a morning flight.'

'When was the last time you visited him?' Pete looked straight ahead, his eyes locked on the grave. The giraffe.

'Don't...' *Him.* The words sent a tremor through her gut. She recognised the sensation. It woke her late at night. Sometimes, it caught her unawares in public; like when she walked past a family or heard a child's unabashed laughter. It wasn't painful, at least, not in the way that most people understood pain. It was more like a restless spasm, working through her insides, cordoning off her organs so that she was split into her raw parts, unable to function as a whole. She would have preferred a more traditional pain. The sort that culminated in screams and tears. The spasm had no release. It just made itself at home. Crouched, uncomfortable, between her stomach and her heart. Circulated its concoction of guilt and anger and shame through her blood. 'It's not him. It's a grave.'

They sat in silence for a few moments and she gripped the bench with both hands, wanting more than anything to leave. 'You come a lot, then?'

'Most weeks.' Pete nodded, slow and calm. 'We talk. I tell him about what's going on... anything I see that I think he might like. There was a hot air balloon over the heath the other day.'

'If you're trying to make me feel guilty–' She heard her voice snap. This was so typical. So repetitive. He never understood how she needed to be. How she needed to do things her way. She stood to leave. 'This was a mistake. I shouldn't have–'

'Visited your dead son?'

His words scraped through the air, catching her neck like a rough noose. She stopped, her head hung low, but couldn't bring herself to meet Pete's face. She knew the look he'd be wearing. That crinkle of confusion at the side of his eyes. The curl of pity on his lips. And the worst: the tautening of his cheeks that suggested he was apprehensive, even fearful, of her. She didn't need to see that look again. It was one of the reasons she'd left. She listened to him get up and move to stand behind her.

'I'm sorry, Sofia. It's just...'

'You don't understand it.' She turned, her eyes tracing the hard, dusty ground. 'You don't have to understand, Pete. I was happy to sit with you here. But you can't make me feel how you feel. You can't force me to believe that this... this...' Her voice wavered but she swallowed the air down. 'This isn't him. He's gone. That's what I need to believe. Otherwise...'

She didn't finish her sentence. Through the early silence tore the sounds of her ragged breaths, her fingers clawing at her own chest, her belly. She could almost feel the blood beneath her fingernails again. The grief.

'Okay.' His voice was soft. She raised her eyes and saw that he was crying. Even after all these years, it was unbearable to see. Without thinking, she wrapped her arms around him and held him close, breathing in the smell of his neck, wondering how something could be so intensely familiar and alien at the same time.

'Sorry,' she said. She didn't add what she was sorry for. Sorry for leaving him? Sorry for never coming home? Sorry that the only way she had found to live was to forget? Like an empty vessel.

He sighed and stepped away from her, removing his glasses. 'Look, we can talk somewhere else. I just... you're right. I shouldn't have asked you to come here. It was selfish.'

She almost agreed. She wanted more than anything to be far from here. Far from this awful stoney reminder. Instead, she arranged herself, limbs stiff, back on the bench. 'We're here now. And... if anyone's calling anyone selfish...'

He gave a low laugh and sat beside her. 'Can't be selfish if you don't let anyone in.'

She closed her eyes and let the words bristle against her skin. He was right. He was wrong. There was no point in getting into it now. 'You had something?'

He paused for a moment as if torn between what to say, before reaching into his rucksack and pulling out some files. 'I'll send it all over to you, but here are the hard copies. Take a look.'

She opened the folder and studied the statements. 'This is payroll for the Balcombe Group.'

'That's right.'

'I won't ask how you got these.'

'Very wise.'

She allowed herself a small smile and scanned the first few pages. 'Irene Kanatas. She was a cleaner at Saturn House... wait...'

She ran a finger down the numbers and frowned. 'She was unpaid? What? For six years, she's basically been paid one euro a month. I – we – missed this.' She gritted her teeth, annoyed.

'I'm guessing she wasn't someone who could afford to volunteer?'

'No.' Sofia continued to leaf through the file. 'This is... look, again, Iraklis Barlas, the desk manager. He's being paid basically nothing. Why? Why does he stay there?'

'No idea. It's weird.' Pete shrugged. 'But, like I say, I've been tracking Domenico Bonarelli for a while. He's got a lot of high-profile friends in a lot of high-profile places. A guy like that, on the international jet-set scene... there'd be rumours.'

'And what have you heard?'

'That's just it. Nothing. Not even a whisper. He runs the most exclusive club in town, parties with the rich and famous, funds them, yet I can't find a single person – staff, ex, caterer – who has a bad word to say about the man.'

'If there's no smoke–'

'Then it's likely charcoal fire,' Pete finished. 'Deadly unless treated with caution.'

Sofia closed the folder. 'Katerina met Tatiana Kanatas, Irene's daughter, last night. She's convinced there's something going on. I'm with her.'

'Trafficking?'

Sofia nodded, squinting as a cool breeze lapped against her

face. 'Maybe. Lots of young, pretty girls. Lots of rich men. You don't exactly need to be imaginative. Thing is, there's no obvious trail, no suspicious links with high-risk countries, no red-flag transportation, no connection to anything underground, organised traffickers...'

'Yet, three murders, one of them possibly a copycat, or not. It could be the same killer.'

'Something on that scale would need infrastructure. It would be traceable – a network of traffickers, helpers, communications. We've found nothing. And this Saturnalia party.' She let out a frustrated groan. 'My colleague's convinced it has something to do with some ancient ritual, if you can believe it.'

'The same colleague who blew The Awakening open?'

'That's the one.'

'You rate him?'

'Yes. He's going through some stuff, though. He has an imagination. But he's thorough. Logical. If I'm honest, the whole investigation has turned into a bloody mess. I'm not sure any of us are working to our best abilities. I've missed something, I'm sure of it.' She gazed down at the folder. 'This is something. Why would the Balcombe House Group not pay these, specifically these, employees? Both of them had daughters who worked at the hotel previously. Tatiana's in London, Eleni's dead. That can't be a coincidence.'

'Yeah...' He folded his legs and massaged his forehead. A morning mist had rolled in over the terraced roofs that stretched from the foot of the cemetery. 'Perhaps they *needed* to remain working there.'

'You mean like a debt? Something about their daughters?' She watched the mist glow orange for a while then lowered her gaze to look at the grave's inscription. *Lucas Sampson. February*

2009 – *July 2013. Loved forever. Mummy and Daddy will see you soon. Night-night, little egg.*

'What else?' Her eyes fixated on his name. She knew she should look away. This was the start of the spiral. The oily slope down to the gaping abyss. But there was his name.

Pete shifted beside her. 'What else?'

'You said you told him about the hot air balloon. What else?'

Pete cleared his throat before replying. 'I walk through Regent's Park in the mornings, if I have time.' He pointed to the giraffe toy. 'I see the giraffes over the trees. He'd have loved that.'

She nodded, her lips pressed shut and tight.

'There's a water fountain that kids like to play in by King's Cross. The water shoots up without warning... it's fun. I tell him about that, you know, just stuff. Just stuff to talk about.'

She didn't reply. They sat in silence for close to a minute. Pete was patient, like always. She flicked the file with her fingernail in a quick, restless rhythm. She shouldn't have let her curiosity pique. She didn't need to know about the waterpark.

'We arrested someone for the sniper attack. I think there was something going on between her and Domenico, judging from the note we found on her. The interesting thing was that she was a victim's girlfriend.'

'Alek Knox?'

She raised her eyebrows.

Pete sniffed. 'He was social media famous here. The press have a bit to say about him.'

She squinted into the horizon. 'Right. Well, let me know if you find anything that suggests Domenico and Innes were in a relationship. Any connection at all.'

'Like I said, it's radio silence out there.'

'You always find something.' She turned to him, her face warm against the breeze. 'You know, I keep thinking about the cleaner, Irene. She had a photo of her daughter in her cottage. I doubt she knew where Tatiana was, if she was safe. As a parent, you'd do anything, wouldn't you, to keep your child safe? No matter what their age?'

'You know that as well as I do.'

She shuddered at that. The briny smell of hospital corridors mingled with the cemetery air. Had they, though? The amount of phone calls, the desperate begging for third, fourth, fifth opinions. Could she have pushed harder? Fought more? She bowed her head, a nausea gurgling in her belly. 'That's what I thought. Yet, I don't think she looked for her, by the sounds of it. All those years. Her daughter disappears without a word and, instead of doing anything about it, she continues working at Saturn House, for free.'

'You're wondering why a mother would do that?'

'There's something I don't understand, clearly.' Sofia smacked her lips, remembering the footage of Irene from Lily's office. 'Something was bothering her… enough that she attacked her boss. Clearly, something was upsetting her.'

Pete hung his head, removing his glasses as he rubbed his eyes. 'I'll ring you with anything I find. You won't be back for a while, I take it?'

She stood. For a few seconds she observed Lucas's gravestone, the nausea lurching up in a hot wave through her lungs, groping at her throat. How did Pete leave here, after their chats? Did he kiss the grave goodbye? Did he place his hand on it? Touch the cool, relentless marble? Another thing she didn't need to know. She didn't want to remember him like this. Just like when the local paper had taken his photograph in his hospital bed at the children's hospice fundraiser – she had hated it. It hadn't looked like him. Pete had emailed the paper asking for it not to be printed. She wanted to remember him as he had been for the majority of his life. Happy. Laughing.

Pete sniffed.

'Not sure. Probably not. Good luck with... with everything.'

He remained seated as he placed his glasses carefully back over his nose. 'Sometimes, Sofia, parents can't keep their children safe. Then, they need to cope with the next best thing.'

Stuffing the folder into her handbag, she turned towards the steep path without saying goodbye, allowing the thrashings of grief to release in useless tears as she hurried down the hill.

Inversion

'Did you get a name, any identifying information at all?' Katerina did not like Michail's tone. 'We had no jurisdiction in London, Michail, as Sofia has explained.'

The afternoon light settled through the kitchen window in orange patches. A car trundled past on the dusty road outside, casting a shadow between them and the opal sea. London seemed so far away, as did the unidentified girl, walking unsteadily into the crowds. He was right; she should have done more to protect her. But she hadn't been quick enough. Clever enough.

Sofia raised her face and, for the second time today, Katerina thought that she seemed fatigued, her eyes glassy and dull.

'She's right, Michail.' Sofia took a long sip of coffee and wriggled out of her jacket. 'The purpose of the trip was to find something to work with, which we managed. Katerina couldn't have done anything more if she'd tried. Anyway, by the sounds of it, we'll be seeing both Tatiana and her friend at the Saturnalia.'

Katerina gazed at Michail's board. 'What's that? You've added something.'

'Good spot.' Michail circled a photograph of a teenage girl. 'As I already mentioned, the girl who ended her life by suicide at the *Lykeio* was Eleni Barlas, Iraklis's daughter and Maria's sister. Upon further investigation, it turns out that she had a tattoo on her ankle of the sickle symbol. Maria told me that she had a boyfriend who was a guest at Saturn House in the months leading up to her death. I asked Lily to run a search and Teddy Menkopf would have been staying for a long period at around the same time.'

'You think he was the boyfriend?' Sofia asked.

'Almost certainly.'

'Did Maria say anything about mistreatment? Did her sister mention that she was unhappy?' Katerina stared at the photograph. It was silly, but she felt the same looking at it as she had speaking to Tatiana and her friend. It was as if she could sense the sadness, the desperation.

'Her behaviour changed.' Michail flipped over the paper on the board. 'She began to talk a lot about how women shouldn't have rights, how they should be happy with their *place*–'

'Like Alek,' Katerina finished. 'It's what the sickle represents, isn't it? Some weird misogynistic ideology. The girl I saw in London was wearing a sickle necklace too. It's like it's the icon to some club.'

'It seems so.' Michail nodded grimly. 'I've been doing a lot of inquiry into it. Remember the term "unveiled"?'

'It's what Domenico said. You said it had something to do with that Roman Saturnalia festival.'

'Correct,' Michail said. 'I discovered that when you search *invelatus* and Saturn together on the internet, the only reference seems to be, as you say, the Saturnalia.'

'You said something about the priests wearing their heads

uncovered?' Sofia leaned forwards on her elbows, unusually interested in Michail's more academic inquiries.

Michail seemed a little taken aback by her interest too. He paused for a second, holding his pen in mid-air, before nodding enthusiastically in her direction. 'Precisely, Sofia. In fact, upon further investigation, it seems that this unveiling of the priests' heads was more symbolic than merely clothing choice. It represented an inversion of values, of social practices. For example, the slaves were served dinner by their masters and...'

'Inversion of values?' Sofia looked to Katerina, who was already following her train of thought. 'Like how Eleni inverted her values before she died?'

'Or how Innes stopped drinking and partying when she met Alek?' Katerina added, remembering Innes's strange reaction to the empty bottles in her hotel room.

'Jesus, do you think that these rich, powerful men see themselves as *slaves*?' Sofia rolled her eyes, but her lip quivered in disgust.

Michail was one step ahead of her, his head bowed, scrolling quickly on his iPad. 'Alek's social media posts certainly point to that. *Enslaved* to misguided feminism... *stripped* from their rights to live as men should.'

'Ugh, it's disgusting.' Katerina leaned back in her chair, shaking her head. *How could someone like that have gained such a following?* As soon as the question entered her head, she shivered. More than anyone, she knew precisely how easy it was to be taken in by insidious, persuasive, hateful words. They acted as perfume first. Intoxicating with their sweet, alluring fumes. Then they turned to poison. Infectious and merciless.

'Agreed.' Michail tapped the side of his thigh with the pen. 'It's the same sort of rhetoric that Teddy posted. And, based on my research, seems to be a popular philosophy amongst a certain group of men.'

'Assuming that he was Eleni's mysterious boyfriend, I think we can gauge that he brainwashed her before she killed herself.' Sofia's eyes moved slowly from side to side, as if making some calculation. 'Were his death an isolated incident, I'd be looking closer into the Barlas family.'

Michail breathed heavily, as if frustrated, before appearing to curtail his irritation. 'But remember that Iraklis Barlas has a strong alibi, as does Maria. Additionally, neither Iraklis nor Maria know who this mystery boyfriend was. If they had, they would have notified the police.'

'Still...' Sofia's eyes narrowed. 'It would be wise to leave no stone unturned. Katerina, will you talk to the local station about Eleni's suicide? See if they noted any messages between Eleni and who we're assuming is Teddy? If he was grooming her, which seems likely, then he was probably careful, but it's worth a try. Also, just double-check there's nothing suspicious about either Iraklis's or Maria's behaviour around the time of Teddy's murder? I know...' She held a hand up to Michail. 'I know we've already triple-checked, but, like I said, they're the only two people to have a motive for wanting Teddy dead.'

'*If* it was an isolated murder,' Michail repeated, his eyes growing a little dark. Katerina looked between her two colleagues: he was dangerously close to displaying insubordination. Based on Sofia's mood today, it seemed like an unwise move.

Sofia levelled her gaze at him. Surprisingly, she didn't raise her voice when she spoke. 'As I said, it's just a precaution. I agree that Alek and Irene's murders make it unlikely this is anything to do with the Barlas family. I just want to make sure that we've explored everything thoroughly. Yiorgos is also running checks on all of Eleni's school friends. They have possible motives too.'

Michail seemed to perform a strange dance in response,

where he moved from one foot to the other. Sofia sighed, resting her chin in her hands. 'What is it, Michail? Go on.'

'It is imperative that you both understand that I would never do anything to jeopardise an investigation and that I understood, under good authority, that the Barlas name had been cleared and removed from any active inquiry.'

Sofia glanced uncomfortably in Katerina's direction. Clearly, she had an idea about where this was going. 'Michail, if you could get to the point?'

'Ah, yes.' He purposefully avoided looking at Katerina, which made her think that she also had a good idea about where this was going. 'I have entered into a friendship with Maria Barlas. Yesterday afternoon, we met and shared a glass of wine. She willingly offered me information about her father to aid the investigation. I, of course, have not shared any sensitive information with her.'

'I see.' Sofia, who also seemed to be avoiding looking at Katerina, sighed. 'Well, these checks are just precautions and nobody is under investigation at present. Do you have plans to see her again?'

Two red patches appeared on Michail's cheeks. 'Yes. This evening.'

'Right.' Sofia shrugged, and looked to the ceiling, seemingly exhausted. 'Keep an eye on comms, but I don't see any reason for you to cancel any plans just yet. In any case, it's usually best to act normally when in doubt. Raising suspicion doesn't benefit us.'

'I am in no doubt about Maria's innocence in this matter.' Michail spoke the words with such sincerity, that it almost brought tears to Katerina's eyes. She gulped, hoping that her face didn't reflect the burning sensation she felt creeping up her neck.

'Right, well, I'll get on with that.' She stood to excuse herself.

'I have one more question before we leave.' Michail looked straight ahead, his back straight and his jaw tight. Katerina wanted more than anything to shut herself in her room and disappear into her laptop. It was irrational, of course. Michail could see whoever he liked. But that didn't help ease the thorny weight that had appeared in the pit of her belly.

'Pistachios. Did either of you notice pistachio trees growing on the Saturn House grounds?'

'I'm not an expert.' Sofia looked completely puzzled.

'No...' Katerina closed her eyes, trying to visualise the hotel. 'No. Olive trees, but no pistachios. Why?'

'That's what I thought.' Michail didn't offer any further information.

Michail took a long, deep breath. Tonight, the air seemed thicker. He could taste, very slightly, the saltiness from the gentle sea spray. Maria had booked a table arranged a few metres away from the others, positioned on the sliver of concrete that reached out over the water. Of course, this meant that the waiting staff had further to walk, however, he appreciated the privacy as he waited.

His finger traced the diagrams in his notepad. *Sickle. Saturn. Inversion. Speakers.* He was close. That, he could sense. But it was like there was an invasive mist intruding his thoughts, billowing into a cloud as soon as a theory sharpened and turned. He took a quick sip of wine and placed his head in his hands. The missing items were also bothering him. Teddy's phone and clothing. Iraklis's key card. Statistically, there was little hope of finding them now.

He checked his watch and frowned. Maria was uncharacteristically late by quite some margin. This wasn't entirely encouraging behaviour and, worse, he found his mind wandering to the many occasions at which Katerina had demonstrated poor time-keeping. He had, against his better judgement, learned to accept and even embrace this trait. He shook his head, realising that his lips had twitched into a small smile. Inexplicable. He had made it very clear that he could have no emotional attachment to Katerina. He had moved on, as required. Based on their last interaction, he was almost certain that she wanted even less to do with him.

He jumped as his phone buzzed. Maria. 'Maria! Your lateness is no problem at all. In fact, I have ordered a glass of–'

A muffled sound came from the other end of the line. His stomach tightened. 'Maria? Is that you?'

'Yes... yes, sorry, Michail. It's me.'

He relaxed slightly but there was a blunt pause as he tried to work out how to proceed. 'Excellent. Like I said, your lateness is no–'

'Do you think... do you think you could just come here?'

Michail felt his head jerk up. Her voice sounded throaty and hoarse, as if she had been crying. 'Here?'

'*Baba's*? He's at work and... look, I understand if it's a bit much. Second date...'

'It makes no difference to me.' He motioned for the waiter to bring him the bill. 'But is there any reason for the change in location? You sound upset.'

There was a pause at the end of the line. Michail stood abruptly, the pit of his stomach tightening. Something seemed unusual, which was rarely a good thing. 'Answer yes or no if you can: do you need help?'

He tensed as he awaited her reply.

'No! God, no!' She eventually gave a broken laugh,

signalling that she was most likely not in imminent danger, at least. The Barlas house was a short walk from the main town; he could walk there in less than fifteen minutes. 'So are you coming here?'

He could see no reason why not. 'Yes. Certainly. I'm leaving now.'

With that, he downed his wine and set to a brisk, not-quite-urgent walk.

Katerina was squished against a wall in the corner of the police station, scrolling through the paperwork relating to Eleni's suicide. There was little more distressing than the black and white documentation about the death of a child. It was sad, terribly so, but the detached format of the statements, the way that they recounted the final hours of a young life, seemed to glare from the screen, so hollow and cold.

She seemed happy, like normal.
There was maybe something troubling her.
Some guy… older.
We had no idea.

Her friends' recounts read like a bad film script. Insufficient and clichéd. There was nothing here that told her anything new. She clicked onto the next set of notes, searching for any reference that might point to Teddy. Nothing at all.

She almost missed it. Her eyes had glazed over as the words moved, generic and useless, up the screen as she moved to the bottom of the document. However, she caught it at the last moment: an exchange between Eleni and Irene.

Eleni, did you manage to ask about what I told you? It's very important.

Then, on the next day:

Please reply to me! I'm counting on you. I'm sorry to ask, but I have no other options. She listens to you. If you could just ask...

That night:

ELENI?! I'M ASKING YOU FOR HELP! PLEASE. YOU MUST DO THIS FOR ME. IMAGINE IF THIS WAS YOUR FATHER!

Eleni had replied five minutes afterwards:

Will you stop messaging me? I've said I can't, okay? She's just abroad. If she wanted to be in touch, she would. Just stop messaging, okay?

She seemed to have blocked Irene's number from that point onwards. Katerina studied the exchange again. Obviously, Irene was trying to find out where her daughter Tatiana had disappeared to. *She listens to you.* Who was she talking about? Who did she want Eleni to speak with? Tatiana? Someone else?

Katerina made a note and continued to look through the files. There wasn't much else. Nothing had been treated as suspicious, there was certainly nothing to indicate that the Barlases knew who Teddy Menkopf was. Michail was right: Maria had nothing to do with any of this. The stab of disappointment hardly caught her by surprise, which was stupid, she knew.

Her phone ringing made her jump. She shook her head, attempting to sharpen her mind, and answered the call.

'Katerina Galanis?' Her eyes continued to scan the screen for any other odd exchanges. She shook her head silently, annoyed at the distraction of the phone call.

'It's the ticketing office at Saronic Ferries in Piraeus. We had a request about a ticket from one of our customers?'

Katerina sighed, hanging her head. 'Go on.'

'Maria Barlas? She purchased a ticket on Thursday 24th July for the afternoon crossing. Er, at 3.40pm.'

A dull ringing sound shifted between Katerina's ears. She breathed in, her throat dry. 'Uh, can you double-check that? She told us that she got the next morning's crossing? The 25th?'

'It's definitely her. We've checked our CCTV footage too, to be sure, since you sent us through a photograph. Definitely the 24th at 3.40pm.'

Katerina's eyes flicked to the time in the corner of the computer screen. Michail would already be on his date. She managed a 'thank you' to the man on the other end of the line and began running to the car as she frantically called Michail.

Entasis

The Barlas house was a small white square building at the end of a narrow street. The buzz of the diners in the numerous restaurants was still audible, though nobody ventured this far up the road. Despite the relatively central location, a distinct feeling of abandonment rattled about the discarded beer cans and empty plant pots.

Maria opened the door before Michail had a chance to ring the bell. She looked worse than she had sounded on the phone. Her make-up smudged black beneath her eyes and she held her body in a tense hunch. As if she had something to be embarrassed about, she bowed her head, avoiding his gaze.

'Maria, is something wrong?'

She ushered him into the house, placing a hand between his shoulder blades to guide him into a small living area. Unsure how to behave, he stood in between the two couches, which faced the television, and waited for her to offer an explanation. He noticed that his right-hand fingers began to tap against his thigh. One. Two. Three. Then again, on the left. He clenched his eyes closed, and then again. There was no need to feel overwhelmed. This was a perfectly normal scenario. He forced himself to hold his hands still by his side.

'You're humming.' Maria walked to the kitchen and set out two wine glasses on the counter. When he didn't reply, she nodded in his direction and said gently, 'I sometimes sing without realising it too. Did you know you were–'

'Yes. I sometimes hum when I haven't syphoned effectively,' he replied. 'The case has taken a great deal of my concentration.'

Maria cocked her head to one side, as if considering what he had said with great thought, and then handed him a glass of wine.

'You must be wondering why I'm in such a state...' She sniffed before taking a long gulp of her drink. 'I'm sorry...'

'No apology is necessary. I don't share your reticence about having a second date at your childhood home.'

She laughed as they settled onto the couch, but, like the archaic warrior smile, her laugh was empty and hollow. It wasn't a wholly unpleasant sound, but one that felt like an imitation, as if it knew what it should be but lacked the heart, the humanity. He studied her face, which remained pinched with what he calculated as some kind of anxiety. 'If it is not too personal a question, may I ask what's troubling you?'

For a moment, her eyes widened, panicked and sharp. Then, without warning, she planted her forehead in her hands and groaned. 'It's just all so... it's all so messed up. A total mess.'

It was as if the Maria he had met previously dissolved before his eyes. Her arms barely held her head up as she wept into her hands; they seemed limp and devoid of the life, the tenacity, which used to course almost demonstrably through her veins. 'Is it your father? Has something happened?'

'Oh stop! Stop, will you!' She flung her head upwards,

looking to the ceiling, a retching sound escaping her throat. She lowered her voice. 'Stop being so concerned about me. I don't deserve it.'

One. Two. Three. His fingers tapped against the side of his thigh again. *I don't deserve it.* Setting his glass on the table, he scanned the room. It was homely; decorated with care. Maria's prints hung on the wall below the staircase: five landscapes showing the same scene of the view from behind the Temple of Apollo, each printed using a different colour. The single column reached up into the sky, the swirls of the sea below it depicted through impressively rendered incisions, curling back into spirals and licks through the block colours. She undoubtedly possessed a lot of skill – the details were conceived in such minute, punctilious movement.

The colours blended, red, orange, pink, green, into a murky grey. He blinked, refocusing his eyes. The volute patterns emerged more clearly. He pushed himself from the couch and walked towards the prints. 'How does one achieve such detail, here? The incisions, they're exact.'

His eyes fell to the volute patterning at the top of the columns. The meticulous width, the steady curvature that wrapped around the space so confidently. He realised he was shaking his head. This could not be. *The cave, the feeling of being cut loose, let go into the atmosphere, split into chaotic, random little pieces.* His chest tightened and he breathed, slowly, fighting to find a sliver of reason. A sensible explanation.

'Maria?' His lips moved over her name as he turned to face her. 'I said how–'

He was cut short when he saw what she had placed on the table. The small room began to move, at first, slowly, as if the walls were shifting, breaking free from their bonds, bending towards him. *One point six one eight. One point six one eight.*

One point six one eight. His numbers. He hadn't thought about them for a whole year. His signals of order, of what was right. They expanded in his mind, pushing like early saplings, virile and bright. *One point six one eight. One point six one eight. One point six one eight.* Without being able to help himself, he turned to look at her prints again. His phone vibrated, but his hand didn't seem to move. The single column. Out of context, alone. Its curvature, its *entasis* laid bare and obvious without the rest of the temple. His stomach began to churn as he reached for his phone.

'No–' The device flew from his hand; Maria's arms were wrapped around him from behind. She was crying. The hot, serrated breath burned against his neck. She was shouting inexplicable things. She was begging him to listen to her. He lurched forwards, his hands groping the air before him, knocking two of the prints from the wall as he fell onto all fours. Her screams grew louder. 'Please! Please! You must believe me! I didn't mean to! I just... I'm *telling* you now! I thought... I thought...'

He clawed at the hands around his neck. 'Stop.' His voice was small and choked. 'Stop. Stop.'

'I didn't know it was him! I didn't know it was him until...! Michail, you need to believe me! I never meant... I need to tell you, I need your help–'

His phone buzzed unceasingly from somewhere behind him. Grey clouds began to close in from the corners of his eyes. 'Maria, please–'

A horrible, helpless scream erupted next to his ear. He clenched his eyes, ready for whatever blow was about to come. A feeling of weightlessness overtook his limbs. His ears rang, the remnants of her voice streaming and distorted. He opened his eyes, seeing first the broken shards from the prints. Then, turning, he registered two things simultaneously. The first, the shadow of Maria disappearing through the front door. The second, a phone, a key card, a pair of salmon-coloured chinos, and a pink shirt displayed on the coffee table.

'Maria!' He pushed himself from the floor, following her out onto the street. She was already seated on her motorbike. 'Maria!'

She turned to face him; her lips parted. Then, the ringing in his ears erupted into thunder. A heat, fast and ravenous, pushed him back into the door-frame. He fell down, gasping. The sound could only have lasted a second or so, but he seemed to be caught in it, hearing it in minute detail. The pull of metal, the crunch, the fire eating air, the tearing, the crackling, the burn.

'Michail!' Katerina's voice cut through the racket. 'Michail?'

He didn't speak. The heat on his face continued to burn and lick with hundreds of tiny tongues, all whispering and jeering in nonsensical languages. He blinked up at Katerina, whose face appeared between his and the ceiling.

'It's okay, Michail. It's okay, we're here. We're here.'

———

Sofia gripped her coffee cup as she read the email thread. 'Jesus, we only had to look at her work emails, the comms with Alek are easy enough to recover. Look at this: *Alek, I know you're a misogynistic pig, but surely even you can't support this. Have you even bothered to look at what they're doing? They're using you. Imagine the press when this gets out...*'

It was dark outside, and the moon's reflection on the black water fell in sharp shards. The four of them were squeezed around the small kitchen island.

'That explains him wanting to come clean,' Katerina said, sending a concerned glance in Michail's direction. So far, he'd said very little, apart from to request that he be the one to break the news about Maria's death to Iraklis. 'She hit upon what he cared about: public perception. Better to break the story, repent, and continue. By the looks of these emails, he subscribed to the Saturn ideology, but had no idea what he was actually promoting. He was a pawn. Him pretending not to know Teddy makes more sense. By the time we spoke to him, Maria had sown the seed. He was distancing himself, I bet, in case the police blew open the operation.'

'Agreed. But Maria's emails are all very vague, still. I mean...' Sofia scrolled down the emails. 'There's reference to girls, so I think we're on the right track with our trafficking narrative. But this gives us nothing in terms of how they're pulling it off. Where are the transactions, the handovers? Again, this isn't proof of much at all.'

'Look.' Katerina pointed at the screen. '*Innes is acting suspiciously, I think she knows something's up.*'

'There you go.' Sofia took another gulp. Tonight looked set to be a long one: she needed all the caffeine she could get. 'There's Innes's motive.'

'Any news on her release?' Yiorgos was hunched over his own laptop on the other side of the table. He spoke without looking up.

'Still in custody, which is good, although whoever blew up Maria is still obviously at large. As for Irene's murderer...' She looked at Michail and let her voice trail off, unwilling to start another argument. He was adamant that Maria had not killed Irene. They didn't have time to waste on the same back and forth.

'Oh–' Sofia held up her phone. 'Pete sent these through today. Innes and Domenico outside of Saturn House a couple of weeks ago. They certainly look very friendly.'

Yiorgos glanced up and laughed at the photograph of

Domenico and Innes in a tight embrace. 'Useful. I told you that we're struggling to get much of a background on her? She's slippery which means I'm becoming less dubious about her sniping proficiency.'

Sofia thought back to her conversation in London with Domenico and how he'd been flanked by 'bodyguards'. 'It's fairly obvious that Domenico – the Balcombe House Group – is at the apex of some sort of organised criminal behaviour. Right now, I wouldn't underestimate anyone.'

'Look at this.' Yiorgos turned his laptop around to face them. 'Maria wrote this to Lily around a month ago: *Hi Lily, Just going through the accounts...*'

'Her advertising agency had Saturn House as a client,' Katerina remembered. 'That's how she knew Lily.'

'...right... *just going through the accounts, and there are a couple of inconsistencies with the drinks business.*'

'She must mean the pistachio business,' Sofia said.

Yiorgos nodded. '*There are huge sums coming in for single bottles of liqueur, which can't add up. Can we catch up about this?*' He kept reading, then raised his eyebrows. 'Look at this, two days later to Alek: *I think I know what they're doing. I need to come to the island to know for sure. You mentioned there's a guy called Teddy staying? If he's involved, then I can try and get it out of him. I'll need to be discreet: my father doesn't like me anywhere near that place.*'

Michail let out a soft grunt. 'I don't understand.'

Sofia forgave him his slowness. He'd suffered a huge blow; yet again, his trust had been misplaced and abused. She wasn't sure that he'd recover from this. She spoke gently. 'I think it's clear that Maria entered into a secret relationship with Teddy to find out, well, to find out what we want to know: *how* and *where* this operation is being run.'

'Yes.' Michail raised his head, his eyes dark. His face looked completely ashen, like his skin had been blanched and drained. 'That much is obvious. What doesn't make sense is *why* she killed Teddy.'

'Michail.' Katerina bit her lip. 'Remember that Teddy was responsible for her sister, Eleni's death.'

'Yes, thank you, Katerina.' For the first time ever, Sofia detected an iciness in Michail's voice. 'I am not questioning that Maria is our culprit. The wounds on Teddy's wrists are consistent with the scalpel used for lino printing, plus this sort of wound would have loomed large in her mind due to her sister's suicide – Teddy's wounds were symbolic, like the archaic sculpture, as I explained. Within the full context, it's obvious. My theory was fully formed, I just didn't apply it to the right person. I have no doubt the weapon will be found in the Barlas house. What you are *not* asking is how Maria–' his voice wavered, ever so slightly over her name, '–knew what Teddy had done. I highly doubt that he would have shared with a new girlfriend how he drove a much-younger lover to suicide. So, how did she know? When did she discover both his identity and hand in her sister's death? Plus, why steal her father's key card to go back into the room? It doesn't make sense.' The kitchen fell very still. He added, 'Are we assuming that she was the crying female heard on the night of the murder?'

'Impossible to say for sure, but, perhaps.' Sofia shrugged, her shoulder blades pulling down her back like lead. 'Sometimes, we can't know everything, Michail. We just need to work with what we've got. It doesn't look like she planned to kill Teddy, I admit – she made too many mistakes. Her father's key card being the first, as you point out, Michail. Then, keeping the evidence. It wasn't a slick job; I think she panicked.' She took a deep breath. 'I can now see why Irene was so anxious about being asked about hearing the crying. My guess is that she saw Maria on that night, perhaps even suspected what she'd done. Irene didn't want to implicate herself.' She didn't add that if Maria had seen Irene on that night, it was yet another motive for a second murder.

For a moment, it looked like he might sink back down into his stoney silence, when the darkness in his face was penetrated with something resembling his old self. 'Yiorgos. Yiorgos! Read the email about the pistachios again.'

The change in tone was such a shock, that Sofia gaped. Then, catching up, she nodded at Yiorgos to do as he said.

'Erm, okay... *the drinks accounts aren't adding up...*'

'Yes, yes, keep going.'

Yiorgos frowned but continued, '*Huge sums...*'

'The pistachio trees!' Michail jumped up, almost causing Sofia to spill her coffee. 'The pistachio trees, or lack of, at Saturn House. Lily said that there were pistachio trees on the grounds, yet I have never seen one. Surely, an entrepreneur specialising in pistachios would know what the tree looked like?'

Sofia didn't follow. 'The pistachio trees? But—'

Katerina began typing quickly. 'Here, Michail. Lily's website.'

They gathered around the screen, Sofia still at a loss as to what Michail was getting at. The website looked professional, with varieties of pistachio liqueurs displayed on the homepage. '*Full-bodied, great for sipping with friends,*' Katerina read. '*Creamy, full of flavour and fun. Young, under-developed notes...* no... it can't... oh my God.'

Katerina's eyes widened with horror. It was disgusting, so much so that Sofia didn't want to allow herself to believe it. However, as she read the descriptions, the numerous descriptions, it became more clear, more audacious. 'Click on one of them.' Her voice was low, disbelieving. 'Try and buy a bottle.'

Katerina obediently clicked on a tab. A new window popped up, reading: *A great choice! Our medium-sweet, half-aged variety is a popular one. Please enter your code below to complete your transaction.*

'Code?' Katerina looked at Sofia. 'I've never been asked for a code before for an online purchase.'

'Bet you've never bought anything like this.' Yiorgos stood with his arms folded, his face contorted with disgust.

'Innes's password,' Sofia suggested. 'What was it, the numbers of Saturn?'

'81726.' Michail's fists had formed into two tight balls. His eyes were locked on the laptop screen, shiny and unblinking.

'That's it!' Katerina's mouth fell open as the next tab loaded. '*Payment of £40,000 is due today. We run many events at which you can collect your purchase, ensuring the utmost privacy and security. Details will be released upon completed purchase. As always, we ask you to keep this quiet from those people in your life who remain unenlightened. You have unveiled freedom. You may live unveiled and unshackled. We look forward to welcoming you at our next event.*'

'It's a front!' Sofia grabbed the laptop and brought it closer to her face to make sure she wasn't seeing things. 'It's a front. This is how they're accepting the money. The events... Lily! She's the main driver behind this! That simpering, annoying woman... I didn't think she had it in her.'

Katerina stared at the screen, her eyes black and hollow before the light it emitted. 'She's been stringing us along. When Tatiana first went missing, Irene messaged Eleni Barlas. She said, "She listens to you". I bet she was talking about Lily.' She covered her mouth with her hands and looked at Sofia. 'The

Saturnalia. That's where the girls will be. That's where they'll be traded.'

'It's tonight.' Sofia felt the useless panic in her gut rise. 'The music, Michail...'

He nodded, clearly already one step ahead of her. 'They blast the music outwards as a scapegoat. Everyone complains about the sound, but nobody can hear what's actually going on inside. On the face of it, it's just a wild party. They've been hiding in plain sight. Pretending to be one thing, when they're another.'

'We need to go.' Sofia grabbed her jacket and was halfway out of the house, calling for backup when she stopped. The dark beach stretched out before her, as if beckoning her to think. 'We have to blow this open tonight. We need proof. We need photos, evidence that this is trafficking and not something these girls have entered into willingly–'

'Which means we can't just burst in,' Yiorgos finished. 'They're organised. They'll have a protocol for a police raid. We need to be clever, otherwise we'll lose the opportunity.'

Katerina, who had been chewing on her nail, stepped forwards. 'Hear me out. Nobody has paid much attention to me, if at all, at the hotel. If... if I dress up, change my hair colour, I can infiltrate–'

'Out of the question,' Sofia interrupted.

'It might be our only option.' Yiorgos sighed, leaning against the door-frame. 'We only have tonight, then who knows when we'll next pin them down. Whatever's going on behind those walls was bad enough for them to have killed Maria and Alek over, maybe more. We don't have time to waste waiting.'

Sofia looked at her colleague, who, as the moonlight hit her face, resembled a ghostly creature. However, her lips were set and hard. She wanted this. Nodding slowly, she agreed. 'Okay.

We can get together a disguise. We'll be on surveillance just outside, full comms. Does that make sense?'

Katerina gritted her teeth, her shoulders tense and ready. Sofia noted that Michail had uncharacteristically not offered an opinion. In fact, he was avoiding looking at Katerina altogether. 'Let's get on, then.' She turned away from them to make some calls, ignoring the cold stone rotating in the pit of her stomach.

Saturnalia

Katerina barely recognised herself in the reflection of the glass doors. She wore a long blonde wig, which was surprisingly natural, coupled with light-pink lips and dramatic eye make-up, enough to cover up her bruising. Sofia had found a dress that somehow managed to alter the appearance of her physique, making her seem flatter in the chest. Since the Saturn House staff had only ever seen her wearing uniform, she was quietly confident the disguise would work. She'd climbed over the wall where the outward-facing speakers were. Sure enough, they boomed so loudly on the exterior that her bones reverberated to the beat.

'Katerina? Confirm you can hear me?' Sofia's voice questioned in her ear, clear and sharp.

'Yes,' she said, keeping her words to a minimum. The arched walkway leading to the pool at the back of the hotel seemed deserted, but she didn't want to take any chances. 'No security on this end yet.'

'Good, keep your wits about you, there's bound to be some. The guests seem to be either entering the front in their cars or the side by speed-boat. Remember, don't go underground. We'll lose contact. I'll keep in touch here.'

'Got it.' Taking a deep breath and throwing her shoulders back, she swung the glass doors open and walked towards the pool, along the walkway that snaked through the olive trees. As the lights of the pool grew nearer, she noticed two men dressed in black flanking the pool's entrance. She closed her eyes, forcing herself to remain relaxed.

'Evening.' She looked at each man from beneath her eyelashes, making sure to let her smile linger. 'I appear to have lost my way. I got off the boat, had a look at the beach and before I knew it... lost!' She giggled, the muscles in her throat tightening.

From here, she could hear what the exterior speakers had been muffling to the outside world – the PA system on the other side of the beach was being used for some sort of announcements. *'The Saturnalia wishes you a night of freedom and unbound desires. If at any point you get bored, or need anything to assist you, find a member of staff and they will be happy to oblige. Remember, rules do not apply here. Like the ancient ritual, this is a night of inversion. We know how the woke rhetoric has affected you. You are our guests. Now, you can let go. Claim what is rightfully yours. Let Saturn, your masculinity, rule. Be sick! You are one of the very few to have realised that there is another way...'*

Their eyes scanned her chest, taking in the sickle-shaped necklace that hung about her neck. Hopefully, it had been worth rifling through Teddy's personal effects. Voices intermingled through the blue night air; it didn't sound as if people were partying hard. The conversations sounded muted, serious. She blew out through her front teeth, attempting to seem impatient. Eventually, one of the men nodded her through. 'You should stay with your guardian.'

'Oh, I know! I'm an idiot. I'll find him now.'

They looked at one another, and, for a moment, she was sure they were going to pat her down. However, after an agonising pause, they beckoned her to move onwards.

The pool was almost unrecognisable. At the far end was a huge sculpture, lit up in blues and reds, showing the symbol of the sickle. The water shimmered in bright multi-colours, making it seem thicker, an alien substance. Baskets laden with bottles of champagne were stationed around the water. A couple – a middle-aged man and a girl who looked like she couldn't be more than eighteen – shrieked with laughter, rolling about beneath the steam. Shadows enveloped the girl's body, so that her head floated, untethered, above the water. The man grabbed one of the bottles and popped the cork into the darkness, before pouring the liquid into his mouth as he stroked the girl's face. Katerina held her face in her best neutral expression. There was no point intervening; like Sofia and Yiorgos had said, they needed solid proof of wrongdoing to stand any chance of bringing Domenico and his gang to justice.

'Unsold, so far, but she's a pretty little thing...'

Katerina headed to the source of the voice: a woman speaking. Where the pool opened up to the back entrance to the lobby, a platform had been erected. No musicians were playing. Instead, Tatiana Kanatas wielded a microphone, prodding a woman who stood next to her. Katerina recognised her as the girl from London – she didn't seem as intoxicated today, although her eyes remained vacant, shining blank in response to the torches lighting the area. A small group of men gathered before the platform. 'Twenty! No, thirty grand! You must be dreaming... she's only worth fifteen...'

The girl looked above their heads, ignoring the jeering, and her eyes settled on Katerina. A jolt of anxiety whipped, restless, at the base of Katerina's spine. The girl's stare didn't flinch. Did she recognise her? She stepped backwards into the shadows of the foliage, hoping that no one had followed her gaze. Tatiana pointed at one of the men – the highest bidder – and tugged on the girl's arm, encouraging her to follow him. The girl cocked her head to one side, her eyes still set on the shadows thrown by the olive trees. Katerina prepared to run, as Sofia had instructed if her cover was blown. She whispered, 'Tatiana and the girl from London are here...'

'Do they recognise you?'

The girl finally turned her head away, a dreamy smile clouding her face as she was shoved into the bidder's arms. Katerina swallowed hard, fighting the sickening sensation. 'No. No, it's okay.'

Tatiana clapped her hands, apparently pleased with her sale, before beckoning up another girl to the stage. 'It's like a modern-day slave market,' Katerina whispered. 'Tatiana is selling them. I reckon she's a fixer; she lures them in.'

'Sounds about right; this sort of scum often relies on using victims as bait,' Sofia replied. 'Locate Domenico. His plane landed at the island airport this morning. He'll be there. Also, have a look at Lily's office. I have a hunch that any incriminating documents will be stored there.'

Katerina watched the man lead the girl from London away, his fingers caressing the base of her spine like fat, rough spiders. 'She looks so young.'

'Focus on what you're there to do. The best way to help them is to gather as much evidence as possible.'

It felt as if her disguise was becoming more and more translucent; her thick dark hair seemed to push on the inside of the wig. She realised her hands were trembling and pressed her nails into the side of her thighs. She had to do this. She had to prove herself. Her last conversation with Michail echoed around her head. *This is good for nobody. She couldn't continue to work with him. She was getting in the way.* He hadn't contradicted her. The only reason that he'd tried to make it work between them was because Sofia had ordered him to. He had no feelings left for her, professional or otherwise. And who could blame him? As her last shift as his partner, she would make him proud. At least he would remember her as something useful, someone worth having known.

She headed towards Lily's office, slipping quietly through the other side of the greenery, trying not to walk too quickly. The lobby had been bathed in red lighting which reflected off the marble surfaces almost too vibrantly. The colour was so deep that she had to squint. Whispers and groans crept along the hard walls. Her eyes adjusted and she noticed that dark bedding, pillows and blankets, had been positioned in the corners. She stopped as she realised that naked bodies writhed on top of them, the flesh dyed red against the black of the bedding. Tears started to burn at the back of her eyes. Was this what the girl from London was being forced to do? Had she been led into one of these dark corners to be set upon by one of these disgusting men?

She continued down the main corridor until she arrived at Lily's office. Drawing out Iraklis's key card, she held it over the sensor, holding her breath. The light flashed green and beeped twice as the door swung open. She checked behind her shoulder. 'It worked. I'm going in.'

———

Sofia pushed the headphones against her ears even tighter, her spine straight and alert. The van was warm, yet goose-pimples erupted all over her body. Michail and Yiorgos were silent on either side of her. 'We need something that proves the pistachio business is a front. Right now, all we've got is proof of extortionately expensive bottles of booze and an odd delivery method. There must be some records indicating which girls are for sale and to whom they're being sold.'

'Got it.'

Katerina's voice sounded small and awfully far away. Sofia, for the thousandth time, thought about telling her to just get out of there. But Yiorgos was right – this felt like the last chance they'd have to help these girls. She screwed her eyes closed and shook her head, speaking to Michail and Yiorgos. 'I can't work out Irene and Iraklis.'

Yiorgos's head jolted upright – clearly, he wasn't his usual unruffled self either. 'You mean their pay, or lack of?'

'Both had daughters working for Saturn House. Eleni killed herself because of this crackpot ideology and Tatiana got caught up in the organisation, never to return home again. Both the parents don't receive proper payment. Why? If they agreed to work for free to appease Lily, well, *why*? They'd both lost their daughters, why would they do anything Lily wanted them to do? Why wouldn't they go to the police?'

'Sounds like she had something over them.' Michail looked up from his laptop. 'That's the only reasonable explanation.'

'What do you mean? They'd already lost their children. What could be worse?'

He shifted in his seat to face her, his brow creased and serious. 'We assumed that Irene was looking for money because that's what Lily told us, but what if she wasn't? It would be unwise to trust anything that Lily Woodstow has told us so far.'

'Bring up the video again.' Sofia tapped the work surface with her nails, as Michail opened the file. The footage was as she'd remembered. Irene entered the office, throwing herself over the desk at Lily. 'Stop there.' Sofia leaned close to the screen. Irene's arms were outstretched, but it didn't look like they were reaching towards Lily. 'She's going for the laptop.

Hang on...' Sofia rewound the tape again. 'See that! Lily grabs a memory card from the side. See, there! Once you know she's holding it, it looks like Irene's trying to take it from her, not attack her.'

Michail spoke softly. 'She didn't want money. She wanted whatever's on that card. Lily made a simple business decision – two free employees for as long as she had leverage.'

Sofia sank back into her chair, unable to speak. The van, the headphones, fell away, and her nostrils were filled with the smell of sanitiser and urine. She was back at the hospital. Lucas lay on the bed, his small body fed with wires and tubes. She wanted to swap places with him. The conviction was so strong. She spent most of her time wishing it, hoping that, with each blink, she would open her eyes to find she was prone and weak and ill. She would do anything to protect him. Anything. She would do a deal with the devil itself.

But she couldn't control what happened. His fate – and hers – were horribly, brutally torn from her hands.

The fundraiser. The photographer. The images. Those she could control. She could stop them being published. She wasn't ashamed. She was proud of him, so proud. But this wasn't how he should be presented. She would submit photographs of when he was healthy. Somehow, although it was insignificant and stupid, somehow that mattered because it was a small, silly thing that she could do.

'Photographs.' She heard her own voice shake as she dragged herself out of the memory. 'I bet they have photographs of the victims, perhaps videos. There's nothing worse than losing a child...' She slid lower into her chair, light-headed. 'But, if it happens, you can protect their memory. Irene had a photograph of Tatiana in her house? That's how she chose to remember her. Nobody should be able to control that narrative. I think Lily keeps compromising photographs of the girls for leverage. That's why Iraklis and Irene worked for free. That's why they said nothing. They dedicated the rest of their lives to their daughters' memories.' Her throat grew thick and she gulped down a hot mouthful of saliva, willing herself not to cry.

Yiorgos cleared his throat. She had never discussed her personal life with him, although she had the impression he knew more than he let on. 'That makes sense. Katerina?'

'Yes?' Her reply sounded in Sofia's headset too.

'There's a memory card somewhere in the office; we think it contains explicit images of the victims. It might be in the computer–'

A short yelp sounded, followed by the sound of a loud intake of breath. 'Katerina? Can you hear me?'

'Sof–' Katerina's voice cut off and the line went dead.

The ground was cold against her cheek. Katerina's bones trembled as if the warmth was being shaken from them. Her shoulders hurt; something was pulling them backwards. She realised her hands had been bound behind her back. A low groan escaped her mouth as the pain from the back of her head emanated across her whole skull. The room was dimly lit, with a faint smell of damp.

'Officer, so glad you could join us.' A pair of expertly pedicured, stilettoed feet appeared before her eyes. 'It's usually polite to await an invite, you know...' Lily softly rested her toe against her cheek and rolled her so that she lay on her back. Nausea rushed through her as Lily's grinning face swam into focus, '...but, if you want to be a part of it so much, we are, of course, happy to oblige.'

'Sof...' Katerina tried whispering Sofia's name. Surely, they'd have heard that she was in trouble?

'Ah!' Lily gave a tinkly laugh as she pulled Katerina to a seated position, letting her fall like a rag doll against the wall. 'We found the device. There's little to no chance they'll find you down here. They could search the place from head to toe and still...' She tutted. 'It's our little secret hideout. You're very lucky to see it at all, actually.'

The room was huge. The walls were whitewashed breeze-blocks and the floor was tiled in black. Narrow doors led off one side of the room, which looked like they led to further chambers. On the walls hung implements that made her stomach churn. A number of different-shaped knives, as well as leather gags and tools that she didn't recognise.

'Our most profitable offering,' Lily whispered, a strange, excited undertone twitching beneath her voice. 'You wouldn't believe how much our patrons pay for stuff like this. And why not? They deserve a little fun, don't you think?'

'This is a torture chamber,' Katerina managed. She had broken into a cold sweat; her teeth chattered uncontrollably. 'Nobody deserves this.'

'Some do.' Lily spoke insistently, like a petulant child. 'If you have enough money and power then you can walk like a god on this earth. That's what we provide. Liberty.'

'What about the victims?' Katerina squirmed against the wall, trying with all her concentration to slip free from the bindings.

'Those little sluts? Oh sorry, sorry...' She placed a hand over her mouth, mimicking embarrassment. 'We can't slut-shame anymore, can we? We can't say anything that might suggest that the little rats are anything less than sweet, innocent angels, can we? You know, at first, they *lap* up the lifestyle. Shameless, every time. The jets, the parties, the yachts... you'd think they'd been born into it. I hardly think they can complain about a little slap and tickle as payment. It is the oldest industry in the world, didn't you know? They should be glad – it's not like they bring anything to the table apart from their bodies. Most of them would be working behind a bar for the rest of their lives. They're lucky to even have exposure to our calibre of client.'

There was a sound of screeching metal and the main door swung open. The girl from London appeared in the doorway, her eyes downcast. The man who had bought her guided her, both hands resting on her shoulders, towards one of the open chambers. Katerina wasn't sure whether the girl had seen her, but she watched until what sounded like a bolt slid on the other side of the door. 'Please. Help her. She looks terrified. You're a wom–'

Lily laughed, throwing back her head to expose her thin throat. 'A woman? Is that it? I'm other things too, you know: smart, discreet, dedicated. You might try some of those on for size. Honestly, I am always, *always*, surprised by how dense and pathetic women can be. Maria, for example. If she had just had the sense to keep her snout out of our business. But no...' She imitated a pig, pressing the tip of her nose upwards. 'Asking me about the accounts, sneaking about here with that drip, Teddy. She really thought she could outwit me, us, I think! She didn't even have the sense to keep quiet when she killed him–'

Katerina's head was now thumping with pain. She forced herself to stay upright, her eyes on Lily.

'–I heard her crying, like I told you. I was honest about that. When I went to investigate, I saw her with that idiot, Irene. She'd got there first and, idiotically, decided to help. They were so panicked about what Maria had done, they didn't even notice me watching them, right there at the bottom of the stairs! Talk about amateurs. God knows what happened! Some weird sex game gone wrong? Who knows!' She looked delighted at the prospect. 'Anyway, anyone could have seen them dragging the body to the beach... it was honestly comical. Farcical! I wouldn't have thought any more of it if Irene hadn't charged into my office. *I've had enough! You can't get away with this any longer! Maria Barlas is onto you, she knows what you are!* Blah, blah, blah. Literally, all her cards laid out. Could she be any more stupid? Good to have it on video, though, wasn't it? Diverted the attention for a while.'

'You killed her?' She knew nobody else was listening to the conversation, but she needed to hear it, for her own peace of mind.

Lily shrugged. 'Domenico didn't think it was necessary, but after Innes told me about Alek's silly emails with Maria–' She rolled her eyes. 'I realised that Irene would be kept in the loop too. They all had to go. Domenico gave me carte blanche.' Her smile suddenly shifted to a much darker shade, one that Katerina had never seen her wear before. 'My specialty. I told you, I'm not like other pathetic women. I was glad Maria had been so... creative! It was fun, emulating Teddy's murder, slicing that old crone.'

Katerina stared at her. She was still wearing the same sickly smile, but it had become sharper, somehow. Her eyes had widened, and they glistened, excited, electric as she recounted Irene's murder. A cool lick of fear cut through the waves of nauseous heat; she wriggled her wrists desperately behind her. 'You killed Alek too? And Maria?'

Lily's grin grew wider, as if hearing Katerina say it aloud delighted her. 'You didn't look into me, did you? It's why Domenico likes me. I'm sick...' She laughed as she said the word, lifting up her skirt to reveal a small sickle-shaped tattoo at the top of her thigh. 'We're all sick! It's fun, isn't it? But nobody would ever suspect posh, harmless Lily. This is by far the best contract I've ever accepted. Beachside luxury hotel... it doesn't get much better.'

'You're ex-military? A contractor?'

Lily smirked down at her and crouched, taking her chin between her fingers. 'You almost caught me. I loved it, it's just too easy sometimes; the thrill of being cornered, the sound of your skull cracking against the wall–'

Her face blurred in and out of focus as Katerina pieced together what she was saying. 'It was you? Above the fish restaurant? What... you were framing Innes? You planted the note, the money?'

Lily bent her neck one way and then the other, her smile dropping suddenly at the mention of Innes. 'She'll never tell tales. She knows what I'd do to her if she started singing. Prison is preferable.' She chuckled, the noise coming from deep in her throat. Sitting back on her heels, she looked up at the ceiling. 'I know Domenico has his flings, but her? Innes? Damp, dreary Innes? She dropped the note by the pool like she *wanted* me to frame her.' She levelled her gaze back at Katerina, biting her lip with excitement. 'It worked, didn't it?' She counted her fingers as she continued. 'And then Maria takes the blame for Irene and, as she should, Teddy. It's perfect, isn't it! So perfect...'

'My colleagues will be searching for me. They know I'm here–' Her words sounded hollow. It must have been at least half an hour since she'd lost comms with the team. Why weren't they here yet? A small, viperous voice whispered in the back of her mind: *They've left you. They don't care. They'll be glad to see the back of you.* She shook her head and the pain erupted, new and red, behind her eyes.

'I told you, they won't find you.' Lily spoke as if she was teaching a child, her fingers stroking Katerina's hair. 'You see, I still need someone to take responsibility for the motorbike bomb. You really are perfect, Officer. I've done my reading... such a fascinating character you are. Darker, much more twisted, than I ever could have hoped for. Here's your story...' She leaned forwards, pressing her mouth up against her ear.

'You, deranged after your last disastrous boyfriend, overwhelmed by returning to work, develop an obsession for your colleague, Sergeant Mikras. However, like all good romances, the road to love is not smooth. You see, he's into Maria. Beautiful, fun, whimsical Maria. You can't stand it...' She pulled Katerina's hair, tugging her head towards the ground. Katerina let out a small grunt of pain. 'So, you plant a bomb on her bike. You're a police officer; you're au fait with all the ingredients. It's easy. They'll find the paraphernalia in your room after a tip-off, plus, you'll kill yourself, overcome with shame at what you've done.'

Katerina choked out the words. 'They won't believe it. They know I'm here. The team, they won't–'

Lily cackled and dragged Katerina upright again, driving her head against the wall. The pain was all-encompassing, bright light erupted somewhere behind her eyes. She winced, feeling tears pour down her face. 'It doesn't matter whether they believe it or not! Why are you so *dense*? Why are you *here*? All alone, recklessly running about! You need evidence, don't you? They'll have no evidence against me, against Domenico, against anyone *apart* from you. They've already overlooked your, may I say, obvious involvement with that corrupt boyfriend last year. Do you think the authorities will give you or your team's opinion of you a second chance? Do you think anyone will listen to them after last summer? I shouldn't think so. So, you see, you're exactly what I need.'

A clear, pure thought cut through the swelling ache that was now pushing and pulling at her entire body. Lily could kill her, she would die, her reputation tarnished forever. That was bearable. But a young girl was locked behind the bolted door opposite suffering unimaginable terror and pain. That wasn't. Throughout the hotel were similar girls, all who needed help. She could take the blame for Maria's murder. She could die. But first, she had to help these women. She had to put an end to this.

'Fine.' She looked Lily directly in the eye. 'Fine. You'll be doing me a favour... I... I'm worthless anyway. You're right; I should never have been given a second chance. If I were you, I'd untie me, though. The longer my hands are tied up, the more chance there is of bruising. That will look suspicious.'

'You must think I–'

Katerina writhed, giving one large tug at her wrists. 'Every time I struggle, the more obvious the marks will be. They'll see them straight away.'

Lily grimaced, apparently annoyed at herself for being unable to find a decent counter-response. She blew out through her teeth, spitting slightly, and reached to the small of her back, drawing out a handgun. Holding it to Katerina's temple, she hissed, 'Turn around then.'

She traced the gun against Katerina's skull as she pivoted around, waiting for her hands to be freed. As soon as she felt the sag of the bindings, she threw herself to the ground, swinging her legs around so that they drove into Lily, knocking her off-balance. The gun skidded across the floor tiles and Katerina, without looking back, threw herself in its direction, scrambling to get a hold of it. Lily's weight was suddenly on her back, nails clawing at her face. She used the momentum to catapult Lily overhead, sending her head-first into the brick wall, a strained, ragged groan escaping her lips. The metal instruments clanged as she smashed into them. Katerina launched herself at Lily before she could get up, and swung the back of her gun into her head. Lily slid to the floor, a thin trickle of blood dripping down her face.

'What the–' The narrow door opened and the man who had bid for the girl emerged. She raised the gun at him, her heart hammering against her ribs.

'On the floor. Now. On the floor. Hands behind your head.' He looked like he was about to call out, when she screamed at him again. 'I said on the floor!'

His chubby face hung heavy in disbelief as he lowered himself down. Katerina nodded at the girl. 'Get the handcuffs from the wall. Tie him up.'

The girl gawked at her, her arms hanging limp and bare at her sides. She was wearing her underwear. Katerina noticed that bruises laced their way up to her collarbone. 'The handcuffs, please.'

The girl nodded and unhooked the cuffs from the wall. Katerina held the gun steady in one hand, making sure they'd been secured properly. Placing the key in her shoe, she raised the gun to the man's face. 'Get up. Back in the room. Now.'

'What? No... I... help! Help!'

Katerina stamped her heel into his bare foot, turning his words into empty cries of pain. 'Now.' She shoved him through the door, her stomach turning as she noted the room: a narrow, surgical-looking massage bed and bare walls. 'You're disgusting,' she whispered, before retrieving the girl's crumpled clothes and shutting the door behind her.

The girl was shivering in the main room, hunched over, her arms folded across her middle. Katerina handed her the dress. 'You. I thought it was you, outside. You're from London.'

'That's right,' Katerina moaned, swaying as she checked the main door. Her surroundings had begun to spin, ever so slowly. She needed to act quickly. 'I can help you. Do you know the way out of here?'

The girl looked at Lily, who was still slumped in the corner. Her face hardened, her lips forming a straight, thin line. She gave a brisk nod before replying. 'Yes. But they'll see us and then... they won't be happy.' Her voice trembled.

'What's your name?' Katerina extended a hand and led the girl to the main door.

The girl looked at her feet and mumbled. 'Helen. But please–' She stepped away, looking back at the room where her buyer was tied up. 'You don't understand what they'll do. They're untouchable. I've disobeyed. They'll kill me...' She began to shake; her pale face seemed vacant, faraway.

A sinking feeling reminded Katerina that her presence here had put Helen in more danger. She had to find the memory stick that Sofia had mentioned. 'I know how to end all of this, Helen. Just trust me, okay? But we need to move quickly.'

Helen looked like she was about to refuse, but then bit her lip, her eyebrows moving closer together in a tight frown. 'This bit's hidden. They only let the high-paying clients in here. It's a secret lift, behind the statue in the foyer.'

'The one of the god, Saturn?'

She nodded. 'You push down on the sickle and it opens up.'

She remembered Michail telling her about what Lily had said about the sculpture in the lobby. *They rub the top of his stick and it brings them good luck.* Lily had directed their attention straight to the dragon's mouth and they hadn't even noticed. Katerina gripped the gun in both hands, keeping as steady as possible. 'Stay behind me. I'll keep you safe, I promise.'

The lift was small and clinical, with mirrors on all sides. A smeared handprint had been left in one of the corners; it looked like it was pressing the glass from the other side, trying to pop the frame and escape. Katerina viewed her reflection. She was certainly no longer in disguise – her hair fell in a damp mess past her shoulders. Her face was puffy and bruised. The best they could hope for was that the foyer was empty. If anyone was waiting for the lift... she steadied herself, legs hip-width apart, ready to fight. It ground to a stop and the doors slid open to let the red light flood the mirrored space. Nobody was there.

Katerina let herself breathe and motioned for Helen to stay behind her. They stayed close to the wall, hidden as much as possible in the shadows, and made for Lily's office.

'Can't we just leave?' Helen whispered, barely audible, behind her. Again, Katerina felt that sinking guilt – the poor girl had been through enough. This was the last thing she needed.

'Just a few seconds. I need to find something.' She reached into her bra, realising that she hadn't checked if she still had the key card. Thankfully, Lily hadn't strip-searched her. It beeped successfully, as it had before, and she ushered Helen into the office. 'We don't have long. Look for a memory card. Try and think where you'd keep something important or incriminating. Ransack the place if you need to.'

Katerina checked the computer, daring to hope that Lily had left it in her USB port, but it was empty. She scanned the small room: a bookshelf of self-help books, various cosmetics strewn about the desk, her laptop. She spun on the spot, her eyes raking every corner of the room, desperately trying to find a sign for where someone like Lily might keep her perverted spoils. Her eyes fell to the mid-sized plant in the corner. It was new; it hadn't been in the original footage. She was certain. 'There, the plant.' She dropped onto her knees and began digging in the soil. 'It's a pistachio plant... it has to be...' Her fingers hit something firm and plastic. The memory card.

'Come on, we can go–' She turned to Helen and her words were cut short. Domenico held her by the neck, a gun to her head. Helen's mouth fell into a silent 'O', her eyes pleading with Katerina to help her.

'Let her go.' Katerina placed the gun on the ground and held up her hands. 'Let her go, she has nothing to do with this. Take me. I'll do whatever you need.'

Shouts came from outside. 'Police! Police! On the ground! On the ground!' Katerina kept very still, resisting the urge to scream for attention. She couldn't do anything to put Helen at risk.

'Domenico, it's over. The police are here. I've got all the evidence they need. You can't–'

'I can't? Right now, our members will be obeying your colleagues' instructions as respectfully as anyone could. The girls have been briefed on what to say. They will tell the police that they were delighted, lucky, to have been invited to such an event. Tatiana will explain how they are professional models, and that she is the underage girls' chaperone. She can be very charming. The girls won't divert from their stories because they have nowhere else to go and they have a... let's call it a *healthy respect* for the system above them, isn't that right?' He nuzzled his face into Helen's neck. She didn't pull away, although her body seemed to shrink in on itself. Her thin limbs twitched in tiny terrified tremors. Katerina stepped forwards. 'No.' He pointed the gun at her chest as he dragged Helen towards the door and closed it, ever so gently. 'We're sound-proofed now. You stay where you are.'

He took a deep breath through his nose, closing his eyes, as if he could not be more relaxed. 'So you will see why I need the memory card you have in your hand. Very clever finding it, but you're not quite clever enough.'

He pushed Helen to her knees and pressed the gun into the back of her head. She was shaking; silent bulbous tears spilled to the floor. 'You wouldn't be stupid enough to kill her in the middle of a police raid–'

'She's a nobody. No family, no one to miss her.' He smiled; his face perfectly placid. 'I've got lawyers, the best money can buy. It's worth my while to deal with a little "tragic accident" to protect my business.' He kept his eyes on Katerina as he moved the gun in a fluid movement downwards and shot Helen in the foot.

Her screams caused Katerina physical pain. Again, she tried to fling herself to Helen's side, but Domenico pointed the gun at her. 'Now, before I hurt her other precious foot, please give me the memory card.'

Helen whimpered on the floor, her breathing ragged and forced. Katerina pictured Michail, Sofia and Yiorgos making their way through the hotel. They'd surely be here soon. This was the last place that they'd received comms from her. She just needed to stall Domenico. A further gunshot stunned her. She barely registered the sound, barely believed it. Helen screeched in agony, the sound peeling through the air in high, frantic wails. He'd shot her other foot.

'Stop!' Katerina realised that she too was screaming. 'Stop it, you monster!'

Domenico was laughing, his head thrown back, his neck convulsing. 'Give me what I want and I'll stop.'

She didn't think about what came next. Katerina felt her body launching through space before her bones connected with Domenico as she rode him to the ground. She didn't see whether he was still holding the gun; there was no time to check. She flung open the door, screaming for help, as she dragged Helen into the corridor. Police torches approached from the far end. 'Help! Help! Over here!'

'Katerina!' Michail called to her. She squinted behind the lights as she moved forwards, conscious of Helen's screaming as her legs dragged against the floor. 'She's here! Sofia! Yiorgos! She's here!'

The ground was shifting now, moving in slow, heavy rotations as she stumbled towards him.

'Michail... she's hurt... here...'

Her eyes met his. She smiled, glad that she had done something right, and slid the memory card towards him. As he picked it up, she was confused. His expression was not what she expected. His eyes were not relieved. He was not smiling. His gaze looked at something behind her shoulder. She opened her mouth to ask him what the matter was, but, for some reason, no sound came out. It was as if time had stopped. Sound had stopped. She smiled, an intense quiet falling about her, cradling her. He shouldn't look so frightened. His face shouldn't be so red, so upset. Everything was fine. Everything was fine. She had got what they needed. The girls would be safe.

The last things that Katerina Galanis's brain processed was the image of her partner's face, the sensation of his hand in hers, the sound of his voice telling her that she would be okay. Then, whatever essence that made her: the thoughts, the memories, the likes and dislikes, all the shame and pride and hope and dreams, left her body for good.

Maria
The day of Teddy's murder

Teddy rattled the cocktail shaker, tensing his pectoral muscles as he flashed her a smile. Maria rearranged herself on his sofa and stretched out her legs in an attempt to seem natural. She hadn't counted on him being such a party animal. By the time they'd got back from the harbourside gig, he'd already been wasted. She needed to find a way for him to slow down; at this rate, it would be impossible to get any information from him. She stood, smoothed down her skirt and walked towards him. 'Shall we try out your tub?'

'Bit late for that, no? I was hoping...' He placed a hand on her waist. She laughed, stepping away from him.

'Come on, we've been dancing all night. The water looks amazing.' She slid open the terrace door and began to undress. The steam wafted from the surface of the water in volute, intricate curls. Against the darkness, the patterns looked like they were carving out the sky. She lowered herself into the warm water and looked expectantly at him. Perhaps she could get him talking once he was in the water.

He raised his eyebrows and took a swig straight from the cocktail shaker. Wiping his mouth, he followed her lead.

'It's pretty out here.'

'Should be for the price tag.' He swam closer to her, pressing his body against her side. 'You're special, I can tell...'

'Special, me? How?' She glanced at the side of the pool, noting there was no space for her to move away from him. He moved his face towards hers, caressing her cheek. She fought the urge to brush him away.

'All those girls tonight at the harbour. Drinking, dancing, behaving like little...' his mouth half-formed a word she didn't recognise, before he shook his head, '...like they own the place. Imagine if men acted like that. We'd be called hooligans. You're classy. I like it.'

She turned to face him, thinking carefully about what she should say next. 'You find it difficult to find the right type of girl?'

His lips curved into a gentle, mocking smile. 'Do I look like the sort of guy who struggles to find women?'

'No...' She placed her arms around his neck. Even in the water, the smell of his aftershave was overpowering. 'I'm just wondering where someone like you usually finds dates. I bet you don't normally pick up local girls.' His face hardened. For a second, she thought she'd been too obvious and ruined it. However, he shrugged and shoved his arms beneath the surface, wriggling out of his trunks.

'I think we've talked enough...'

She stayed where she was, allowing him to push against her and kiss her neck. The tiling seemed very solid and compact against her spine. Her mind raced through how she might extract herself from the situation. She needed information about the accounts, about Tatiana, about what was really going on here, about Eleni. This place had become such an all-encompassing presence in her life. A client, a mystery, a source of fear and suspicion. If she could get her hands on the proof; she needed to go to the police...

Beneath the water, under the glittering pool lights, she saw it, there, just above his ankle. He moved against her with more force now, making the water swell in gentle ripples. But, even through the splashes, she could see it clearly. The tattoo. The same as Eleni's. His lips found hers, but she pushed him away, causing water to overflow onto the terrace. He laughed, shocked, misreading her. 'Feisty...'

'No...' She scrambled out of the pool and stared down at him. The air suddenly felt like it was suffocating her. She pointed, her gaze unwavering at it. 'The tattoo. On your ankle. You – where did you get it?'

'Oh? You like it?' He thrust his hips forward so that he floated to the surface, brandishing his leg. 'It's one of my favourites, actually, same as my necklace.' He reached to the back of his neck and pulled around a small charm of the same symbol. 'Got it with an ex. She turned out to be a disappointment in the end – annoying little thing, really.' He shrugged. 'She was a local too, since you asked! Younger than you.'

Maria had never known what people meant when they described losing control. However, that is just how she would describe the following two minutes. She was silent. All her strength gathered and pulsated in her arms. She held him down as he thrashed. She pushed and pushed and pushed, her face looming over his, her eyes glassy and unforgiving. Until he fell limp and loose, all she saw was Eleni. She didn't know why she dragged him out of the pool. She didn't know why she ran to her bag for her painting supplies. It was a primal feeling, one that had no words, no reason, no thought behind it. She wanted to mark him. To stain him in the same way he'd stained Eleni. She wanted him to feel her pain, match her anguish. She cut him carefully, in a suspended, methodical daze. Sculpting the skin, his head in her lap.

The first sound to escape her lips was when she cried. It was like waking up. She found herself in the corridor, wet and shivering. The horror was overwhelming. She needed to call the police. That's what she kept telling Irene Kanatas, who was cradling her. She needed to call the police. She needed to tell them what she had done.

But that isn't what she did. The foyer, the promenade, the beach. His body was heavy and wet in the bin liner. Irene was talking, saying something about how Lily needed to pay. *Too many girls had been affected. Too many tragedies. She would bring her down. Tonight. She would bring her down.*

But the blood. The room. I...

Suddenly, she was alone again. *You'll need to clean the room. I can't be a part of it, understand? Use the supplies in the cupboard. You can do this. Be thorough. Sweet-pea? Understand?*

She nodded, a quick, continuous movement, staring at the body strewn on the sand. She could do this. She had to do this. But then, the chill of realisation. Teddy's key card. His clothes. She'd left them in the room. How would she get back in?

Had she been thinking straight, she never would have used her father's key card, hung up behind the door to his office. However, it was the quickest way. Irene had disappeared, fuming, ranting about Lily. Everyone else was asleep.

And so, her father's card in hand, she ascended the stairs, ready to clean up her mess.

Cat

Michail sat at a café on Iraklidon. He stirred his coffee three times to the right, then to the left, then to the right again. It was a beautiful day. His eyes trailed along the patches of shrubbery until they rested on what was still his favourite building. The Parthenon. It still towered above him. It was still truly a monument of peace. Only now, it was tinged with a deep sadness, which he was certain would never abate. He took a slow sip of coffee and let his eyes fall searchingly at the bend in the street.

There she was, running up the street, belt askew, shirt pressed moderately, though not expertly, sweating already, breathless and rushed. 'Michail! I am sorry!'

'Again,' Michail replied to the blank space in front of him, wondering if his voice had always sounded so flat, so disapproving.

Her image smiled and he felt a phantom slap on his shoulder. She repeated after him, 'Again.' He could hear the playful lilt in her voice as if she was here.

She sat down on the chair beside him – although, of course, the chair remained untouched beneath the table – chattering about her sisters and her mother and her aunty and some other irrelevant business. Michail held a hand up, remembering what he had said perfectly. He formed his lips over the word and said it silently. 'Stop.'

She blinked at his hand and patiently lifted her own before grasping his. He knew, he remembered, that she had then placed both their hands back on the table so they could get on with their business. But, for now, he was happy to sit with his hand in hers. She knew, he realised, even at the very beginning, how to calm him. She knew him.

'Michail?'

He bowed his head as Sofia pulled out the chair. The scene before him faded, disintegrating into the chatter of the tourists. 'Major Sampson, I expected to see you at headquarters?'

She smiled at him and he noticed she was back to wearing her characteristic red lipstick. In fact, she seemed less tired altogether; the dark circles beneath her eyes had disappeared. 'I thought I'd enjoy a coffee with you first. I had a feeling you might be here,' she said.

'Ah.' He looked at his cup, his chest tightening. 'Of course, you must have been aware that this was our meeting place.'

'Yes.' She gestured to the waiter to bring her a coffee. A silence grew between them and Michail was given the distinct impression that he was expected to fill it.

'I believe you are assessing my emotional state before my first day back?'

'If I were, how would you describe it?'

'I would assess it as "Below Average".' He stirred his coffee again, mainly so that he didn't need to look Sofia in the face. 'Of course, I am being proactive. I am reading, jogging...' He glanced at the Parthenon again. 'Being back in Athens helps.'

Sofia shifted in her seat. 'It's probably not at the forefront of your mind, but Domenico, Lily, and all the major players are facing what I'd tentatively call iron-clad charges. Tatiana is complicated, Innes is cleared of murder but not much else. Helen, the girl who...' Her voice trailed off. 'The girl we found Katerina with, she heard Lily's confession from the next room. With the memory card, it's pretty much a done deal. She saved countless young women. Sorting through the images, the videos,' she grimaced, '...well, some good came out of it.'

He looked at the table. 'Yes. She helped them. Unlike me. I... I was misled again, by Maria—'

'We all missed Maria.' Sofia tutted, as if she was annoyed at herself. 'There was no reason to suspect her, Michail. She'd been nothing but helpful. That was sort of the point. She was trying to help us as much as she could without getting caught herself. I think she finally realised that, unless she confessed, we'd never stop Lily and Domenico. Teddy's murder kept throwing us off the scent.'

The prickly memory of his lips against hers, her laugh in his ear, the view of the sea below and the Temple of Apollo behind them crawled into his mind. He winced, wishing he could erase every moment he had spent with her. The whole thing was a brutal kick to Katerina's memory. *Katerina.* The great, gaping numbness filled his head with white noise. 'We should never have let her go in.'

She sighed and leant back in the chair. 'We made the best decision we could at the time. She wanted to help, Michail. And she did. I know—'

'I didn't tell her how I felt.' The words spilled out of him, completely unprecedented. 'I didn't tell her. And now I can't.'

'You shouldn't blame—'

'Incorrect. I am to blame. I was perfectly aware that syphoning my feelings was the right thing to do. Instead, I locked anything to do with her away. I was cold. So cold that I am certain she took risks that she should not have.' He took a sharp puff of breath. 'And now... now there is nothing I can do.'

He didn't expect Sofia to respond; there was nothing logical that she could say. He was right. His actions, his lack of emotional maturity had made Katerina feel like she had to prove herself. It was his fault that she was gone. He closed his eyes to ensure Sofia didn't notice his tears forming. To his utter surprise, she reached forwards and grabbed his hand. Looking up, he realised she was crying too. 'You know, until very recently, I would have agreed with you about that. But...' she took a long, slow breath, '...I think you can tell her, Michail. Syphon, if that's what you call it?'

'Correct.'

She laughed, although it was a sad sound. 'I thought for a long time that it was better to ignore lost loved ones. It felt easier, more... detached. I was wrong about that, Michail. I... you should remember Katerina, because when you remember someone, you can talk to them, in a sense.'

He had never seen Sofia behave in such a way. He squeezed her hand, hoping it would convey gratitude. For a short while, they sat in silence. Then, having woven its way down the Acropolis foothills, a small tabby cat circled the table and, without invitation, jumped onto Michail's lap and nestled into his uniform, purring gently. He frowned and moved to brush it off him, when Sofia chuckled. 'Let her be. Cats can sense it when you need some support.'

He sat very straight as the animal looked up at him. Its yellow eyes stared into his, unflinching, like it was sorting through his thoughts. He raised his hand very slowly, frightened that he might scare it away, then lowered his hand to stroke its head. The purr grew more intense. 'She liked cats.'

'Yes.'

He tickled it behind the ears and chuckled as it rubbed its

furry head against his hand, begging him to do it again. His laughter shocked him; he had not made the sound for a long while. The cat, considering its job done, jumped down from his lap. He stood, smoothing down his shirt. 'We'll be late if we don't leave now, Major Sampson.'

'All right, let me just finish my–'

'Out of the question.' He folded his arms. 'It is our responsibility to maintain the smooth and orderly running of the Special Violent Crime Squad.'

She raised her eyebrows but smiled at him, giving him a small nod. 'Understood, Sergeant Mikras.'

Every year, towards the end of the summer, small groups of tourists wait at the water's edge in Aegina for their return trip to Athens. The heat is still lava-like and heavy, although the breeze of the sea rolls in at dusk, bringing relief to tired, be-sandaled feet and rouged cheeks. Were one of them to be particularly observant, they would notice a serious-looking policeman disembarking their boat before they board. A few others follow him, yet his are the first feet to hit dry ground.

If the observant tourist were to continue watching, they would see how his lips tremble ever so slightly, as he surveys the town from a distance. It seems like he might change his mind, turn around, retrace his steps, and run back aboard. But then he would have nowhere to place the bouquet of flowers. Nor would he have anywhere to recite his note. So, he marches, his head held high, his chin jutted forwards, onwards. Of course, the tourist doesn't see what happens next. They don't see him walk the long way at the side of the dusty road, one steady foot after another, ignorant of the beads of sweat dripping down his forehead, for about one hour. They don't see him stop, abruptly, swaying backwards slightly, in front of what looks like a boarded-up, deserted hotel on the beach. They don't see him kneel in the sand, unconcerned about his uniform, place the flowers before him, then carefully unfold a piece of paper.

He takes a deep, brave breath, and begins. 'Katerina...'

THE END

Afterword

This second installment of the Hellenic Mystery series was, again, such fun to write. I urge anyone visiting Athens to take the short boat trip to Aegina – it's a beautiful spot. I would spend a night or two there, however, it's very easy to treat it as a day trip from Athens.

A few artistic liberties have been taken with locations; the geography of the island itself is mostly accurate and true to life. It is well worth visiting both the remains of The Temple of Apollo and The Temple of Aphaia. Both the east and west pedimental sculptures from The Temple of Aphaia (which help Michail solve the case) are on display in the Glyptothek in Munich. The 'Mask Gallery' in London's National Portrait Gallery exists, although the stairways and the vaults beneath the gallery are embellishments.

Also by V.J. Randle

The Athenian Murders

Acknowledgements

Thank you to Betsy, Fred, Tara and Hannah at Bloodhound Books for all your support and enthusiasm – it's a pleasure working with all of you. Also, to the incomparable editor Abbie Rutherford, thank you for your eagle-eyed insight and sensitive suggestions. If anyone is in need of a superb editor, I would endorse Abbie any day.

To my Dad, Ethan, who always reads the first draft of my books and offers his unparalleled narrative and structural thoughts, thank you.

Thanks to my husband, Will, who provides calm and perspective for me, especially amidst book releases!

About the Author

V.J. Randle is the author of The Athenian Murders and The Saturn House Killings. She read Classics at King's College, University of Cambridge before teaching Latin and Greek for over a decade. She has given many a tour of Hellenic sites over the years, both in the capacity of educator and holiday-maker. If you spot an excitable woman in a maxi skirt waving her arms about on top of The Acropolis, chances are it's her. Do say hello!

She now lives and writes in the North-East of Scotland (via a brief spell in Canada) with her husband and cat, Athena.

A note from the publisher

Thank you for reading this book. If you enjoyed it please do consider leaving a review on Amazon to help others find it too.

We hate typos. All of our books have been rigorously edited and proofread, but sometimes mistakes do slip through. If you have spotted a typo, please do let us know and we can get it amended within hours.

info@bloodhoundbooks.com

Printed in Great Britain
by Amazon

44286480R00169